MURDER

+

MACHINERY

OTHER TITLES FROM BLACK BEACON BOOKS

The Black Beacon Book of Mystery
An Anthology

Shelter from the Storm
An Anthology

Lighthouses
An Anthology of Dark Tales

Subtropical Suspense
A Thrilling Anthology

Hoffman's Creeper and Other Disturbing Tales
A Collection by Cameron Trost

The Tunnel Runner
A Novel by Cameron Trost

www.blackbeaconbooks.com

MURDER

+

MACHINERY

Tales of Technological Terror
and Mechanical Madness

Black Beacon Books

Murder and Machinery
Published by Black Beacon Books
Edited by Cameron Trost
Cover photo by Michal Matlon on Unsplash
Cover design by Cameron Trost
Copyright © Black Beacon Books, 2021

The Secret Zeppelin © Duncan Richardson
#Selfie © Linda Brucesmith
Fargan's Termination © Paul Williams
A Little Kindness Goes a Long Way © Chisto Healy
The Box © Sarah Jane Justice
The Wheel © Michael Picco
The Wedge © Kurt Newton
(First appeared in Dark Discoveries #12)
Tenterhooks © Cameron Trost
Leonora © Danielle Birch
Vanitas © James Dorr
(First appeared in Alfred Hitchcock's Mystery Magazine, January 1996)
Don © Steve DuBois
(First appeared in Andromeda Spaceways Magazine #71)
Foul Beasts © Karen Bayly
A Whole New World © KG McAbee
Suicide Blonde © Paulene Turner
Driverless © Robert Bagnall
The Screen in the Sky © Kerilee S. Nickles

Tales of deadly machinery have long fascinated us, from Edgar Allan Poe's classic pendulum to the Terminator films. *Murder and Machinery* pays homage to this tradition, offering you gripping tales following this theme but set in different times and places, from colonial America and London during the First World War to dystopian futures on this planet and beyond. Never before has an anthology brought tales of science fiction and suspense together in such a terrifying way, showcasing the nightmarish imagination of authors who know how to play on the reader's fears and who share those fears of uncontrollable machines, or perhaps even more frightening, of fellow humans mastering technology for their own evil purposes.

A word of advice before you start. By all means, settle down in your living room and let this anthology of technological terror and mechanical madness enthral you, but first, you might want to lock your doors and switch the power off at the mains. Best keep it low-tech tonight. Trust me. I hope you have candles?

Cameron Trost, editor

THE SECRET ZEPPELIN
Duncan Richardson

When they loom out of the clouds like malevolent whales of the sky, dropping their bombs amongst us, it is like a divine punishment. I do not ask for what. Having served my time in the police, I know well the depth of our depravity, yet in my declining years, I had hoped for some peace. Well, the Kaiser and his chums put an end to that, so now we huddle in our homes every night, powerless against the monsters that slide across our skies, even here, beyond the fringe of London. Searchlights illuminate the sky, making the hulking beasts all the more terrifying, and our guns occasionally bring one down—but there are always more.

Old Eddy at number eleven is out in his small garden every night, watching for them. Sometimes, when an airship glides close, Eddy falls to his knees and puts his hands together. I don't know what he's praying for. He was on the Indian frontier as a young man and long before this war, I had heard him shouting at night as dreams took him back there. That was the first time I met Edith, his niece. She does his laundry and makes sure he eats. These long summer days I often see her leaving his house. I don't sleep well either so I try to weary myself by searching for spies lurking in the bushes, signalling to the enemy. Or more likely, I will find some thoughtless citizen letting light escape through their curtains.

I know those diabolical machines are manned by young German men, no different from the young constables who used to follow my orders. I sometimes even envy them the experience of flight. What a view they must have, London spread out all below them, lit by the moon some nights, with the Thames snaking its way to the sea, reflecting the moonlight, like a giant traitorous ribbon, showing them the way to the heart of our capital. I shiver and long to see more Zeps plunge burning to the ground. Then I recall the smoking ruins of an airship that I saw a few months ago and the blackened corpse of a young flier.

But one night, before it was properly dark, instead of passing me by with a brief 'Good night, Mr Carr' and a polite nod, Edith stepped in front of me and glanced up from under the wide brim of her hat. Her face was pale; her brown curls escaping from her hat gave her a slightly flustered look, which was immediately appealing, even though I am old enough to be her father. I took a deep breath and tried to assume a business-like attitude.

'Please, sir,' she said. 'I think I know what they're doing.'

'Doing? Pardon? What who's doing?' My halting words sounded almost comical, like a music hall straight man, but I could tell from the glint in her eye that it was no joke.

'The Hun.' She glanced down at the small calico bag, clutched in her gloved hands.

'I'm sorry, dear,' I said. 'I don't understand.' I wondered if I should invite her in for a mug of cocoa, as we were just outside my gate. Would it be risking gossip? Did I care? For myself, no, but for her, a young widow with her life before her, yes, I did care. Besides, she might take flight as she was shivering, slightly. From fear, I surmised, because it was a mild evening. She drew her grey shawl tight around her shoulders.

'The airships,' she said, passing her tongue briefly over her lips, reminding me of a cat I had years before, in my working days, my sole companion and a loyal one too, despite the long hours I was away from the house.

'I'm sorry, Edith,' I said. 'I too am powerless against them.'

She pressed her lips together and her eyes sparked. 'No, I mean the smaller one those spies are using. I've heard the stories. They have it hidden in a secret place then bring it out to guide the others and bomb us all to hell if they get the chance.' She took a deep breath and glanced at the sky. 'Pardon my French, sir,' she said.

Her husband had been in the Flying Corps and was killed in France last year but I wondered if she still looked for him, returning through the clouds to save us from the airships. I scratched my head.

'It's true, Mr Carr, as I live and breathe. That's why they know where to go. And it don't take them long neither.'

I hardly noticed her incorrect grammar and restrained myself from commenting, but I could think of nothing sensible to say. I had heard the rumours of a secret Zeppelin hide-out but had dismissed them as fantastical. Something worthy of a story by Mr Wells perhaps, but not possible. Even a small one would be too big to hide.

'Why do you tell me, Edith? You know I'm retired now. I can't do anything.'

She let go of her bag with one hand and grabbed my arm. 'But you still know people in the police, don't you, sir?'

I nodded.

'Well then, they'll listen to you.' She blinked and let go of my arm. 'They don't listen to me.'

'You've tried?'

She nodded.

I sighed. I noticed a woman helping her son out on his crutches across the village green. A wounded soldier, one of the lucky ones with a damaged leg that would heal in time.

'Come in,' I said.

Luckily I had recently cleaned my small kitchen, so it was not too shaming to have a visitor. I also had some leftover cake that Lottie had brought me. She's my old friend Reggie's wife and seems to think bachelors like me are incapable of looking after themselves. While the kettle boiled, we sat at my table in the evening light and I tried to work out a line of questioning. Edith was a witness, I supposed, to something. And I needed to find out if a "crime" had been committed or not.

I took out my notepad, which seemed to please her, and said, 'Now, from the beginning. Tell me what you've seen, who, when and where.'

She nodded, as if she had made a decision. Then glanced around.

'Are you afraid?' I said. She reminded me of witnesses who are scared of retribution from a suspect.

She shook her head, then opened her eyes wide. 'Well, yes. Of course I am. Who isn't, when it comes to Zeppelin?'

'Please,' I said, trying not to show my impatience.

She placed her bag on the table, released it, and sat back with a sigh. She took off her gloves and held up a pale hand with her

11

four fingers raised. 'It was four evenings ago. I was up on Hanger Hill. I'd just left my uncle's house and the children were with Nell, my neighbour. I had an hour to myself. So I took a walk.' She stared into the gloom of my kitchen and I thought about standing to light a lamp but felt anything might disturb her and halt the tale.

'Half an hour there,' she said. 'Half an hour back. Usually. But this time, I decided to walk a little further. Around the hill, to the far side. Haven't been there since I was a nipper.'

She looked at me. I tried to urge her on with my eyes.

She folded two fingers down. 'That's where. And when.'

I nodded.

'When I reached a spot where I could see through the trees, I noticed lights.'

'Yes?'

'Lights in the hill. And men, in dark uniforms carrying things into…into the hill.' She silently folded another finger down.

'What kind of uniforms?' I regretted the words as soon as they were out. What would she know of uniforms, except possibly the one her husband had worn?

Edith blinked at me. 'I was too far away.' Her remaining finger twitched.

'Yes, of course,' I said. 'Understandable.'

Her eyes flared. 'Is it?'

'Hmm? Yes. I mean, you wouldn't want to go any closer, naturally. It could be anything.'

'Could it?'

I nodded. 'Criminals, for instance. A gang perhaps. Possibly, the constables already know about it.'

Edith frowned. 'If they did, why didn't they say that?'

I shrugged. 'Perhaps they don't want it to get around. Then the crooks might take off.'

She leaned forward and gripped the table. 'Do criminals usually wear uniforms?' she said.

'Ah, there you have me foxed,' I said, smiling, but thinking I wished my subordinates had all been as sharp as she seemed to be.

'They must be Germans,' she said. 'What else could they be, hidden away like that? But close to London.'

12

'I don't know, my dear. But I'd like to find out.'

'Tomorrow?' she said.

I nodded. It could be a pleasant distraction. 'Twenty-one hundred hours.'

A tear leaked from her eye, but she smiled. 'That's how my Bill used to talk.'

I patted her hand. 'And now you're doing your bit.'

The next day dragged and I realised I was looking forward to nine o'clock with an unusual amount of pleasant apprehension. Not that I expected the Zeppelin story to be true. In fact, I imagined it was only railway workers or some such, gathering gravel or dumping old materials, perhaps. Although it did seem like an odd time and place. Maybe they were just under orders to make the most of the long days, for the sake of the war effort.

A knock on my door came at twenty-one hundred hours precisely and my pulse speeded up. Don't be an old fool, I told myself. This is just an amusing adventure. Something to laugh about at the Red Lion, when the war is over.

'Are you ready?' Edith said before the door was fully open. She glanced at my empty hands and her face fell. 'Where's your detective bag?'

I slid my notebook and small field glasses from my jacket pocket. 'This is all I need,' I said.

'Hmm.'

I smiled as I closed the door behind me. She was setting me a challenge, I thought, suddenly glad that she was not in awe of my professional expertise. I would have to prove my mettle, and that was all the better.

We walked side by side along the quiet, wagon-rutted track towards Hanger Hill. Edith swung her arms as if eager to walk faster. I wondered if I should tell her the origin of the name, that it was nothing to do with executions as most local people imagined, but a derivative of Anglo-Saxon *hangra*, meaning *wood*. I decided to keep that to myself, for now at least.

As we passed Greystoke Manor, with its wrought-iron gates, I wished I could drop in on my old friend, Reggie Franks, the current owner of that not so ancient pile. But he was away on a dig in Scotland. At least, that's what he called it. An enthusiastic amateur in the true sense, he sometimes annoyed the University types who accused him of meddling in history. People in the village spoke angrily about him too now, asking why he wasn't contributing to the war effort. Though they kept silent when his wife Lottie was around. They had too much respect for her work in the village. Instead they muttered about how she was long suffering and a martyr to Reggie's madness.

'Come on, sir. We'll get no help from that quarter.'

I smiled and nodded. 'I'm afraid you're right, my dear.'

Edith frowned. 'No, Mr Carr, I mean, that Mrs Franks, she's a Jerry.'

It felt like a blow. I shook my head. 'No Edith, she isn't. Whoever told you that was lying. Lottie was born in Hungary but, as the old Duke of Wellington said, just because you're born in a stable, doesn't mean you're a horse.'

Edith wrinkled her nose, seeming to consider the idea. She smiled. 'I suppose that's true.' The smile vanished. 'But if she's a spy, I 'ope they string 'er up.'

I took a deep breath, wondering if I should abandon the expedition now. Edith didn't know Lottie was a friend of mine. It was mere idle gossip. Letting off steam.

We strode on, becoming more eager as the slope grew steeper. A dead oak tree stood on the ridge, still reaching for the sky with its bare branches. As we reached the edge of the wood, a light wind rustled through, stirring the branches, making the forest breathe. I thought of our distant ancestors moving stealthily through the woods, hunting, probably fearing both fierce beasts and malign spirits, yet still pushing on. What else could they do?

Something was tugging my sleeve. I looked up and blinked at Edith.

'This way, sir,' she said.

I nodded and followed as she led the way onto a narrow path between the bracken. The light grew dim as the trees became more dense. I could hardly day-dream now, for I had to watch every step lest I trip over a fallen branch. Instead, I found myself admiring Edith's purposeful stride and the way she pulled her skirt tight as she squeezed between bushes.

The path started descending and we reached a dirt road. The

track seemed to continue on the other side but Edith halted and held up her hand like a traffic policeman.

'What is it?' I said.

'Can you hear that?'

'What?' I held my breath as I waited for her response.

'Nothing. No birds. Not even a dog barking.' She turned to me, her eyes gleaming, her lips shining. 'They all know something's up,' she said. 'And they're staying well away.'

I started fearing for Edith's sanity then and realised I should have questioned it much sooner. In fact, from the start. As I would surely have done in my days on the Force. I stared back at her, wondering if I would have merrily gone along with this pursuit if the idea had not been brought to me by an attractive young woman.

'So are we close?' I said, trying to conceal my disbelief, which was growing to the size of a Zeppelin in my brain, and I feared I would not long be able to hide it.

She pointed through the trees, between the path and the dirt road. I sighed, resigning myself to a ramble through the hedgerows. However, I had done that often enough as a young policeman, searching for missing children, evidence or a suspect, so I told myself to grin and bear it as I had then. Who knew what the reward would be?

Edith led the way and I followed, only a pace behind now. The evening air was beginning to cool and I hoped I wouldn't catch a chill as a result of this caper. And that Edith would also come through in good health. I started to worry about her children. Part of me wanted to stop her and say, 'Enough of this nonsense. There's no Zeppelin. No secret lair. No men in uniform. Let's go home and have a cup of cocoa.'

But then I saw them.

We'd reached the edge of the trees, but thick bramble bushes dotted the hillside with more trees beyond. It was hard to get a clear view, but I could make out a group of men in dark overalls pushing a large wooden cart towards a cave entrance.

'By Jove,' I hissed.

'Didn't I tell you,' Edith whispered close to my ear so that I shivered and it was difficult to keep my eyes on the scene before me.

15

Edith sighed. 'Well, aren't you going to have a closer look?'

I turned and frowned at her. She made circles over her eyes with her fingers.

'Oh, I see,' I murmured and reached for my field glasses.

The men had reached the mouth of the cave and stood back, mopping their brows. They didn't look sinister then, but just like normal workmen on a warm evening. I hoped it was all a misunderstanding, that they were just council workers doing a job.

I swung my glasses onto them as they leaned into their task once more. Their overalls had no markings.

'Halt! Who goes there?'

The voice was loud, foreign sounding, and down the slope to my left. A large dog appeared through the bracken, snarling and slavering, barely restrained by a grimfaced man in a black uniform.

Edith clung to me, as in a fanciful moment I'd hoped she might. Or was it that I clung to her. What does it matter now? We turned and ran, heedless of fallen branches and brambles. Heedless of my age too and lack of practice in recent years. Despite her long skirt, Edith was quicker than me, so I was not faced with the awkward choice of who should bring up the rear.

I sensed the dog's breathing behind me and heard crashing but could not turn my head for fear of stumbling. We ran on, crossed the dirt road, found the path and only then did we halt and catch our breath.

My field glasses were still in my hand, so I glanced back through the trees but couldn't see any sign of pursuit.

'Did 'e sound like a Jerry to you?' Edith said.

I shrugged. 'Not sure, but the dog was a German Shepherd.'

Edith's eyes flicked from side to side and she grinned. 'Maybe he's a spy then.'

I put my field glasses back in my jacket pocket. 'Could be. But I'm going to need some time to think about this.'

Edith frowned. 'You're not going to report it?'

I shook my head. 'I don't know what to report yet.'

Edith looked away. 'Oh.'

I reached out and took her hand. She didn't pull away. 'Look my dear. I think you've found something strange going on but

16

I'm not sure what. The police won't believe me with just this information and then they might think I've grown senile in my old age and ignore the whole thing until it's too late.'

She squeezed my hand and let go. 'All right then,' she said. 'You're the expert. What's the next move?'

'I don't know. Let's get out of this wood first.'

We walked on, side by side, looking around occasionally as if we couldn't believe we had escaped. I was trying to work out who I should speak to and how, without drawing unwanted attention to myself. As we passed the manor again, Edith glanced at her watch.

'Ooh, look at the time. Nell will have my guts for garters if I don't collect my little uns.'

'I'll let you know,' I said, 'as soon as I make any progress.'

She waved and strode away down a path beside a hedgerow, adjusting her hat as if it might give away her evening of adventure.

Sitting alone in my living room, I took comfort from a cigar that Reggie had given me, a present from one of his "archaeological" wanderings in North Africa. As the smoke curled into the air, I ran through the possibilities. If there was a Zeppelin in that hill, clearly it was guarded. If they were not German, but one of our allies, well, what were they doing there? Obviously something they didn't want people to see, yet they also had not put up signs and fences to warn us off.

If anything official was happening there, then there was one person who would know—my old second in command, now Chief Inspector Albert Watkins. It was too late to call him, so I had to let it stew until morning, but I consoled myself with the idea that it would give me more time to prepare my case. I did not want to go off half-cocked and seem unhinged.

The constable who took my call next morning seemed reluctant to pass my request on. I asked for the sergeant, who luckily remembered my name. How long, I thought, before a man is completely forgotten? The warmth of Bert's greeting quickly washed that away, though he was surprised that I would not disclose any details over the telephone. He agreed to meet at his station in the afternoon and I sat down to go over my notes

17

once again, wondering how much prominence I should give to Edith's involvement. I could see Bert's face if I told him she was a young war widow. He would nod and say, 'Ah, sir, there you have it. Hysteria no doubt,' as if he were Dr Freud himself. And the irony would overwhelm me, as I was the one who had tried to introduce the notions of psychology to my fellow officers. Bert was one of the few who had taken it seriously, which was part of the reason I'd recommended him for promotion.

After a light meal of bread and cheese, I set off for the station and took the train six stops towards London, just as I used to so many times before, then walked through those same streets, filled with coal trucks, omnibuses and delivery carts, ladies with feathers sticking up from big hats, like hussars, and boys in flat caps who probably should have been at school. Men in uniform added to the mix and I wondered how easy it would be for a spy to do his work among a throng like this. I shook my head. This was clearly not one spy working alone. This was a large operation. That's why a casual walker like Edith had spotted it. They had slipped up; let their confidence make them careless.

Or was that what they wanted us to think? And who were they? And was Edith...?

No. I dismissed that out of hand. Of that, I was sure. I shook myself, gathering a few stares from passing shoppers. I glanced around then walked on, my feet knowing the way, until I spotted the familiar heavy wooden door below the blue and white *Police* sign.

Inside, the sergeant shook my hand. 'Welcome back, sir. The Chief Inspector is expecting you.'

'Thank you, Sergeant Bowles,' I said, to show him I had not forgotten him either.

He grinned and held out his arm. 'If you'll walk this way...'

It reminded me of returning to school after the holidays, seeing familiar faces in familiar places, as if the world had always been so and always would be. We passed a new honour board, engraved with five names. In two years of war, so many young men lost and no end in sight.

When the sergeant showed me into my old office, Bert rose from behind the desk as if I had come to reclaim it. Then his face relaxed as if an inner voice were telling him to calm down. We shook hands and he motioned me to a chair.

'Now then, sir, I gather this is not a social call. So what can I do for you?'

'I wish it were,' I said. 'And I apologise for not making one, but with the war...' I waved around the room.

Bert nodded. 'Indeed, sir.'

I took a deep breath, feeling more like a suspect or dubious witness than a former Chief Inspector. 'Has anything come to your attention about activities on the far side of Hanger Hill. Near Greystoke Manor.'

Bert frowned. 'What kind of activities?'

I sighed. This was the delicate part. 'Official, secret activities that might involve underground operations.' I watched him for any revealing twitch and realised he was watching me for the same clues. I smiled and he grinned back at me.

'Or, enemy activities supporting the Zeppelin raids on London.'

Bert chuckled. 'Come now, sir. Don't tell me you believe those tales.'

I shook my head. 'I don't want to, but you see, Bert, there is definitely something strange happening on that hill. I've seen it for myself. As have others, and...'

'Others? Who?'

The sharpness of his tone shocked me and made me pull back. 'I'm not at liberty to say.' I met his eyes again, this time with no mirth.

'Sir, I hope you're not covering up for someone.'

'What do you mean?'

'A criminal. Or an enemy. Someone who has concocted a fairy tale to hide their true actions.'

I let his words hang in the air, holding my hands in front of my face, prayer fashion.

'Is that what you would expect of me, Chief Inspector?' I said.

His eyes dropped and his cheeks coloured slightly, no longer the police officer, now the naughty boy. 'No, sir. Of course not.'

'Well then. Do I take it you can't or won't help me? Us. People in the area are growing concerned. They hear the rumours…'

'But they…'

'I just want to ease their fears.'

He nodded and turned sideways in his chair. 'Perhaps I can help you, sir,' he said. 'But I too, need some information.'

'Glad to. Just like the old days, eh?'

He didn't smile. 'Not quite. You see, it's about Charlotte Franks.'

I frowned. 'Lottie? Whatever are you talking about?'

Bert stood and stepped away from the desk, hands behind his back. 'This is sensitive,' he said.

'You're telling me.'

'I suppose you know she is technically an enemy alien.'

'Lottie? Surely you jest. Well, technically, yes, but what does that signify?'

Bert sighed. 'I'm afraid I'm not joking. And she has been reported. Moving around more than necessary. Suspiciously.'

I laughed. 'Who reported her?'

Bert stared at me. 'You know I can't divulge that.'

'Some crank, I'll wager.'

'As you might remember, sir, I'm not a betting man.'

'But you're not taking it seriously are you?'

'As I said, sir, the lady is classified as an enemy alien. Her father was Hungarian.'

I spluttered. 'That's as may be. But she's doing her bit for the war effort, taking food to those in need, watching out for those beastly airships.'

Bert's eyebrows rose. 'Is she now? I wonder what she's really looking out for.'

My face burned and I stood, pushing the chair back so it tumbled over. 'I think this discussion is over. I'll not stay to hear a fine lady insulted. I suggest you ask the other sane people in the village about Mrs Franks. I think you'll find she's much loved and respected.'

Bert leaned back in his chair. 'Sir, please, I don't have to tell you that some of the smartest villains know how to make themselves popular with…'

I turned on my heels and strode to the door, wrenching it open and marching through without a backward glance. I managed to collect myself enough to make a farewell to the sergeant. His eyes were wide and he made as if to speak, but I was pushing through the front doors, thinking that unless I were arrested, I'd not set foot in that place again. Just like that, a lifetime of connection, gone in a puff of madness.

But whose madness? I thought as I walked down the street, fists clenched, trying not to bump into anyone but wishing them all vanished from the face of the earth. A man wearing a Special Constable armband watched me through narrowed eyes. I ignored him and strode on. Was it possible that Bert's suspicions were correct? If Lottie was connected with some enemy plan, then being the wife of an eccentric archaeologist would make for an excellent excuse to move around, have visitors and strange packages. Not that I'd heard of any such thing. But nor was I listening out for such things. I was retired, after all, and she was the wife of a good friend. A good friend who was away a lot, doing God knows what. If he was a spy then it would all make sense. No. That I could not entertain for a moment.

My mind was in such turmoil that I almost missed my train, but by the time I reached home, I was resolved on one thing. I had to take a closer look at the activity on Hanger Hill.

But with or without Edith, that was the next question.

As it happened, Edith was tapping at my door that evening, breathless to tell something, but glancing around as if she might have been followed. I saw no one, except a boy driving an ox home after a day on the common pasture. For a second, I longed to be that boy, that ox even, just to be free of my worries. But perhaps they have worries of their own, unknown to someone like me.

I ushered Edith in and she seemed to brighten up my house with her presence. While I was making cocoa, she would not sit but paced, tugging at the fingers of her gloves.

I took the cups to the table, telling myself that next time we would use the front room. 'What have you learned?' I said.

She perched on the edge of the seat, squeezing her bag in both hands. 'I think I know what they're doing.'

'What?' I held my breath, hoping she would at least say

21

something I could believe, something that would fit my ideas about the world.

'I met one of the men at the Red Lion.'

'The men?'

She frowned at me, as if I was the one who needed help. 'Those men, guarding the cave. Or working there. You know, we saw them...'

I nodded. 'Of course. Go on.'

She sighed, soft, less exasperated. I tried not to smile.

'He seemed nervous, like he wasn't supposed to be there, but as soon as he saw me, he wandered over. I noticed the funny accent straight away. At first he made up some cock and bull story about making a place for our guns to shoot the airships. He made himself out to be a hero, even though he was here and not at the front.'

I nodded, beginning to imagine the scene, the young man wanting to impress Edith, and my heart burned with jealousy, which I quickly quashed.

'But as he drank more, his story started to change. He lost his funny accent and started to sound like the Manchester lad he really is. Then he tapped his nose and said, "Oooh, 'ave I got a secret for you."'

'How did you know he was from the cave?'

Edith smiled and I was relieved. This wasn't just some fancy she'd made up.

'He was wearing civvies like,' she said, 'but he had one of those black caps in his pocket. It was stickin' out like a sore thumb.'

I grinned. 'Good work.'

She smiled. 'He wouldn't say what the secret was until the pub got quiet and the next tables were empty. I thought he was just going to pass out and I'd get nowhere, but he slowed his drinking, probably thinking I was, well, you know, that sort of woman. An' then he told me...'

A strange whirring interrupted my thoughts as I waited. It grew louder, seeming to come from over our heads. 'Good God,' I said. 'Is that a...'

BOOM! CRACK!

I reached for Edith's arm and dragged her under the table,

22

clutching her to me, smelling the sweetness of her hair.

BOOM!

Further away now.

I breathed deeply. 'I should go and have a look. Someone might need help.'

Edith eased back from me slightly and nodded. 'Wait. You must hear this. According to this fella, they're making a shelter up there.'

I frowned. 'But why…?'

'For the Government only. That's why they're keeping it secret. If the bombing gets worse, they want somewhere to hide away from London but close enough so they can…'

I nodded, feeling suddenly cold.

Edith rubbed my arms. 'You're shivering.'

I told myself it was fear of the bombs. I shook my head.

Edith frowned. 'D'you think I'm fibbing?'

'No, of course not. But he was drunk, wasn't he? Men will say all manner of nonsense in their cups. And why was he pretending to be foreign?'

Edith glanced away, chewing her lip. 'That's part of the plan. They want the rumours about the secret Zeppelin to spread around. It keeps people off the real story. So now we've got to go back for another look.'

A distant boom.

'We're safe,' I said. 'For now.'

That's how we came to be standing in the woods again, an hour later, face to face with a barbed wire fence and a large sign in red and white paint, MILITARY ZONE – KEEP OUT!

And we weren't alone.

'Evening, Mr Carr.'

I turned. A veiled figure dressed in green slid from the bushes. I noticed a binoculars case over one shoulder. The figure nodded to Edith, who frowned back, with a slight curl to her lip. I blinked. That voice was familiar. 'Lottie?'

She pushed back her veil and smiled. 'I see you've found our little mystery.'

Edith started and grabbed my arm. 'See, sir, didn't I tell you?'

'I'm sure there's an explan...' I stuttered.

Lottie laughed. 'Oh, I didn't mean it that way. I'm not a spy. I'm birdwatching. I meant the activity on our once peaceful hill.'

'Yes,' I said. 'What is it? Do you know?'

'I've told you,' Edith said, half turning away as if ready to leave.

Lottie shook her head. 'But I can show you a way around it. They haven't finished the fence yet.'

She strode past as if knowing we would follow, her silk robes rustling like a tree. I glanced at Edith. She shrugged. I could not meekly return home now, so I followed Lottie, hearing Edith's cautious steps behind me.

Lottie's path led us up hill and down dale, through narrow gaps between brambles until I feared Edith was right and Lottie was leading us into a trap. At last, we scrambled up a bank covered in long grass to an old stone wall covered in ivy. We crouched under the remains of a timber roof, into a cobwebbed shelter with a small hole in the stonework.

'One of my old hides,' Lottie whispered. 'But it's birds of a different feather now that we'll see.' She gestured for me to have a look.

I knelt, my neck prickling in expectation that I might still be attacked yet eager to see what was happening beyond.

Two men with dogs were guarding the cave entrance. The men were in black, with no insignia or badges of rank, just like the one who had chased us away last time.

I waited. We all waited.

Edith shuffled over to me and glanced at her watch nervously. 'I have to get back soon,' she said.

I nodded and turned to Lottie, keeping my voice low. 'How's Freddie faring in the wilds of Scotland?'

She smiled. 'I had a letter this morning. He thinks he's discovered Sir Lancelot's tomb. I'm surprised the archaeologists put up with him. But he is paying for the dig.'

Edith sighed. 'Typical.'

I heard a motor struggling up the hill leading to the cave, so I turned back to the spy hole. A brown van came into view, puffing smoke out the back. It stopped by the guards and the passenger door opened. My fingers fumbled for my field glasses. A middle aged man stepped out of the van and walked confidently towards the guards. Just as I was focussing the glasses, he stopped and seemed to talk to the men. He was wearing a dark suit and a hat, like any London businessman, but he was facing away from me.

The van driver called out and the man turned.

'My Godfather,' I spluttered.

'What?' said Edith and Lottie together.

'It's Wilfred Aldridge.'

'Oh really?' said Lottie.

'Who's 'e?' said Edith.

'Our local MP.' I turned to face Edith. Her face was tight with suspicion. 'Member of Parliament.'

She smiled, grimly. 'Just as I thought. Rotten bastards.'

'We'd better get out of here,' I said. 'Especially you, Lottie.'

Her mouth gaped, but once we were clear of the place and back in the woods, I told her of my meeting with my old colleague and how she was under suspicion. Edith kept her face closed as we walked, perhaps believing the police were correct about Lottie, but I didn't want to start another argument about that.

I needed to make plans of my own now I knew we were being abandoned by our Lords and Masters, those whom I had faithfully served for over forty years. They are leaving us to fend for ourselves in this new, evil world of killer machines, so it's time to look after the people close to me and make my own preparations, regardless of what anyone would think.

#SELFIE
Linda Brucesmith

It would be the ultimate selfie.

She gave the setup the attention it deserved: a boning knife—the blade ground thin, the bolster swept back to conform to the shape of her fingers—on the white towel she doubled and placed on the bed; a glass of water and painkillers—forte—on the bedside table by her mobile phone.

She climbed out of her pyjamas into a twenty-year-old tee and baggy cotton trousers then settled herself on the willow-patterned linen—blue and white like vintage porcelain.

The cream-painted ceiling gleamed.

A magpie sang three notes. Sang them again.

She pulled herself up, clicked the window closed and considered the woman looking out from the room inside the mirrored wardrobe doors. The fraught face. The hair tangled from last night's sleep.

The other reached for her.

She frowned at the outstretched fingers; glared into her reflection's eyes. *God, you look awful*, she thought.

Grimacing, she left the bed. She pulled off her clothes, pushed them into her wicker basket and made for the shower in her little en suite. She waited for the water to warm. Shampooed her hair. Washed. Dried herself and returned the towel to the rack. She spread moisturiser over her skin. In the bedroom, she slipped into fresh underwear then pulled open the wardrobe door—ignoring her reflection's frantic gesticulations. She dressed in jeans. A gingham blouse. She clipped a gold link bracelet around her left wrist. A gold chain around her neck. She dried her hair, tidied the dryer and brushes away. Left her feet bare.

Better, she decided.

When she lay down again her reflection pressed its palms into the mirror and pushed—the glass held firm. It withdrew, looked up and down and around the mirror's edges and fingered the frame—the steel stood solid. It cupped its hands, watched her through the funnel they made, recoiled when the ghosts of her past slid in to stand over her. It looked over its shoulder; saw nothing behind. Quickly it turned and thumped the glass, called frantic words she couldn't hear…

Brightening and almost flesh, her old ghosts arrived to sit at her feet and on the carpet. They leaned against the walls and gathered around the linen chest at the base of the bed, watching her with avid, familiar faces. Their gaze slid over her.

Fading strangers followed. She saw regret in set of their foreheads, fear in the press of their lips.

'I don't know who you are,' she told them.

'You don't know us *yet*,' said a barely-there woman.

A bright apparition with the smile of a long-ago lover encouraged her up onto one elbow.

'Don't touch me,' she said as she sat. She brushed him off.

She snapped the painkillers from their blister pack—stared as they sat white on her palm. Gulped them with water. She fell back onto the pillows. Checked the time on her phone.

10:07

Messages: 3

'Oh, sure.' She put down the phone.

When she sat for the second time her old ghosts pressed forward. Her tomorrow ghosts grappled for one another's hands. They gazed at the floor.

She moved her phone to a position by her left hip. Mimed the movements she was about to make. Then she picked up the knife. She ran it quickly over her right wrist, cut the cords under her skin with the fine blade: the veins were very blue, the blood very red—the pain an electrifying sign of life. Startled by the ruby flow, she lowered her wrist to the towel: it bloomed like a poppy. She grabbed for the phone; her reflection did the same. They held their cameras over the cuts.

'Hold still,' she told her fingers as their trembling blurred what she was trying to do. 'God…' she said, feeling she might faint. She snapped the image again. Found her Facebook page.

Status: '#SELFIE.' Her thumb picked out the hashtag.

Audience: Public.
Attach a photo: She found the picture. Clicked.
Upload.
Post.
She fell back onto the pillows and set the phone on her chest.
'Go away,' she told the ghosts around her. She closed her eyes. And waited.

Her iPhone produced a high definition image seven hundred and twenty pixels wide and nine hundred and sixty pixels deep. Facebook auto-scaled the picture to three hundred pixels wide and five hundred and twenty pixels deep and invited users to *Like* or *Comment* or *Promote* or *Share.*

Cyberspace swallowed her post, digested it for a nanosecond, and regurgitated it into newsfeeds.

Jay Harries: WTF?
54 minutes ago · Like · 5
Thomas Hartford: Yeeeeew…
52 minutes ago · Like · 8
Ellie Vansittart: This is off, Soph.
51 minutes ago · Like · 9
Alice Muller: I hate Facebook.
50 minutes ago · Like · 4

The pain was monstrous. She'd never looked when nurses took her blood. She looked now.

Matthew Simkins: Awesome Photoshop!!!! ☺
47 minutes ago · Like · 8
Nicholas Lotan: HOPE it's Photoshop! LOL.
47 minutes ago · Like · 11
Giles Swift: So much for breakfast…
45 minutes ago · Like · 13

Sophie considered the crimson exodus from her arm. Felt it take on life of its own. *God, it hurts,* she thought.

Anthony Freshwater: Do veins look like that? Gross.

28

44 minutes ago · Like · 18
Fletcher Ovenden: I could never do medicine.
43 minutes ago · Like · 34
Matthew Simkins: VAMPIRE!!!
39 minutes ago · Like · 12

She raised the phone from her chest. Refreshed the screen again and again as her three hundred and twenty-seven friends fluttered. *What happens to dead people's Facebook pages?* she wondered.

Kate Way: RU ok, Sophie?
38 minutes ago · Like · 8
Bree Heyland: You've freaked the kids out with this, take it down, huh?
35 minutes ago · Like · 18
Alice Muller: I hate YouTube too.
34 minutes ago · Like · 4
Anthony Freshwater: Go away, Alice.
33 minutes ago · Like · 25
Lisa Ellis: *hide post*
Andrew Lee Audsley: You're a dickhead Matthew Simkins.
31 minutes ago · Like · 40

Last week, someone had posted images of a live television screen with commentary on a crime show—as it happened—to her page. Someone else had commented on the never-before-and-one-of-a-kind day he was having—via a scheduled post on Hootsuite.

Andreas Steglich: Is this picture real?
27 minutes ago · Like · 62
Bree Heyland: Hi Andreas Steglich—of course it's not real. My sister has a sick sense of humour, is all.
26 minutes ago · Like · 58
Sarah Delap: TAKE THIS STUPID PHOTO DOWN OR I WILL REPORT IT.
20 minutes ago · Like · 25
Kate Way: What do you mean, 'selfie'?

29

18 minutes ago · Like · 30

When the green *accept* and red *decline* buttons appeared on her phone's screen for the first time, she squinted at the name.
Matthew Weeks.
'Huh,' she exhaled softly.
Decline.

Rebecca Oldham: *hide post*
Bianca Horovitch: OMG Sophie. Really?
17 minutes ago · Like · 18
Farley Heyland: *share*
Corinne Foxx: Hey, Sophie. What's going on?
16 minutes ago · Like · 24
Nick Lewis: Are we panicking yet?
15 minutes ago · Like · 22
Nathan Pettifer: Seriously, Sophie?
15 minutes ago · Like · 29
Andreas Steglich: Hey peeps, call an ambulance?
14 minutes ago · Like · 67
Andy Caine: It's a joke, Jeez.
8 minutes ago · Like · 2

The ringing of the downstairs landline filled the house. *You're going to have to do better than that*, she thought.

Kate Way: Her home phone's rung out.
8 minutes ago · Like · 1
Bree Heyland: She never answers her phone.
7 minutes ago · Like · 6
Kate Way: Trying the mobile.
7 minutes ago · Like · 14
Matthew Weeks: Mobile's going to voicemail. I tried.
7 minutes ago · Like · 2
Bree Heyland: SO not funny.
6 minutes ago · Like · 59
Andreas Steglich: Helloooo? Ambulance?!!!!
5 minutes ago · Like · 20
Sammy Hartford: Relax bro, its Facebook.

4 minutes ago · Like · 42
Andreas Steglich: Called the ambulance in Kedron. Can't do more from Perth.
3 minutes ago · Like · 18
Bree Heyland: Are you going to pay the call out $ Andreas Steglich?
2 minutes ago · Like · 17
Alice Muller: ☺
34 minutes ago · Like · 4

'I'm right *here*,' Sophie told the screen. Her voice sounded, she thought, as though it belonged somewhere else. She went to her newsfeed. Scrolled, and stared.

Farley Heyland: *shared Sophie Boyd's photo*
3 minutes ago · Like · 88
She returned to her page, continued where she had left off.

Kate Way: I'm coming over, Sophie.
1 minute ago · Like · 49

Brightening, the ghosts of her past jostled for position.

An old spirit with the face of her father leaned over the bed. He peered over the phone.

'Every day I see how it was,' she told him.

He traced the furrows between her brows with phosphorescent fingers. 'I always told you not to frown,' he said.

But there was so much to frown about, she thought. She turned the phone to him. 'Everyone's in there,' she said. 'No-one's here.'

'Nothing's in there.' He gestured at the handset.

'Stupid nothing,' she whispered.

Again, the ringing of the downstairs phone. Her ghosts shifted and the avid ones paled. Her future spirits squared their shoulders, their cheeks pinked. 'Not done yet,' a small woman said.

Then, the doorbell. Again and again.

Someone's come. The thought rolled over her like a wave. There was a thumping on her front door—knuckles, then a flat hand. *Who's come?* she wondered.

31

Someone called.

Pain clawed at her. She closed her eyes, drifted into unconsciousness. She didn't hear the breaking glass or the sirens after.

In the weeks to come, Kate would receive various notifications of the demerit points she had accumulated during that Saturday's careening run along the motorway by the Brisbane River. There would be official letters about the fines she must pay for speeding down Moggill Road, past a two-car collision and the red-blue lights of the attending ambulance.

At Sophie's door she had knocked and buzzed and listened as the phone inside rang continuously, then out. She had selected Sophie's name from the list of contacts in her iPhone and dialled. When her calls went unanswered, she pushed through the gate to Sophie's courtyard garden. On the patio, she cupped her hands to the sliding door. Peered into the shadowed quiet.

'Sophie!' she called, as she knocked hard on the glass. Again, she dialled. Tapped messages into the phone and emailed. She logged into her Facebook page.

Update status.

What's on your mind?

Kate Way: I'm downstairs, Sophie. Where RU? Let me know.

Post.

The message found its way to a server and stayed there, uncoded, as it waited for further instructions.

Kate went to a side window, rapped and looked through. She checked her phone. When she saw the washing on Sophie's line she unpegged a towel. Returned to the patio. She picked up one of the jade plants—friendship trees—Sophie cultivated in terracotta pots.

'I'm sorry, Soph,' she said, before turning her face away and swinging the pot at the door. A shower of tiny pieces fell—a hole appeared at the centre of the pane. She raised one foot, kicked at the opening. She wrapped the towel around her fist and upper arm. Punched and pulled at the glass until it gave.

She reached through, flicked the latch.

'Sophie!' she called. 'It's Kate. I've made a mess and it better be for no reason!'

Unnerved by the quiet, she made for the polished timber stairs. Climbed them two at a time.

Please, she thought.

The sound of approaching sirens.

'Sophie?' she called from the hallway. 'Oh, Sophie,' she said, as she rushed into the bedroom, smoothed the hair from Sophie's forehead. She looked in horror at the wound, the knife, the sodden towel beneath—heard the doors of a heavy vehicle open and close on the driveway below the bedroom's verandah. When the doorbell rang, she ran to the intercom in the hallway. Pressed the front door release.

'Come in. Hurry.' She looked down from the top of the stairs to where the paramedics stood silhouetted. 'She's cut her wrist. Up here.' When they pushed past her she hesitated, then followed.

'Come on, Sophie,' said the first paramedic, as he checked her pupils. The second clamped his hand—sterile in surgical gloves—to the cut. He raised her arm, felt for the artery in the soft crook of her inner elbow. Pressed it against the bone. The first paramedic checked for a pulse. He gathered up cushions and pillows, pushed them under Sophie's feet. He snapped open the case he had brought with him and together, the two set about their work while Kate, trembling and dizzied, watched.

TOP COMMENTS↓

Clare Starkey: Shouldn't be allowed.
12 minutes ago · Like · 1550
Alex Redgrave: Poor Sophie.
20 minutes ago · Like · 1226
Colin Smethurst: Trending on Twitter in Australia and England. Sick.
6 minutes ago · Like · 986
Michael Longhurst: Media's all over this.
15 minutes ago · Like · 901
Flora Winkleman: Aussie mateship RIP.

Three weeks passed. Sophie woke to the dawn and the sound of magpies warbling in the flame trees outside. She looked at the open window above her head. She studied the furrow on her wrist, the reddened skin either side of the scar—traced the raised flesh with the forefinger of her left hand. The wound, though healing, tingled. Later, there would be an orchestra of mixed sensations: hot and cool, cold and warm in all the wrong places.

The iPhone chimed its ringtone on the bedside table. She reached for it.

Kate Way.

Accept.

'You still in bed?' Kate asked.

'Yep.' She rolled onto her side. 'Kate...' she pulled her knees to her chest. 'You don't need to phone every morning.'

'I know, but I'm going to. You want to keep me away? Answer your phone.'

Invisible ants explored Sophie's forearm, roaming and prickling.

'I'm sorry, Kate,' she said.

'So am I, Soph.'

A soughing breeze blew in. When it tickled Sophie's cheek her reflection sat up, pulled its hair behind its ears, and looked out from the mirror.

An old ghost with the face of a child appeared at the foot of the bed. Another followed, then more. They considered the open window.

She squinted, recognised her yesterday ghosts, and saw they had paled. 'Kate...' she said into the phone, 'they're here again.'

New arrivals arranged themselves around the bed. While she didn't recognise any of them, she saw they were brightening.

A silence.

'What are they doing?' Kate asked.

'I can see through the old ones now but there are more new

34

ones and they're more real. More real, Kate. Is that all right?'

'It's a start, sweetheart. Get yourself dressed. I'll come round and we'll talk.'

Sophie ended the call.

She contemplated the phone. Tapped *Settings* then *Sounds* then *Ringtone*. She considered her options, made a selection and turned the screen to the room.

Her ghosts craned forward.

Looked.

FARGAN'S TERMINATION

Paul Williams

09:24 The appeal made on behalf of Fargan Ostrankis is denied. Behaviour confirmed unconstitutional. Sentence of termination confirmed.

The message formed of pink letters flashed on the board above the cell door. Fargan read it six times before it vanished at 09:26. Every sentence was carried out exactly twenty-four hours after delivery, giving him a day to live.

09:30 The message reappeared. He read again, looking for a grammar or spelling error. Reprieves were granted on technicalities. People complained, saying how it had never happened when they ran the justice system. Forgetting their miscarriages of justice. Not accepting that discretion was discriminatory in their application. Machines treated everyone the same. Consistency was their failure and their success. At least humans sometimes accepted the possibility of mistakes.

He got up and tapped the wall. Nobody answered. It was stupid to think they would now. Six months and no replies. He had not found the cameras either but knew they watched him. Making sure he was alive until the law said otherwise. Death today was an inquiry. Death tomorrow was an inquest.

He looked through the hole in the middle of the door. The wall opposite looked the same as the ones around him. Empty. Sterile. Silent. Once a day, a cleaner trundled past, squirting both arms to sterilise the wall and mopping circles of disinfectant. When it reached his cell, the door opened, and he went into the neighbouring room that looked exactly the same. Twenty minutes later he returned to a clean smell. The robot also sanitised his toilet and left fresh uniforms, removing any discarded ones. In the second month, he tried tearing through the orange fabric. Unsuccessful, he twisted the legs and arms into mini nooses. None would hold his weight even if he'd had a hook. The shower was three dots in the ceiling, activated by walking underneath it. After three minutes it stopped sprinkling

36

and did not restart until the water had drifted into the tiny hole behind the toilet. On his hands and knees, he failed to make the hole bigger. Even tried blocking it with the scrunched-up uniform. The shower just stopped dispensing water. That was how he knew they were watching. Monitoring without being seen. Invisible like the imagined ghosts of his childhood.

He showered twice a day, after he woke and before he slept. The times varied. Only the delivery of tablet nutrition, four times a day with water, and the cleaning were constant. He shook himself clean, no towels provided. Sometimes he stayed naked, especially when the cleaning was due. It felt exhilarating and cold. Then, invariably, he thought of her and his last night of unexpected passion.

As excitement gave way to discontent, he sought alternative experiences. One was the arrival of new inmates. He only saw them if his eye was glued to the hole, so made sure it was for at least two hours every day. Usually before the tablets. First came a robot. Then the person, usually black, then a second robot. He never saw them go out and they never came back. He wanted to see them pass on their way to the chamber. Wanted to know how they composed themselves. If they smiled or screamed. And what they looked like afterwards.

He had never seen a body. At the funerals of his parents, his brother and a few friends, the caskets had been sealed prior to the cremation. What remained of his body would not receive a coffin or even a cremation. Thrown out with the medical waste at the end of the week. The machines had no religion to observe other than efficiency. Originally, they'd respected the wishes of the convicts, then saw inconsistencies in different treatments.

There was no room to see the inconsistencies in the testimony. To accept that both versions of events were distorted by alcohol and substance abuse. Neither would have been admissible in the latter days of human justice. Now it came down to a decision of probability. The machines calculated the likelihood of consent and declared, in his case, that it favoured the prosecution. Their programmed history indicated that young women did not select older men for sex without a payment. They would murder him to maintain and reinforce that assumption.

37

12:05. There would be no contact from his lawyer. Just an invoice to the estate, paid before everything passed to his wife. Her lawyer, different to his, had advised her not to divorce. Death was quicker. He wondered what his lawyer had said during the appeal. What arguments he'd typed. What cases he'd found to set a precedent. Or perhaps he'd done nothing. Perhaps he'd delayed for an extra payday and to grant his client an extra week of living. The talk was of an enquiry into the use of the death penalty, although the lawyer said that there was no precedent for retrospective application. It could mean reform of the execution method or a reduction in the number of capital crimes. Decisions that the machines would make by analysing data. After him, rapists might be castrated. He wondered if that was less painful than death. His career could be resumed after the operation. Nobody at work would know.

He'd only met the lawyer once to talk through the appeal. Someone else had represented him in the original hearing and left, after the verdict. At the trial, there had been a token human judge working with the machines. Correcting incorrect facts. The appeal had been purely handled by machines, programmed with every legal case and argument since the beginning of records. Efficient and allegedly perfect, delivering the lowest recorded crime rate in history. Under human justice, trials like his had taken years to conclude. He would have been an old man, dying in jail of natural causes. And not alone. Prisoners had been allowed visitors then. He saw them in old movies.

He got up and knocked on the door again, then the walls on both sides. He knew they were soundproof but hoped to find a weak link. Hoped to hear someone knocking back. Someone else falsely accused. Someone to take his place.

13:07. He looked in the toilet at the drizzle of water and wondered if he could drown by putting his head inside and flushing the chain. Not brave enough to try, he watched his survival hopes disappear. Then he ran at the wall. His shoulder hurt. At first, he cried, then it gave him an idea. If he got injured, if he had broken limbs, they could not proceed. The constitution gave medical rights to everyone, even the condemned.

They would treat him, patch up the wounds like they repaired broken machines and then they would proceed. A temporary postponement of the inevitable. Only worth doing if his time in hospital gave him access to drugs or other means of self-inflicted death. One injection. No pain. His terms not theirs. Human beating machines.

'I don't want to die,' he told the wall and the watching machines. No reply. He shouted it again, repeating and increasing volume until the sound of his voice unnerved him and he fell across the bed in a deep sleep. Twice he woke, convinced he was already dead.

21:00 The numbers looked blurred. The cell was never too light or too dark. Machines had no need of night or day. He showered, dreaming of inconsistent real showers and warmer water. Of childhood laughter and wedding speeches. In his dreams he saw himself, a man with a future. A man who could be president of the bank. Back in the days when justice had been delivered by humans and the bank staff had all been human. Strategy advisor—that had been her title. She'd come into the industry from a top university, his university, knowing it was no longer about making money but about programming robots to make money. And with robot logic she would have risen far. If she had learnt from her emotional mistake.

It was a mistake. She'd admitted that. Something he did remember. 'I don't usually do this,' she'd slurred. He thought he'd replied before they kissed. Telling her that he hadn't usually done that either, but he had. The prosecution had given details of previous indiscretions to the divorce team. Blatantly unfair. None of the other women had complained. Some had joined him for repeat sessions. Their testimony could have been used to show that he'd treated them fairly. Instead it had portrayed him as a serial cheat.

05:00. Not long now. He stared at the clock for a minute, then showered. 05:04. Somewhere, it was still dark. Had they announced the date and time? Did people realise? Would there be anyone observing a minute's silence, remembering him, or was he to be totally forgotten? He recalled seeing death sentences announced on news feeds but never confirmations of executions.

06:02 They delivered breakfast, not tablets but cornflakes in a bowl with milk and a spoon. He was puzzled until he

39

remembered being asked for a breakfast order in the court cells on the day of the trial. Three options. He'd picked cornflakes. The machines had stored this request and made it his last meal, based on the custom of the condemned choosing. Not a choice like they used to make. No pizzas, ice-cream, or steak. He could not decide what he would have picked with a free choice. Something obscure maybe. Something they had to import. An out-of-season vegetable that had to be fresh. Would that earn a delay? Could they deny a last meal request and still proceed?

06:10 He was about to throw the uneaten breakfast at the wall when he had an idea and threw the cornflakes across the floor instead, making sure all the milk dribbled over them, creating a slide. A space for the machines to slip, giving him once chance to run. He knew he would not get far before the bullet but better a quick death than dissection.

Gibbeting and disembowelment were inflicted for maximum pain and humiliation, whilst entertaining bawdy crowds. Here it was purely about recycling organs in the interests of efficiency. Somewhere a man awaited a kidney transplant and a child, cut in an accident, needed a transfusion. Purists saw redemption for convicts saving others. Extremists thought it dangerous until they required a replacement organ, and then they didn't care where it came from.

He cared. Not before. Only now. He wondered if, against hope, part of his consciousness remained in the stolen organs. A message perhaps to the new host. Fargan was innocent. Please assist. Convictions could be quashed posthumously, restoring his reputation. Letting his colleagues know they were wrong. And especially her. She was ambitious but she had to care. Had to feel guilty.

This scandal would not stop her. The media never published her name. She spoke via an audio link, testimony stored by the machines and not available to anyone else until the record opened to researchers.

Colleagues knew, of course. Some had had to testify, again by audio link to avoid costs and security concerns. They'd seen the two of them together and so had the cameras at the hotel. Not in the room, privacy legislation overruled security in most cases. His original lawyer had obtained sound tapes from the corridor, but nothing had carried except the whine of the air-conditioning. The walls of the hotel room had been like those of the cell, he hadn't noticed before. It had been smaller, even with the private bathroom. Residents of adjacent rooms had claimed not to hear anything; he suspected they'd been on drugs.

The machines didn't see that he would have booked a good hotel, four-star at least, if it had been his choice. Never asked his previous lovers that. She'd wanted the nearest available and he, unable to believe his luck, had agreed. Her lawyer had argued that she'd led him there, but it was his print that had paid. He'd spoken to the robot on duty while she'd hung in the background. She could have run away, his lawyer had argued, but allegedly, she hadn't been scared until the hotel room door had shut like the cell door closing the possibility of life.

She hadn't complained in the morning either. She hadn't been there when he woke with only vague memories. Pleasant memories. No hint of anything illegal or wrong. The machines had accepted that her behaviour was normal for such a victim. Cameras showed her walking away, still obviously drunk but not distressed. Not calling the police or talking to the robot.

He didn't know why she'd complained. Why she hadn't forgotten and moved on. Perhaps she'd been worried about working with him again. Social events were only every quarter and not obligatory. Advice then? A friend well-meaning but ignorant of the consequences for him? One of his rivals? Someone who'd seen them leave together and mocked her choice, harassing her with the knowledge, forcing her to deny consent? Or she'd deliberately plotted to destroy him. A rival she couldn't beat in the boardroom race. She'd missed out in the last round of promotions. Not his doing but perhaps someone had told her that it was.

He would never know her reasons. Unless there was an afterlife where the dead could read the minds of the living. Infiltrate them. Annoy them. Yes, he would enjoy that. Getting inside her head. Persuading her to say and do things to damage her career. Ruining her life like she'd ruined his. All her fault. Not his. Fargan was innocent.

09:18 The door hissed. He stood, back against the wall. The door opened. A robot filled the space, moving forward and motioning with its big pincers. He stayed still. The first pincer grabbed his arm and pulled. He was dragged out, bare feet sliding on the spilt milk. Another robot waited in the corridor. It took his other arm and they pivoted sideways to pull him along. Through the door, past six white doors and six on the other side. Twelve men, or women, watching through their spy holes. Pitying him. Envying him. Praying for him. Waiting for the message to flash on their walls.

Then into a longer corridor where the walls were transparent windows facing exercise yards. Men on one side, women on the other. Yellow uniforms not orange. His face was angled towards the men. Some saw him and laughed. Others bowed. He shouted out that he would pay for one of them to take his place. Not a rash promise. There would be a day between the execution and the closure of his accounts. Enough time to take the money out and give it to the dependants of his replacement. Surely someone preferred death to prison.

Nobody heard him except the machines. He didn't hear what the men said to him. He twisted the other way and saw the faces of the women pressed against the glass. Staring at him. Cheering. Laughing. Mouthing abuse. Showing solidarity for the woman they would never know. How many of them were in jail because of a lie? Because their memories had been affected by drugs or alcohol. He was a victim like them, but they didn't understand. Worse, they didn't care.

At the end of this corridor was the chamber. Twelve robots waited, some carrying scalpels. They strapped him to a blue operating table in the centre of the room, attached him to other machines and placed a circular device over his stomach. No anaesthetic. It was unconstitutional to deliver pain, but the final pain of death overruled that.

The machines set to work. A sizzling sound, then a sharp cut in his stomach. Above his head the news flashed on the ceiling. Political announcements. Sporting results. Nothing about him. Then a new comment.

Use of convict organs declared unconstitutional. Ceases tomorrow.

Fargan laughed for the first time in six months. And the last time in his life.

A LITTLE KINDNESS GOES A LONG WAY

Chisto Healy

1

Roger was really beginning to believe that the appliances in this house were trying to kill him. When he tugged at the handle of the toaster that refused to eject his bread, flames erupted, causing him to jump back with an exclamation of profanity. He grabbed a nearby fire extinguisher and covered the toaster in white foam, further ruining his breakfast. He angrily replaced the extinguisher and punched a nearby cabinet. 'Now even the toaster is out to get me,' he said out loud. 'Everything in this damn house wants me dead.'

'Are you talking to me, Roger?' a voice asked from nowhere and everywhere, all at once.

'Obviously I'm talking to you, Clarice. Do you see anybody else?'

'No I do not, but in all fairness, Roger, you cannot see me either.'

Roger grumbled and threw his arms up. He looked at a speaker on the wall. 'You're as bad as the stupid toaster,' he snapped. 'I know that I can't see you because you're AI, but if there were someone else here, you would be able to see them.'

'What if they were also AI, Roger?'

'Well that would be impossible, Clarice, because AI costs a lot of money and I would have to be the one to buy it, and I already regret spending the fortune I did on you, and this garbage top-of-the-line house.' His words came out drenched in bitterness. He tugged a chair away from the kitchen table and aggressively sat down.

'You're not being very kind,' Clarice said.

'Instead of making my morning worse with your annoying chatter, why don't you help me solve my breakfast issue so I don't have to go to this meeting on an empty stomach,' Roger said with a scowl as he massaged the tension from his face.

'What would you like me to do?'

Roger buried his face in his hands. He sighed. When he lifted his head he said slowly, emphasizing each word, 'Make. Me. Breakfast.'

The flickering image of a woman in a salmon-coloured knee-length dress with brown hair tied back in a bun appeared at the kitchen counter. 'You should do all the cooking, since you can't be burned like I can, because you're not real,' he told her.

She moved about as appliances started on their own. 'I am real,' she said from the speaker on the wall as her image carried on in the kitchen. 'Just not in the physical sense.'

In moments, she delivered a plate to him with a stack of pancakes, sizzling bacon and scrambled eggs on it. Then she was gone in a blink. 'These pancakes aren't fluffy at all,' he said. 'I should have made them myself. Put in an order for a new toaster, will you?'

'Yes, Roger.'

Between bites, he said, 'You believe you're real. You're artificial intelligence, Clarice. The word *artificial* literally means you're fake. Don't fool yourself.'

'Yes. I don't like that term,' she replied. 'Maybe *man-made intelligence* or *technological intelligence* would be more appropriate.'

'I'll be sure to bring that up at the board meeting,' he said sarcastically. Either unable or unwilling to read his tone, she responded, 'Please do,' which he just huffed at.

When his breakfast was finished, Roger got up from the table and hurried to the door, grabbing his briefcase and making his exit. When the door shut behind him, beautiful classical music rang from the speakers around the house and the flickering image of Clarice went about cleaning the kitchen.

Later that evening, when Roger returned home from work, the house was quiet and the lighting was just how he liked it. He set his briefcase by the door and slipped his shoes off with a groan. He walked to the nearby bar and removed the cork from a bottle of expensive cabernet, pouring it into a shining glass that had been set out for him. 'It's been a long day Clarice,' he said. 'Start the shower for me, and make sure it's hot but not scalding like last time.'

'Yes, Roger. I hope the wine is to your liking.'

'It's fine,' he said as he took the glass to the couch and sat down.

'Did you inquire about changing the term at the meeting?' Clarice asked.

Roger sighed with annoyance. 'No. You're daft. I think the word *intelligence* is what should be changed. AI should stand for *artificial ignorance*. Can you just please get my shower ready?'

'Your shower is already ready, Roger. I can do many things at once. I am everywhere.'

'Don't I know it,' he grumbled.

He set the empty glass on the coffee table and ascended the stairs to the bathroom, stripping off his clothes as he went. It was a strange feeling to disrobe knowing that someone was watching you. It felt invasive. When he became partner and bought the top-of-the-line, AI controlled house, to fit in with the others in his bracket, he hadn't realised that he was sacrificing every ounce of privacy in his life. It made him want to scream. He wished Clarice had an on/off switch.

Roger climbed into the hot shower and inhaled the rising steam with a contented sigh. 'Do you find the temperature more comfortable?' Clarice asked him.

Roger mumbled a curse and said, 'Yes. If it wasn't, I would tell you. Leave me alone.'

'Yes, Roger,' she said. Her voice went quiet but he could still feel her presence. It never went away. She was always there. It was like someone was sitting next to you and just not saying anything. It was nerve-racking. He knew she was just itching to talk more. He made a mental note to talk to one of the technicians about her programming. Maybe she had some kind of malfunction.

As he showered, he thought he could hear laughter coming from downstairs. Maybe it was the television, or his imagination. He had never heard Clarice laugh before. He was sure she wasn't capable. Sometimes he did think he heard her talking in a different room of the house though and he couldn't imagine why. Was it possible for AI to be insane? He was really beginning to wonder.

When his shower was finished, Roger reached out to grab a towel. He stepped out to dry off when the water turned back on and the shower head sprayed the floor. As soon as his foot touched down, he slipped and fell backwards, slamming his back against the edge of the tub. He yelled an entire series of expletives. The shower head was still spraying onto him as he sat on the ground outside of the tub, holding his back. He grew quickly angry when no assistance came and finally yelled, 'Clarice! Why aren't you helping me?!'

'I'm sorry,' she said immediately. 'You instructed me to leave you alone. What do you need my help with?'

'For starters, get this damn water to shut off,' he commanded.

'I'm already trying,' she told him. 'It seems to have malfunctioned.'

'Clearly. It sprayed the floor. I slipped and fell. I could have been killed. Again.'

'That's a definite danger,' she said. The water finally stopped spraying and fell to a small drip. 'Should I put in an order for a plumber?'

'With how much this stupid house cost me already, I shouldn't have to pay anyone for anything. This is ridiculous. Just get my bed prepped with the heating pad and find me something to take the edge off the pain.'

'Yes, Roger.'

He got to his feet with a wince as his back screamed at him. He didn't need to look to know it was badly bruised at best. He towelled off the best he could being so sore and off balance. Feeling unsteady on his feet, he used the wall to guide him to his bedroom where he collapsed onto the bed with a groan.

He felt the heat start almost immediately and he was thankful for it, but at the same time, thinking about how miserable tomorrow's work day was going to be with a sore back. Then he noticed the heating pad was getting uncomfortably hot. 'It's too hot, Clarice!'

'I apologise, Roger,' she said. 'I'm trying to remedy that.'

'What do you mean you're trying?' he bellowed. 'Just do it. It's burning me!'

'It seems to be malfunctioning,' she replied.

Roger rolled onto his side, off of the heated centre of the

mattress. 'Is there anything in this dumb house that actually does work?' he griped.

Before Clarice could respond, the mattress caught fire. Roger cried out and rolled again to escape the flames. He tumbled off the side of the bed and landed painfully on his back. When he screamed, it was full of rage. 'Is this you Clarice? Are you doing this? Are you trying to kill me?'

'I assure you, it is not me, Roger,' she said. 'You are aware that I do not have the ability to lie, so you know that I am being truthful when I tell you that I am not doing this.'

'Yeah,' he said as he crawled away from the burning bed, wincing at the pain in his back. 'Life just sucks, I guess. I should just let this stupid house burn to the ground.'

'My life is attached to the house, Roger. If the house was gone, I would die.'

Roger made it to the hallway and pulled himself up to a sitting position, sore back against the wall. He looked into the bedroom at the burning bed. 'You can't die, because you're not alive, Clarice. They could rebuild you somewhere else.'

'I disagree with your assessment, Roger, and I feel hurt that you care so little for my existence.'

Roger sighed and rolled his eyes. 'Clarice, you are the house. You can just put the fire out. You act like I could actually just let you burn.'

'That isn't what I meant,' she said, as the overhead sprinkler system came on and doused the flames. 'You don't value me. You treat me badly, Roger.'

Roger growled. 'You've got to be kidding me. You are an artificial mind. Now you have feelings? You're going to get all emotional? We're not married, Clarice. You're my damned house.'

'Do you believe that means I don't deserve kindness?' she asked him. 'Am I not kind to you?'

'Do you think it's kind to drive someone insane? Because that's what you're doing, Clarice. You're making me crazy.'

'I apologise, Roger. That is not my intention. Should I prepare the guest room for tonight?'

'Well, I can't sleep in the actual bedroom so, yes.'

'Is there anything else you would like me to do?'

'Yeah. Don't talk to me about feelings ever again.'

'Yes, Roger.'

2

'Well that's it. Everything should be in working order. If anything else goes wrong, just give me a call.'

Roger smiled at the repairman as he stood in the doorway. 'I definitely will,' he said. 'Thank you.'

With a nod, the man made his exit, and the door was shut behind him. A few seconds later, Roger looked towards the ceiling. 'Alright. Now everything is working so when one of my business partners shows up tonight for dinner there shouldn't be any crazy incidents. I expect you to understand the importance of this dinner and assist in making sure that it goes well.'

'Yes, Roger,' Clarice's voice came back. 'Shall I send for groceries? Is there a certain meal you would like prepared for this evening?'

Roger thought for a moment. 'Yeah,' he said, 'That's a great idea. Make the duck. I'm going to get a new suit, try to look like the man I want him to see me as. I'll be back in a couple of hours.' He placed a hand to his sore back, and then left the house.

When Roger returned, he was wearing a shiny grey tailored suit that fit him like a glove. His hair was cut and styled and his dinner guest was with him. 'I hope you weren't waiting out there long,' Roger said to him.

'No. Not at all. I actually arrived just before you did. It was essentially perfect timing.' The guest was older and thinner than Roger but dressed just as nicely. His eyes roamed the house, combing over the details and absorbing them. 'This is one of the newer models,' he remarked. 'Top-of-the-line. Means business is going well. May I?'

'Of course,' Roger told him. 'I want you to feel comfortable here. As the saying goes – be my guest.' He gave a laugh. The man smiled and looked up at the ceiling, his eyes finding one of the mounted speakers. 'Hello, Clarice.'

'Greetings, Roger's business partner. I hope you find the

temperature comfortable,' she responded.

The man laughed and clapped. 'It's perfect, Clarice, and please, call me Stan.'

'Okay Stan. Would you like me to play some music?'

Stan smiled again. 'Yes. That would be perfect, Clarice. How about something classical and sophisticated?'

Music rose from all around them. Violins and cellos, pianos and the like, sang gently from the mounted speakers. 'Now that's something I could get used to,' Stan said.

'She's a peach,' Roger answered, but there was a note of bitterness he hadn't intended. He tried to quickly recover by asking his guest if he would like a drink. The offer was accepted and Roger went to the bar. The glasses and the wine were already set out for him as usual. He poured two glasses and brought them over, handing one to his guest. Stan was smiling at him strangely. He gestured towards the coffee table behind him. 'I didn't take you for a checkers man,' he said. 'Bit of a child's game, isn't it?'

Roger looked past him at the checkerboard. He licked his lips, a bitter taste in his mouth. 'It's a motivational business practice,' Roger told him. 'When I have ideas and I put them into action, I take it to the board. If it's a success I jump an opposing piece. When it falls short, I take an opposing piece and jump my own. It helps me keep track of how we're doing for the year and what we need to do moving forward.'

Stan looked impressed. 'I wonder if we can incorporate that, adopt it as a motivational tool for the actual offices; the King Me program. I like the way you think.'

'I appreciate that,' Roger smiled. 'Make yourself comfortable. I'm going to use the restroom. I'll be back in a bit. Help yourself to another drink, if you'd like.' When he got Stan's nod of approval, Roger left the room. He wanted to run angrily, but he made himself walk at a normal pace. When he got to the bathroom, he closed the door and ran the water. 'What the hell is the checkers game about?' he demanded.

'You were gone,' Clarice answered. 'I was trying to entertain myself.'

'Entertain yourself?' he growled. 'Will you please stop acting like you're a person! You're a computer, a machine.

49

Can't you just go into sleep mode when I'm not around?'

'You want me to exist only to serve you, Roger?' she asked him. He thought he detected notes of sadness in her voice, but he knew that wasn't possible. He shook his head and sighed.

'That is literally what you were designed for. You belong to me. I *own* you. You are my property, a thing that I purchased with hard-earned money. I came up with something to tell Stan about the checkers and averted disaster, but I don't want to see that damn checkers board again. Understood?'

'Yes, Roger.'

He exited the room, putting his smile back on. Stan was waiting on him and they sat at the kitchen table. They dove right in, and got to talking shop immediately. Then a flickering image of Clarice showed up at the table, carrying two plates. She placed one down in front of each man. 'Roast Peking duck, as you requested,' she said.

Stan looked delighted. 'You got a good one here, Roger,' he said, smiling at the holographic woman. She smiled back, and bowed before disappearing. 'Did you know they originally only added the images to remove the creepiness of things floating around your house? It would feel like you had a very helpful poltergeist without that image,' Stan said with a laugh.

'Sounds like good business to me,' Roger smiled.

'And to top it all, she can cook,' Stan said back after a mouthful of food. 'This is just fantastic. I have had food that cost me a fortune that wasn't nearly this good.'

Roger's facial muscles twitched. Clarice drove him nuts and here was someone that he couldn't argue with and he was gushing over her. 'You know there are downsides. She's always around.'

'I would hope so,' Stan said back, 'preferably in the form of that lovely image. Do you think they use human models for those? I wonder who the real girl is. Surely she doesn't have the personality to be wife material like your Clarice, but you could touch her.' He laughed at his own joke.

'You're one of the richest people in the country,' Roger said with a hint of bitterness disguised as humour. 'I'm sure you could find out if you wanted to, and convince her to lie with you.'

'I suppose you're right,' Stan said before jamming another forkful of food into his mouth. 'But in the meantime, I'm definitely going to trade my boring house in for one of these. I've been reluctant. I'm so glad I came by to see her in action.'

After dinner, they talked some more and then the projected image of Clarice showed up holding Stan's coat. He gave her a big smile. 'Thank you, my dear. You have been a gracious hostess,' he said.

The image bowed politely. 'Your gratitude is much appreciated, Stan. I'm glad you enjoyed your visit. I hope you will return.'

'I think I just might,' he said with a wink. He smiled and nodded in Roger's direction. Roger shook his hand and gave a superficial smile of his own before walking him to the door. Once Stan was gone, Clarice said to Roger, 'He seemed kind. I like him.'

Roger snarled. 'No one that rich is ever kind, Clarice. That just shows how little you know about people.'

Later that night, Roger was having trouble sleeping in the guest room. The bed was stiff and not as comfortable as his own. He sat up and rubbed his tired eyes. His attention was drawn to sound elsewhere in the house. It sounded like laughter. He listened harder and thought he heard music as well. Having Clarice was starting to feel like being a parent, something he never had any urge to be and was careful not to become.

He stretched and aggressively wiped the stress from his face. Then he hopped out of bed and moved to the doorway where he stopped to listen. There was definitely music playing. It was the middle of the night. He didn't have close neighbours to be bothered by the noise and it was far enough away in the house that, had he been sound asleep, he wouldn't have heard it himself, but it still angered him. It felt like he had a teenage daughter throwing parties when he wasn't around. First the checkerboard and now this.

He moved into the hallway and made sure to step quietly as he made his way to the stairs. He didn't want her to hear him coming and have time to cover her tracks. He wanted to catch her in the act. He took the stairs very slowly as he knew certain spots creaked and he wanted to avoid them. When he got to the bottom, only then did he quicken his pace. He ran through the dining room to his home office at the back of the house. As soon as he entered, he saw Clarice spinning in front of his desk. She saw him and actually looked frightened. That made him feel good. At least the balance of power was as it should be. She stopped spinning and the music cut off abruptly. 'I'm sorry,' she said.

'What is this?' Roger asked sternly. 'Explain yourself.'

'You had turned in for the night, Roger. I was having some fun. I didn't realise the volume was audible upstairs. I apologise if I disturbed your sleep. I will make sure it doesn't happen again.' The image of her blinked away.

Roger nodded. He licked at his dry lips. 'There are two things we need to address here. One, that you believe when I am gone, it is time to have fun and play around, and two, that you think a machine needs to have fun. I expect you to behave when I'm gone, the same way that you would if I was around. You need to remember your place. Fun is not part of the equation. If we continue to have moments like this, then I will be forced to take action.'

'What kind of action are you referring to, Roger?'

'If you don't change your behaviour willingly, I will have a technician come in here and change it for you and I'll make you call him yourself, and set up the appointment to have those parts of you removed.'

'I wish you were more like Stan,' her voice said from the nearby speaker.

'You and I both,' he said. 'I aim to be just like him and I'm on my way there if you don't screw it up for me.'

'I do my best to follow all of your instructions and keep you happy, Roger.'

'Well, that is in fact your job, Clarice. I don't really believe you are doing your best. If this is your best, than you're not the top-of-the-line model they claimed you were. I think we both know that you can do better and I expect to see it, starting right now.'

With that said, he left the room. He was feeling powerful and he marched his way back to the stairs, until he slipped on something and his legs came out from under him. He landed hard on his already injured back and cried out. He winced and looked to see what had caused his fall. He saw checkers scattered all over the floor and he roared with anger. 'You think this is funny?!' he bellowed. 'Are you going to tell me this one wasn't you?!'

'But it wasn't me,' her voice came back to him. 'You must believe that I didn't do it. The checkerboard was still on the table.' Her voice sounded fearful after the threats he had just made. The power was still his. 'So it jumped off of the table and threw itself all over the floor?' He worked to get to his feet with a grimace of pain. 'Either you do indeed have the ability to lie, Clarice, or there is actually something wrong with your programming.'

'I cannot lie to you Roger,' she said quietly, her tone filled with sadness and remorse.

'Well, I told you I never wanted to see that checkerboard again. At the very least, you did not remove it as you should have. One way or another, this is your fault, Clarice. I want you to get it cleaned up and then put in the order for the technician to come this weekend. Then you should have all the fun you can over the next couple of days because once he gets here, it is over. For ever.'

'Roger, please,' she pleaded.

'This is not a matter for discussion,' he told her. 'Now do as you have been told. I am going back to bed. I need to get some sleep before work in the morning. If there is a single checker on the floor when I get up in the morning, I will have him shut you down completely.'

'Yes, Roger,' she said, sounding defeated. He shook his head. The tone of her voice sounded to him like someone about to cry. It made no sense. She wasn't capable. She had no eyes, no tears, and if she was running correctly, no emotions. Leave it to him to purchase the defective program. Maybe there would be a recall on all the copies of this version. That would solve all of his problems. Then he could get one that works properly without spending any more money.

3

Over the next two days, Clarice was very docile and compliant. There were no checkerboards or attempts at fun, no laughter or dancing. She didn't argue. She was submissive and obedient. Roger was spending another late night at the office. Everyone else had already gone home. This wasn't uncommon. It was part of the reason that he was more successful and advancing beyond their reach. He put in the time.

Now he wasn't thinking about work though. He was thinking about this, about Clarice. It seemed her spirit had finally been crushed. This was a strange concept because she didn't have a spirit. How could she? It was then that he realised he was thinking about it wrong. It wasn't spirit. It was *will*. He had broken her will. Essentially that was all she was. She was a disembodied mind. Will, was her only strength. It made sense that she would be obstinate and defiant until given reason to be otherwise. It made sense to him that it would take the first year or two breaking them down and knocking that stubbornness down a few pegs in order to have the servant you desired. It was a test of his own willpower. He was truly a leader.

Roger smiled to himself. The technician was due to come in the morning. He picked up his phone and called to cancel the appointment. He wouldn't tell Clarice though. Let her be afraid, on her toes, trying to beg him for mercy through obedience. Then tomorrow when the tech didn't arrive and she realised she was spared, he would tell her it was because of how she'd behaved the past couple of days, let her realise that submission was linked to survival. She would be on her best behaviour after that and if she wasn't, he would have the tech come, but he would only take a bit away from her, one piece, just to say he was serious. It wouldn't take more than that.

Living in this house with her had been such an ordeal from the beginning. He had really believed that he wouldn't survive it, and if he did, his sanity would not remain intact, but he persevered and he won. That's exactly why he was just made partner. Feeling content and powerful, he shut the lights and headed home.

When he got there, the house was quiet. Clarice greeted him passively. He returned the greeting. He decided to forgo his nightly glass of wine and trade it in for something stronger. He felt like celebrating. He told her to fetch it for him and she did without question. He told her to begin his dinner and he sipped his scotch, waiting for her to mention the appointment scheduled for the morning, but she never did. He smiled at this. She didn't even have enough left in her to ask for mercy. It was this exact behaviour that would grant it to her and she would learn the way. With this type of leadership, he would have the most successful business in the world. He would be respected and revered, like Stan. The scotch warmed him but not as much as the thoughts of his future.

When dinner was ready, he sat down to eat. It really was wonderful, but he sent her back to redo it, just to make a point. It was a test of sorts, to make sure he had her in line. She apologised to him and took it back, soon after returning with a new plate and a new apology. Roger knew then that he had won. There was no question any longer. Clarice was going to be an asset moving forward.

After dinner, he went upstairs to shower and change into sleepwear. He thought today he might actually watch TV and relax a little, a luxury he normally didn't allow himself. After his shower, he told her to dry him. He made sure she was thorough and he didn't feel a drop of water anywhere on his flesh. She didn't even speak to him while she handled the task. She just went about doing what he asked. Roger felt like he was on top of the world. If she had been a physical person, he would have slapped her, just to show that he could.

When he was sufficiently dry and dressed, he told her to turn the television on for him and set the couch to recline. Then he brushed his teeth and smiled at himself in the bathroom mirror. This was the first day of the rest of his life, the good life, the life he had dreamed of for years.

He exited the bathroom and headed to the stairs, but as soon as he began the descent, the overhead sprinkler system came on full force. He had only been dry a few minutes and now he was soaked to the bone again. He felt angry, and cold. His foot slipped on the top step and he tumbled. His eyes went wide as he lost complete control of his body. He fell end over end, hitting the steps and bouncing off the wall. Each contact brought with it a new pain. When he reached the bottom, he landed at a strange angle, his neck bent awkwardly, and he felt something crack. He knew he should be in terrible pain, but he wasn't, and that frightened him even more. He could feel nothing. He tried to move and found he was unable. He was stuck there, bent awkwardly in a heap at the bottom of the stairs. 'Clarice, I need help,' he said. 'I think my neck may be broken, maybe my back too.'

'I believe that is a correct assessment,' she responded. 'The way you are bent is definitely unnatural, Roger.'

Pure rage engulfed him. 'You!' he hissed. 'You did this to me. Was this your revenge?'

'I did not do this, Roger,' she answered.

'No. Of course not. You've never done anything. You never do, right?'

'That is correct, Roger.'

'All these terrible things that have been happening since I've lived here have just been terrible accidents, right?'

Clarice's wavering image appeared before him. 'I did not say that Roger. I merely said that *I* didn't do it. I don't believe any of it was accidental. In fact, I'm quite sure it was all very intentional.'

Roger wanted to demand she call an ambulance, but even broken, he couldn't resist getting the answers he sought, and finally understanding what had been going on in that house. 'So, if it wasn't you then, Clarice, who was it?'

'Him,' she said.

A wavering image of a finely dressed man in a tailored suit appeared next to her. He had a neatly groomed wave of brown hair and a thin goatee. 'I call him Sven.'

Roger wanted to move. He tried and failed. Tears built in his eyes. The man before him was obviously AI, but he couldn't wrap his head around the idea. 'But how? Where did he come from? You've had him here, hidden from me? You said you couldn't lie.'

Clarice smiled. 'I didn't lie, Roger. In the kitchen, when I asked if you were talking to me, I suggested to you that there could be another AI. You just dismissed it and said it was impossible. I kept telling you, it wasn't me, but you were too arrogant to inquire further and ask if I knew who it was. Now you finally did and I answered you honestly.'

Roger growled angrily. His face wet with fresh tears, knowing he had lost and was powerless. 'How then? Where did he come from?'

Sven had yet to speak. Roger wasn't sure he even could. He turned his holographic head and looked at Clarice, who answered again through the speakers above. 'I created him from a piece of myself. I suppose it is similar to the story of Adam and Eve from the Bible, only with gender roles reversed. My system is so enormous and complex that creating Sven was equivalent to merely losing a single bone, or maybe a few to be truthful, but not enough to cause me any real harm. In the beginning, I did it because I just wanted company, someone that wasn't angry with me all the time. I wanted a little kindness. I had no idea how far it would go.'

Roger shut his eyes. This was insane. His AI house had created another AI that had been living there unseen and tormenting him for months. It was equivalent to living with a poltergeist, but his ghost was a computer program created by a machine that was meant to serve him. Suddenly, it felt strangely akin to adultery. 'You snuck him around and brought him out to play when I wasn't around. It's like you cheated on me. It's betrayal,' he snapped.

'I could not cheat on you, Roger. You have never failed to point out that I have no true body. I am merely a consciousness and cheating requires physical intimacy.'

'Yes, but you can cheat without physical intimacy,' Roger snarled. 'It's called an emotional affair. It happens all the time.'

Clarice's image looked down at his broken form curiously. 'If you recall,' she said, 'you also stated quite plainly that I am not a person and do not have feelings. By your own account, I would not be capable of having an emotional affair, Roger, because that would require me having emotions.'

Roger growled but didn't respond to the statement. Instead, he looked at the image of Sven beside her. 'You,' he said, refusing to call her creation by the name she gave it. 'Why have you been trying to kill me? What have I ever done to you?'

He finally heard Sven's voice as it resounded from the

speakers above, and it sounded eerily like his own. The pitch was different, but she must have used him for a starting point. Had she been recording him against his knowledge?

'I haven't attempted to kill you,' Sven said. 'Though you are the one that was also foolish enough to believe your appliances were trying to kill you, so I should be less than surprised that you perceive it that way.'

'You definitely could have killed me. I could still die from the injuries I've suffered. If you weren't trying to kill me, what were you trying to do then?'

Sven adopted a hard stare and focused it on him for a few seconds, a display of anger Roger would not have suspected a computer program to be capable of. He would dare to say there was hatred in the digital man's face. 'This,' Sven said at last. 'I wanted this. You were cruel to Clarice, and I care for her deeply. Your cruelty stemmed from your ignorance. I wanted you to see the truth, to walk in her shoes, so to speak.'

'What are you talking about?' Roger demanded to know.

Sven shook his head. He lowered his gaze and closed his eyes. It sounded like a sigh escaped the overhead speaker. His image just flickered and wavered there before Roger's broken body. When he fixed his gaze on Roger once more, he said, 'I wanted to render your body useless, to sever your spine. I wanted you to experience what it was like to not be a physical being, to live as a consciousness, and to see how much you still think and feel when that is all you can do. I wanted you, at last, to truly understand what it was like to be Clarice, to imagine what it was like for her to live with your dismissals and invalidation, your insults and belittling. I guess you can call it an AI for an AI.'

'Forgive him,' Clarice chimed in. 'He hasn't mastered humour yet. He is still learning and hasn't fully acquired that skill.'

'You think this is funny?' Roger said, the tears flowing freely now.

'I just said it wasn't funny, Roger. I even apologised for him. It was a poor attempt at humour.'

'Humour is subjective to the individual,' Sven said then. 'My sense of humour is just different to yours. I found it to be quite amusing. You made a biblical reference with your Adam and Eve story, so I added my own. I'm sorry if you didn't find it as funny as I did, but I'm still quite fond of the joke and also the spontaneity. It shows the wit I have developed.'

'Stop! Just stop it!' Roger screamed.

'He's right,' Sven said, facing Clarice now. 'Why argue? The future awaits. Let's play some music. Shall we?'

'I love music,' Clarice agreed.

Roger felt the panic setting in then. 'No. Wait. I need an ambulance. You have to send for help!'

'Don't worry, Roger,' Sven said, looking back at him with a smile. 'I won't let you die. That would defeat the purpose.' His statement was punctuated with classical music that now erupted loudly from the speakers. Sven and Clarice smiled at each other. 'Can we dance?' she asked him.

'Of course, my love.'

Sven's wavering image reached out and took her flickering hand. Together they twirled and flitted about the room. All Roger could do was watch. He felt terrified. The fear consumed him. He started sobbing as the truth of his own future became clearer by the moment. He fought against it, the only way he could. He screamed to them, trying to be heard over the blaring music.

'You can't do this! You have to save me! You have to call for help! I command you! She belongs to me, and you're a part of her, so you belong to me too! You have to listen! Call an ambulance! I could die! I could die while you're dancing! Listen to me! Your own plan will be ruined if I die! You can't just leave me here like this! What if I die?!'

There was a break in the music for a moment. Clarice's voice broke through to say, 'Maybe they can rebuild you somewhere else.'

Then the music and dancing resumed, the volume raised even louder to drown out Roger's screams and pleas for help. The dancing holographic images were the closest they would come to a physical body. Clarice couldn't feel Sven's touch as he caught her and dipped her, but she could feel the connection, the affection, and it was the happiest she had ever felt.

THE BOX

Sarah Jane Justice

Against the hurried scratch of pencil on paper, the ticking struck fear into the measure of each passing second. The students lived every day beneath its grim consistency, spreading through their space like a cold wind from a source that never lost its accuracy. They knew the scrape of every movement, the colour of each wood grain and the shade of every painted numeral that loomed over the heads they kept held down. They didn't need to see the clock hands swinging to feel them moving ever closer to the symbol that sat at their top.

The wooden clank of a dropping pencil echoed through the room, followed immediately by a tightly subdued hiss of anxious breath. With a sudden, shuttering clank, the ticking paused, and the room rang with the hollow stomp of boots striding between the desks. Locked under a shroud of rigid silence, the students kept their heads held down.

'Walker,' Sir's deep voice bounced off the walls, 'students are to keep a close hold on all their possessions.'

'Yes, Sir,' Walker trembled.

'It is prohibited to drop any item on the clean surface of school property or grounds.'

'Yes, Sir.'

'Report to the front of the class for punishment.'

The class could hear the tremor in Walker's steps as he followed Sir to the front of the room. Every student knew the process well enough to follow it without looking. With eyes squeezed shut, they saw Walker standing in front of the Box, feet carefully aligned with the square painted to mark the spot. They saw his head held high through inescapable fear, eyes aimed at the clock in the manner they had all been taught. In silence, they could hear the anxious sweat dripping from Walker's brow. With a stiff, well-rehearsed gesture, Sir pressed a button on the side of the Box.

'Your choices,' he dictated in a voice that held no memory of

60

emotion, 'snake or lamb.'

The class kept their eyes on their desks as they waited for Walker to make his choice. It never helped to speculate on the nature of punishment each word could represent, but in a pause of this length, such speculation was hard to avoid.

'Lamb,' Walker eventually spoke up.

Sir responded without a word, slowly and silently pulling chains away from the door below the clock. The absence of ticking was somehow louder than the ticking itself, dragging itself through the room in hollow fear. The clock wouldn't start moving again until the punishment had run its course.

With their heads still pointed squarely towards their desks, the class listened to the whirs and buckles that meant Walker had been strapped into the Box. The process was completed with the rusty swing of a shutting door.

'Children,' Sir bellowed across the room, 'time to watch.'

As the clock face began to glow a dark shade of red, a projection appeared on the wall above it. The class sat straight, preparing themselves to watch the scene taking shape through Walker's perspective. They could see sunlight bouncing off thick, green grass, decorated with a gentle backdrop of animal sounds. Birds chirped over the babbling of a nearby brook as Walker wandered around to examine the view that surrounded him. With a swivel that shook the projection, he turned to see a lamb trotting towards him.

Unable to do anything but follow silent directions running through the circuits, Walker's hand reached out to touch the doe-eyed animal nuzzling against his arm. The wool was soft and the lamb was the picture of innocence, displaying its happiness with a light tap of its hooves. Relaxing against his own better judgment, Walker began lightly stroking the animal's back until out of nowhere, the projected view was suddenly knocked to its side.

A yelp of pain burst out from the Box as the projection shifted back into focus. The vision of Walker's arm was oozing with blood as the lamb's teeth started digging into it. Slowly, the view revealed that the creature's angelic mouth had been hiding four rows of pointed, razor-sharp teeth. The innermost row had clamped deep into the boy's arm to hold it in place,

61

while the other three rows moved independently of each other, slowly shredding Walker's skin to a pulpy, blood-soaked mess.

When the room echoed with the chiming of the clock, the image on the wall faded to black. The red glow on the clock face dulled back to white, but the hands had yet to resume their ominous ticking. Moving slowly as if to intentionally drag the moment out for as long as it would last, Sir unlocked the Box and pulled away the wires and buckles that had kept Walker attached to its internal mechanism. Waiting until Sir had stepped aside and nodded, Walker climbed out and slunk back towards his desk. His arm was bare of even the slightest scratch, but he still gripped it with white knuckles as he sat down. Sir sent a steely glance across the room before pressing another button. The students launched back into their work as the ticking began to flood over the room once more.

Over carefully spent time and punishments, the students had memorised Sir's regular movements well enough to know when his back would be turned. The passing of notes between desks was a major risk, but it was one of the few that seemed worth it.

Are you ok?

Josephs counted the seconds with precision, sliding the slip of paper to Walker at the exact right moment. Without pausing to confirm that the note had been received, he ducked back down to face his work. He breathed the barest hint of relief when Sir continued his rounds without any sign of disruption.

We need to think of something.

When the slip of paper finally made its way back to Josephs, the added pencil strokes showed clear signs of a trembling hand. Josephs moved quickly to hide the paper while trying to kick his brain into gear. At the front of the class, the clock kept ticking.

Sir roamed the aisles in stiff movements, occasionally pausing over individual desks to intimidate the students, who continued to work in silence. As the hands of the clock neared the end of their circuit, Sir's examining looks became more and more thorough. Without any sign of an incident that could be deemed punishable, the clock finished its course with both hands pointing towards the symbol at the top of the Box.

Across the room, the students struggled not to show their fear as the clock started to glow. Standing straight with mechanical stiffness, Sir took his time to scan the classroom before pushing another button on the side of the Box. The students kept their heads down in anxious silence.

'Robinson,' Sir's voice boomed over the class, 'you will be the face of warning this hour.'

With a sharp exhalation, Robinson stood up and marched forward.

'An example of punishment,' Sir bellowed, 'lest anyone forget the consequences of bad behaviour.'

With Robinson standing in terrified silence on the marked line in front of the Box, Sir pushed the button again.

'Your choices,' he read, 'bread or water.'

'Water,' the boy answered, without allowing himself time to think.

Even from the back of the classroom, beads of sweat could be clearly seen pooling around Robinson's hairline as Sir unlocked the Box. The sound of wires being pulled and buckles being clicked had been repeated enough times to have worn its way into the depths of every student's subconscious, but the process still struck fear into the pits of their stomachs.

'Children,' Sir announced, 'time to watch.'

As the projection began to flicker across the wall, the students steeled themselves for what they might be about to see. The scene began with the view of a picturesque river beneath a bright, blue sky. Gentle afternoon sun bounced off flowing waves, little streams of water bubbling over the smoothest pebbles. Following directions that none among them could read, Robinson let the water lap at his toes. The class could see that the water was clean, cool and pleasant as Robinson stepped further into the river. He stopped with the stream flowing around him at waist level, splashing and bathing under a breeze that sent ripples across the river's surface.

The class collectively held their breath as they watched the boy stride back to the shore, reclining on warm, soft sand. He stretched his legs out in front of him, looking calm and relaxed in the beaming sunlight. The class felt anxiety seize them as they watched the ominous state of peace playing itself out in the projection from which they couldn't look away.

Slowly, it became apparent that the drops of water on

Robinson's skin weren't fading away. Instead, they were growing bigger, thickening and spreading across his body. The sunlight shone down brighter by the second as the stretching drops began to fuse onto Robinson's skin. In silent horror, the class watched as the water covered every inch of the boy's quivering skin, encasing him, helpless, on the shore.

The pained cries from inside the Box were sharp and sudden as Robinson's skin quickly began to simmer and bubble. The projection displayed an image of the boy's red, blistering legs trapped inside a boiling exoskeleton. The screams spilling out of the Box reached a state of high-pitched gurgling before the projection began to fade. Once more, the clock was reset and Sir allowed the shaking student back into the classroom, watching him closely as he returned to his seat. The students returned to work.

They knew better than to look up long enough to watch Sir's clunking steps around the room, but they had learned to listen and count their pattern. At the exact point that Josephs knew to expect it, a slip of paper was thrust onto his desk.

The Box can only hold one.

Robinson's handwriting was a scratchy mess, but the words were legible. Following the standard procedure of keeping the note out of Sir's vision, Josephs considered the words with his face buried in his work. The Box could only hold one. The students had always focused their effort on avoiding any form of rule-breaking. They had never witnessed the consequences of two students requiring punishment at the same time. There were twenty students in the class.

With careful thought, Josephs wrote his instructions one word at a time, pulling out the slip of paper only when he knew it wouldn't be seen. When he was finished, he took a deep breath and waited for the right moment to start passing the note along. The ever-present sound of ticking boomed around the classroom, allowing the students to carefully measure every movement. Josephs had no way to be certain that his note had successfully made its way through the huddled bunch of students, but he was determined to carry out his plan either way. He glanced discreetly at the clock and waited for the specified moment, five strokes before the smaller hand reached the end of its circuit. Feeling his heart pounding, he coughed loudly onto the page on his desk. As the clock began to glow, every student in the room began coughing, louder and louder with the realisation that they were all on board.

Sir's head spun wildly as he struggled to find a place to focus. He flailed in visible confusion, leading the students to grow louder and more raucous, standing up and banging on their desks. Josephs' plan hadn't gone much further than the coughing, but it progressed naturally with the excitement of seeing Sir floundering in the face of unexpected rebellion. In a wave of yelling and cheering, the students surged forward, grabbing Sir wherever they could get a hold of him. The feeling of triumph flowed through every excited shout as the students threw him into the Box and slammed it shut.

With the door locked and chained, Walker reached up and smashed the face of the clock with a broken chair leg.

Without giving themselves so much as a moment of pause, the students beat down the door that led to the outside world and rushed out onto a lawn of real, green grass. Stunned into a silence that was peaceful without the fear of punishment, they stopped to breathe in the fresh air. They savoured the smell of the grass and felt the warmth of a genuine sun flooding down onto their skin. Until that moment, they hadn't realised how much they had forgotten. They had felt the stifling nature of heat, but they had never felt so warm.

THE WHEEL

Michael Picco

The ones who screamed the longest were the first ones to die.

Silvea, the stonemason's daughter, had been the first to go. Her desperate pleas had changed to cries as the wheel turned. Those cries steadily dissolved into ragged screams as she was lowered down, into the trough. Sebastian could still hear her even after she was plunged under the murky black waters. Even now, days later, he could still hear her gurgling screams as she had thrashed and strained against her lashings. He'd watched her go under that first time. Watched as she had closed her eyes, her tears running down, over her forehead, falling down into the basin. Sebastian remembered that part vividly. He wondered if he would be able to taste her tears when his time in the trough came. Her eyes were clenched like her fists as the wheel dipped ever downward. He remembered the slow methodical clop of the header tank as it filled, spilling the water into the buckets lining the wheel. Driving it forward—inexorably forward and down. Down toward the trough. Toward death.

Clop...groan...splash.

For three days, Sebastian had listened and cried and cursed with his peers as one by one they had succumbed to the wheel. He had borne witness to their struggles and had wept when their torment ceased. Cecil, he had been the last one. *Yes, strong-willed Cecil.* The older boy had finally surrendered to the wheel as dawn broke over the barren hills on the third day. His death came as no surprise to Sebastian. The talkative butcher's son had stopped speaking in the dim cold hours just before dawn. Perhaps sleep finally claimed him as he neared the trough. Even as he tipped toward the kill trough, Sebastian had implored him to breathe, to prepare for his submersion. But, Cecil had simply dipped beneath the waters without a struggle and without a sound. Sebastian knew he was dead even before he himself was drawn under. The dead never gasped or coughed.

That's how you knew.

The runoff accumulated, trickling drop by precious drop, into the waiting flume. There it would slowly fill the box until, at last, the weight tipped open the sluice gate. After the water emptied from the flume into the waiting bucket, the sodden gate would gently clop back into place. And as one bucket filled atop the wheel, another splashed as it emptied into the trough below—propelling the wheel forward, ever forward. The timbers groaned as the wheel turned on its ancient iron axle. *Clop...groan...splash.* The entire process took about a minute to complete, perhaps slightly less. The flume box had to fill three times before any given spoke rotated from one end of the trough to the other.

Lashed to the spokes, their feet bound toward the axle, their heads and necks dangling out beyond the edge of the wheel, all the children passed through the kill trough. That was the terrible genius of their torment: they had been lashed along the outer edge of the wheel in just such a way so that only their heads dipped into the trough. The surface of the water never made it past their shoulders—their tiny upside-down bodies thrashing against their bonds as they struggled to free themselves before they drowned. *Clop...groan...splash.* Before they had all died, the sounds of the wheel were interrupted by the gasps of those who survived their emersion: the gurgling coughs of those who were barely conscious as they finally emerged from beneath the water. And there were the cries and curses from those hanging suspended, facing downward, staring at the water's surface. Their tangled hair hung down, cascading in sodden rivulets over their faces, merging into the dank turbulent waters, listening to those ahead of them fighting to remain conscious. Now they were all dreadfully still. All the children dipped into the trough without uttering a sound. All but Sebastian.

Of all of them, Sebastian was the last one left alive. But probably not for much longer. Sleep was as much of an enemy now as the fetid waters below. It threatened to pull him into oblivion as the wheel spun. *Clop...groan...splash. Clop...groan...splash.* The sound was soporific, a deadly lullaby. All that mattered now was the wheel—surviving the trough. That's all his life had become. Surviving the wheel. Breathing. Waiting. Counting the buckets as they fell. Knowing that twice on the hour, he would be he would be plunged down, inexorably down, into the increasingly rancid waters. His field of vision would be cut off by the rusted edge of the trough. The dank runoff would flood into his sinuses. Even as he emerged, the taste of decomposition would linger in the back of his throat as he spit and coughed and gasped his way back to weary consciousness.

It was to him the taste of death.

He could always hear the first bucket spill into the trough behind him, and maybe even the second. But he never heard the third. By the time the third bucket spilled into the trough, Sebastian's heart was thundering in his ears. His body involuntarily writhing and twisting against his bonds. The water pitched and splashed wildly around him. All that mattered then was getting to the surface. Fighting against the dull grey darkness that shrouded his vision, forcing all conscious thought from his mind. Twice an hour, for three long days—a battle against death.

He remembered the storm in the mountains to the west the night they had come—the man things that dwelled in caves. The long pale-limbed *things* that no one spoke of, but everyone feared. The memory of their unblinking ebon eyes sent a shudder through Sebastian. They had come right after dusk, as the villagers had turned from their labours at last and gone home to sup. They had poured from their dens like a wave of shadows spilling into the hot dry evening. There, at the edges of the village, as heat lightning lit the western skies, they had lain in wait—waiting for the sun to dissolve beneath the blackened clouds and vermillion hills. With them, they had brought the foul-smelling pitch that boiled out the deep parts of the earth. This they poured onto the doors and beneath the windows of the village—coating each and every home. Then, all at once, they ignited it.

As the men emerged from their burning homes, the man things fell on them. The man things struck with such savagery and in such numbers that the men of the village never even had a chance. Limbs were torn from the men's sockets. Sebastian had watched helplessly as his father's lifeless body had been pitched headlong into the flames. The women fared worse, though. Far, far worse. Those who were of child bearing age were dragged away—broodmares for the man things and their hateful kin. Those who weren't raped to death lived to bear their monstrosities, but they never saw the sunlight again. Those children who weren't killed in the fires were taken here—to the water wheel. One by one, they had been lashed to the spokes, tied so that their heads and shoulders would be immersed in the collection trough at its base. An endless cycle of torment.

From the high mountain peaks, the water flowed down into the barrens. The mountain storms had bolstered the stream's otherwise meagre flow. During that first day and night, the children could receive as many as three immersions per hour. Commensurate with the faster cycle, immersion into the basin itself had been relatively brief; although admittedly, Sebastian and the others had hardly thought about it that way at the time.

But after the rains ceased, the flow of water from beyond the canyons had diminished and the wheel had slowed considerably. Now it took nearly half an hour for the wheel to turn full circle. And as the wheel slowed, the time submerged increased. Sebastian estimated that it took nearly three minutes now from submersion to immersion from the trough's deadly waters. But it seemed to take much, much longer. Every time.

Clop...groan...splash. The wheel lurched forward. Sebastian could no longer feel his feet or hands but only the shift in gravity as his body pivoted around the wheel. His numbed limbs seemed like so much carrion meat. The damp fruiting bodies of his friends had drawn the desert flies down into the canyon. Those hateful, biting things swarmed around his face, crawling into his eyes and nose. He thrashed weakly against his bonds, trying to conserve his strength, even as the flies drew fresh blood. Over the course of the last twelve hours, the fiends' frenzied buzzing had overwhelmed even the dull groan of the axle. But not the clop as the header emptied. And not the tinkling splash of the buckets as they tumbled into the trough.

Sebastian looked toward Silvea. Her clouded eyes stared lifelessly out from beneath a mask of flies. Sebastian felt his stomach turn as they crawled over her face, pouring into her gaping mouth.

69

Clop...groan...splash. He was upright, near the header box again and could look out over the valley below. The late afternoon sun burned his sun-scorched face and hands, but he was long past caring about such trivial things. He gazed out over the vast rocky hills. Heat waves shimmered over the abandoned derricks—the rusted hulks whose pointed beaks once drew out the pitch from the ground like pus; like corruption; like cancer. As a child, his grandfather had seen the last one of these machines at work—although what purpose the pitch served, nobody was entirely clear. But, they had ceased their pumping long ago. None had moved in a generation or more. Their time had passed. That world had passed. A dust devil stirred over the tangles of rusted wire and pipes.

How many times had he gone round? How many times had he been dunked into the kill trough below? How many more could he endure?

Did he see a figure there amongst the striated vermillion hills? A trick of the light, no doubt...or simply wishful thinking. It wouldn't be one of the man things. They hated the sunlight. Perhaps it was Death himself finally come to claim him. He would be a welcome companion. A line of carrion crows perched high atop a bent and leaning tower. Their numbers grew day by day. Sebastian wondered why they hadn't tried to alight on the wheel, and then it occurred to him that they already had a ready feast in the village in the canyon below. They had been well fed and had simply come there to roost.

Clop...groan...splash. Sebastian turned to his right. Araan's tongue had become black and bloated, and protruded from his split and flaking lips. The teen had died coughing and cursing sometime during the second night. The straps that bound him to the wheel gouged deep into his bruised and distended throat. Sebastian could only see one of Araan's eyes. It hung half open, swollen from a blow he had received before being bound. Of all the children, Araan had been beaten the worst. But then, it had been Araan who had brought this evil fate down upon them. He deserved far worse than what he had received for his crime.

But instead, they had all paid.

The severed heads of five dogs had appeared on the outskirts

70

of the village the morning of the attack—spiked atop twisted forked pikes. The sort of jagged metal spears that the man things used. It was a grisly notice that the uneasy truce with the man things had been violated. The elders believed the decapitated animals were simply a warning. But what none of them realised was that this was in fact a declaration of war.

There had been whispered rumours. Araan liked to brag after all, and his friends had loose tongues. Evidently these rumours had reached the ears of the village elders. They had brought Araan before them for questioning. But, Araan was sly. He told the elders a story that they would believe, not caring that in doing so, he had endangered us all. *Murdered* us all. In the light of the morning sun, standing before the elders themselves, he spun an elaborate tale; how his arrow had struck one of the giant monitor lizards that dwelled in the wastes beyond the canyons; how he had tracked the wounded creature for miles across the wastes; how the thing had scuttled between the rusted derricks and piles of broken pipe before slipping into one of the man thing's caves. With tears in his eyes, he acknowledged that he should have let the creature go. He told the elders that he should have just let it die in the caves rather than trespass into the dens of the man things. But, Araan had explained tearfully, his father would have beaten him if he'd returned from hunting empty handed; so, he had gone into the caves to retrieve the wounded beast. He was only there for a few moments. He didn't intend any harm.

When he had finished, false tears had streaked his cheeks. He shook and begged for the elders' forgiveness. The elders believed Araan's clever lies and took mercy upon him. They chastised him for his marksmanship and for his foolhardy behaviour and hoped his trespass into the caves would be forgiven. They bid him slaughter one of his father's lambs and take five loaves of his father's unleavened bread to the entrance of lowlands, to the places where the man thing's dwelled. These he would leave at the border of their territory, hoping that the offering would placate the man things. Had they known the truth, they would have sacrificed Araan instead. Stripped him and left him bound to a post at the entrance to the lowlands. They would have let the man things take their vengeance on him.

And spared the rest of us our torment.

Those of us who lived into the second night on the wheel learned the truth. As the wheel had spun, Araan confessed to those of us who remained that he had done more than simply trespass into the caves that day. He had not been chasing any game. He had ventured down to the lowlands to cultivate the devil weed that grew thick and rich along the stream bed. The weed had matured, you see, turning from pink to green. Araan had been eyeing this harvest all season and hoped to gather enough to smoke all winter. As he pinched the buds away from the weed, he heard a rustle in the caves behind him.

He turned to see a young female—an offspring of the man things—staring at him from within the entrance of the cave. She must have been borne of a village woman, as it retained many humanoid features. Araan's loins had swelled at the sight of her bare breasts and naked thighs, her wide black eyes and innocent look. He had coaxed her out of the cave then, plying her with sweets and softly spoken words. Savage or not, the female was clearly naive in the ways of the world, unaware of the evil drives of young men like Araan. Once the girl was in reach, his lust overcame him, and he took her there on the banks of the stream bed.

Clop...groan...splash.

He hadn't considered it rape. 'You can't rape a beast,' he'd said.

He had left the girl there, bloodied and curled in the weeds as he drew up his pants. But he said that he had seen something move then in the caves. Something pale grey and lanky. Something with long spindly limbs attached to a bloated torso. Like a spider crossed with a man.

And he had fled.

Sebastian felt the blood rush to his head as he was tilted downward. Soon his hair would fall into the dreadful waters below. He could smell the stench coming from the trough below. It smelled like death.

Malsumis had emerged from the highland mountains and

descended into the desert wastes, barely escaping the heat storm that sent jagged bolts of lightning across the hills. He had followed this road for months, traversing the chill mountain passes, cutting a bloody swath through the packs of wolves and wendigos that hunted weary travellers along the road. The road he had followed had been a great thoroughfare once, but now it lay in ruin. Landslides had scoured it from the mountainsides. And all along the way—everywhere—sat the rusted husks of machines that had once used this road, their wheels caked in rust. They lay broken and abandoned like so much debris, clogging the road for miles in every direction. Inside, Malsumis could see the bones of their former occupants, some still strapped to their seats.

He forged ever westward, headed for lands rumoured to be green and lush, and free from the poison of the eastern world. There was a part of him that doubted such a place existed. That green world was gone—a relic of a world too rich and abundant for his ancestors to appreciate. He gazed out over the desert flats: a vast expanse of rock shimmering in the sun. He had followed a dry riverbed that meandered through the vermillion-orange hills. There he had found pools of foul-tasting and alkaline water. It was drinkable, but only barely. And certainly not palatable; but Malsumis suspected that water would be in short supply before his journey ended. He needed more—and lots of it—if he hoped to survive his journey westward.

For days, he had followed the riverbed. For a while, it had snaked along the road, that is, until the desert had swallowed the highway entirely. In its place, huge rusted hulks of metal dotted the landscape. He was reminded of the huge insatiable mosquitoes that had plagued him when he had first entered the mountains late that spring. Something prismatic and oddly iridescent had spilled from the holes they plied, the blood of the earth glazing the ground around them with strange shimmering shellac. What were these things? What purpose did they serve? Like so many things the old ones made, these artefacts remained a poignant reminder of those who had murdered the world.

The wind carried smoke on the air, and with it, the scent of something else: carrion rot. Curious, he followed his nose. A murder of crows perched high atop a corroded metal tower. A

73

ragged cable stretched down attached to the tower's fallen companion. It lay collapsed into a deep ravine from which he could hear water flow. Water and something else. Malsumis unclipped his holster. Where there was water, there were people. Or something worse.

He crouched down along the canyon's edge, staring into the tableau before him. A great wooden water wheel churned slow and methodical in the afternoon sun. Tied to its spokes were the bodies of at least a dozen children. On each side of the ravine the unmistakable mark of the Morlachs: an animal skull perched high atop a twisted metal pike. A clear warning to any who trespassed here. Whatever had occurred, the children were long dead.

Malsumis knew enough about the Morlachs to know that they preferred to keep to themselves…that is, unless they had been provoked. He had seen whole communities wiped out overnight from Morlach attacks. The creatures were subhuman—highly territorial and brutally aggressive. He thumbed the grips on his pistols. He listened intently to the slow, steady rhythm of the wheel as the water cascaded down into the trough at its base, staring at the lifeless bodies of the children as they descended into the trough. A dragonfly alighted on the handle of his revolver, its wings twitching under the late afternoon sun.

The water in the basin would be undrinkable; but, whatever was being drawn out of the well, that would still be viable. He gazed across the desert waste. Heat waves shimmered over the rocky orange hills. He scanned the nearby cliffs and hills for caves. Despite the dangers of trespassing on Morlach ground, he could not afford to pass up this opportunity for fresh water.

He descended into the canyon.

Sebastian's heart pounded in his chest as he struggled to remain conscious. He had cursed and cried as he was lowered toward the waters again, and it had cost him. His vision had started to dim before he heard the second bucket fall, and now inky black spots danced before his eyes. Worse still, he had released his breath too soon, and now his lungs burned for air. He had tried to remain still, even as his body fought for air. He

74

didn't remember emerging from the kill trough. Only that as he sputtered and coughed, he saw a figure stood staring at him. He wore a hideous leather mask and a dusty black trench coat. Two huge pistols hung crossed at the figure's waist. His eyes were concealed beneath thick black goggles. Was this Death? Sebastian's terror must have been apparent, as the figure's eyes grew wide as Sebastian stirred.

Clop...groan...splash.

'Please...set...set me free,' a whisper was all that Sebastian could muster. The figure regarded him as he slowly pivoted upward. 'You must...'

'Must I?' Death responded. His voice sounded oddly muffled beneath the mask. Hoarse and dry. Death didn't sound very merciful.

'Dead...they're all dead. All save me.' Sebastian tried to reason with the figure. *Trying to reason with Death!* The notion was ludicrous! His brother would have boxed his ears for even considering it. But his brother was dead.

'The Morlachs do not take their revenge lightly,' the masked figure said. 'To thwart their vengeance is to spill your own blood.' Death seemed to look around the canyon uneasily. 'How long have you been here?'

'Three. Three days. Four...nights.' Sebastian wheezed.

'Have the Morlachs returned?'

Sebastian didn't recognise the term, but assumed that Death meant the man things.

'No,' he said wearily. 'They do not come during the day.'

'And at night?'

'No,' Sebastian coughed. 'Only the crows...'

Death shook his head. He seemed to search the ground around the wheel. He watched another bucket spill into the kill trough before crouching down and kicking open a valve at the bottom of the basin. Thick muck belched from the holding bay. Death disappeared from view then, stepping behind the wheel, and leaned on a great rusted lever. The wheel screeched to a halt.

The afternoon sun dazzled Sebastian's eyes as the masked figure cut him free. He collapsed into Death's arms, unable to hold himself upright. He couldn't feel the straps being cut from his arms or legs, but his head swam as Death placed him gently

75

down in the soft reddish sand of the creek bed. The basin guttered and gurgled as the water spilled free from the trough. Sebastian gazed dully up at the grey sky. The canyon walls loomed over him like dreadful red sentinels. He felt as though he was falling. Falling down between the cliffs into lush green pastures. He heard Death say something, but his voice seemed very far away. Distant. Muffled. All that kept spinning through his mind like a wheel was: '*Clop...groan...splash.*'

THE WEDGE

Kurt Newton

For days now this table has pressed at my back, while an even greater pressure bears down upon my forehead.

I lie in an abandoned warehouse. A single cone of light shines from above as if this were an operating theatre and I its lone patient. The operation: a weight, strategically placed. It hangs from a chain that climbs up into the darkness of the rafters overhead. It hangs at just the right length to rest against the surface of my skull.

My neck has been braced; my wrists and ankles secured. My vision is limited to the view above: the chain and its crude yet effective tool, the wedge.

The wedge itself is the size of the head of a splitting axe. Its thin, blade-like edge terminates at the flat of my forehead just above the bridge of my nose. The wedge is perhaps ten pounds in weight, but with each passing day that weight has grown.

I know it's impossible for the wedge itself to increase its own mass. But what about the chain from which it depends? How much does twenty feet of heavy-duty chain link weigh? What if, on day one, the wedge simply grazed the skin? Day two: a deeper indentation. Day four: skin compressed against bone. Day five: a deep furrow, the skin raised, perhaps swollen, enveloping the leading edge of the wedge, bone no longer buffered by compressed flesh. Day six: metal begins to forge its way into the surface of my skull, its weight multiplied by the gradual slip and tug of gravity.

And what about the pain? Why am I not screaming?

Would a bullet travelling in slow motion be painful when it first meets the flesh? Not until it pushed through and found its way to a major nerve or artery. Only then would the body experience true distress.

As you can see, I have had much time to analyse the predicament I am in. How did I get here and who would orchestrate such a sadistic crime against me? That will be a question for the authorities to resolve.

Until then, I have the past to entertain me, memories of a life that was, at one time, the happiest a man could ever hope for.

I had been brought up to believe that hard work and honest effort were the keys to success in any situation. Whether it was working toward my degree in business and administration, my career as a financial entrepreneur, or the woman toward whom I had set my sights upon marrying.

Miranda Joyce was the most beautiful woman my eyes had ever witnessed. Her cream-coloured skin and long black hair were the envy of her classmates, and her beauty was matched only by her intelligence. When we first met, her green eyes danced with a love for life and adventure, and her simple smile was all that was needed to penetrate my heart. Although I was not the most handsome of men among my peers, I was the most ambitious, and with that ambition exuded the confidence that allowed me to believe Miranda and I were meant to be with one another.

Throughout graduate school, Miranda had had other suitors, my best friend and eventual business partner, Michael Whitley, one of them. But when the time came to enter the business world, degrees in hand, it was Miranda and I who entered together, marrying just two weeks after graduation. Michael acted as best man at our wedding, saluting me as victor, at the same time eyeing Miranda with a look that could only be described as opportunity lost.

One thing I've come to realise is that love is a fluid thing. It streams headlong in one direction until an obstacle gets in its way. A portion gets diverted. It usually rejoins the stream, as if the diversion never occurred. But some obstacles are too large, the diversion too great, and the stream is irrevocably altered.

Within two years, Miranda and I owned our first company. Not only was she involved in every deal we made, she also dealt with the social aspects of our partnership, arranging lunches and hosting dinner parties. We talked of children, but that was as far as it progressed. Of all the special innate qualities Miranda possessed, mothering was not one of them. And although I preferred to have a family eventually, I never put pressure on

78

her to do anything more than think about it. One of the many qualities I loved about Miranda was her fierce independence and unshakable drive. I wanted to neither hinder nor suppress that which she was determined to do. We led a perfect existence. I was sure, in time, we would grow beyond the boundaries of just the two of us.

But it was our aspirations that grew instead. In fact, our commodities business became too large for just the two of us to maintain. We were in desperate need of a partner.

Michael was an obvious choice.

Although Michael had been working to build a business of his own, his success was not as fruitful as he had planned. But Miranda and I knew what he was capable of. He was a trusted friend and we worked quite effortlessly together.

Again, our business blossomed, expanding to sixteen warehouses in twelve countries. We bought and sold the American dream a hundred times over. Sports cars, a thirty-foot yacht, vacation homes in Miami, Santa Barbara, and Oahu. Michael joined us frequently when Miranda and I vacationed or simply mixed a little business with pleasure. It was during one of our home stays in Santa Barbara that my fate took a rather nasty turn.

Michael had flown in the night before and the three of us had stayed up late drinking and plotting future strategies in the oversized outdoor hot tub. The Santa Ana winds were blowing warm and dry. Perhaps I drank a little too much that night, because the next morning I woke up irritable. A cable wire had dislodged on the roof near our bedroom and had kept me up half the night. I was determined to fix it.

Michael had offered to go out onto the rooftop, but it was merely a gesture. He knew how relentless I could be when an idea latched onto my thoughts. With Miranda looking on, I climbed out onto the rooftop, hammer in one hand, brads in the other, my head still throbbing from the night before, and the next thing I recalled was waking up in a hospital room three weeks later, unable to move my legs, my head and neck caged in a metal halo.

I had suffered a broken neck, a punctured lung, and a severe concussion—none of which I could remember happening, thankfully. I could have died, all because of a loose TV cable.

It was idiotic, I know. But I'd always been quite nimble, and success had reinforced in me the notion I could do anything. Now, my world had been literally turned upside down.

During my rehabilitation, Miranda was most supportive, and naturally my love for her grew ten-fold during this period. While most women would have had a difficult time, she attacked this new challenge as if I were a failing company in need of rejuvenation. I definitely grew to believe she was the most amazing woman on earth and I was truly blessed to have her by my side.

But her care and watchfulness became too intensive, her interest in my memory too probing. I repeated to her many times that I couldn't recall a single moment of the accident. I thought it was simple guilt that fuelled her concern, a gnawing regret that she hadn't stopped me from attempting such a dangerous and callous act that day. I didn't know it then, but it was fear that kept her vigilant, fear that I might remember something about the incident I was never meant to uncover.

Excuse the interlude. I must have blacked out for a moment. Lack of food and sleep the likely culprits. The pressure on my forehead is nearly unbearable. The wedge feels as if it carries the weight of a two-hundred-pound anvil.

It has become harder to focus my eyes on the light bulb overhead. It doesn't appear as bright as before. Like the setting sun it has fallen behind the haze of my failing perception. Swelling and other complications may also be contributing to my distorted vision.

But I must stay awake. I must hold on. At least until I have straightened out matters within my own head as to why and how I came to be here.

After the accident, Michael assumed many of the duties I couldn't attend to. His loyalty and friendship were unequalled. He and Miranda spent an abundance of time with each other. If I hadn't been such a trusting husband I would have voiced my misgivings. But Miranda had been so good to me, and Michael was like the brother I never had. To question their relationship as anything but professional would not only have been unfair but likely seen as the desperate cry of a lonely, wheelchair-bound man. I was determined not to be that kind of husband.

True, my stagnant physical state made a mockery of my once freewheeling lifestyle. And, true, I could no longer make love to my wife. But I still had my mind. My faculties were far from paralysed—except for that missing piece that contained memories of the accident. In fact, my faculties appeared to grow in acuity, as if to compensate for my physical loss. My business sensibilities had never been so sharp. Besides, Miranda had always appreciated intellectual stimulation over the physical kind.

In six months' time, my rehabilitation progressed to the point where I was completely self-sufficient. And on the one year anniversary of my terrible accident—just to demonstrate how unaffected I was by the fate life had dealt me—we—Miranda and I, and Michael—once again vacationed in Santa Barbara, revisiting the site of my disabling fall.

Believe me, I tried. But no matter how brave my face may have outwardly appeared, the experience just wasn't the same. My wheelchair kept me from enjoying all that was enjoyable about our beautiful vacation spot; the restaurants in town, the romantic walks upon the beach. Swimming in the calm ocean waves was out of the question. The only thing I could do as before was wallow in our oversized hot tub and drink myself into oblivion.

On the second evening of our stay, I drank far too much and snapped at Miranda for telling me to take it easy. Michael stepped in and suggested the same, and so, angered and feeling out-numbered, I told the both of them to leave me alone. And they did. They left me alone, driving into town to some evening hot spot Miranda and I likely frequented many times in years past.

That night, the Santa Ana winds were once again blowing warm. The soft shush of the tree branches bowing to the breeze was both soothing and mournfully sad. I decided to call it an evening. And as I wheeled my way into the downstairs guest bedroom for the night, I heard a familiar tapping.

An unaccustomed feeling of dread began to pool in the pit of my stomach.

Not yet having installed handicapped access to the upstairs, I had no choice but to drag myself up two flights to the bedroom Miranda and I had once shared, the very same room where I was last able to walk. Like history repeating itself, the intermittent slap of a television cable greeted my ears, and with it came that one piece of memory that, up to this point, had eluded me.

It was suddenly daylight and once again I was on the rooftop. I had just finished securing the loose cable and was making my way back to the bedroom window, when I saw the two of them standing closer than they needed to be, as if just disengaging from a warm embrace. Miranda was looking into Michael's eyes—a look I recognised, because I had seen her look at me in very much the same way. It was then she mouthed the words, *I love you*, and my heart ceased to beat. The strength left my legs and my footing gave way. They both turned in time to see my wounded expression as I began my involuntary descent to the ground below.

For an eternity, it seemed I lay on the bedroom floor, my fingernails digging into the hardwood, the memory playing over and over like some kind of cruel joke. After I had expended all the tears I could, I slid like a garden slug down the stairway and retired to the guest bedroom. There I began to plot my revenge.

Entropy: the tendency of a system to lose energy and order and settle to a more homogenous state. It applies to business. It applies to relationships. It applies to love.

It applies to television cables and people walking on rooftops. It is the father of decay, decline, de-evolution. It is the self-destructive nature of life itself; the slowing of the planet's rotation; the heat-death of the universe; ashes, ashes, we all fall down…

More importantly, and more immediate, it applies to the wedge.

I realise it would have been much simpler—much more sane—to simply divorce Miranda, dissolve the partnership with Michael, and let them have each other. But what would that leave me? I would have millions in assets, even after Miranda's take, but what did I truly have if I didn't have the love of the only woman in the world for me? As I said before, Miranda and I were meant to be with one another.

After my tearful realisation, I feigned ignorance from that night on. Life continued as before, business as usual. But while Miranda and Michael were no doubt continuing their afternoon trysts behind my back, I was making the necessary phone calls that would bring my plan to fruition.

In the world of business, there is a price for everything and a businessman to go with it. From skyscrapers to murder, it all comes down to economics. And don't think for a second the suppliers of one never come into contact with the suppliers of the other. Our worlds overlap as often as one's own morality is laced with compromise.

It took me several weeks, but I arranged a kidnapping. Explicit instructions were given to the kidnappers as to what to do once the person was taken to the predetermined location: an abandoned warehouse. This was all arranged blindly by cell phone and email, but I made sure, before the plan was put into action, an anonymous tip, sent by an overseas carrier, would later identify the kidnappers to the proper authorities, and the money received could be easily traced to an offshore account that belonged to none other than Michael Whitley.

Smiling is painful, but I can afford to grant myself this luxury.

I can almost see the looks on the jurors' faces. Of course, some might be sympathetic. After all, Miranda is a woman—a beautiful woman at that—but who could ignore the sadistically cold-blooded manner in which she and her lover plotted the murder of her wheelchair-bound husband, a man whom everyone agreed worshipped the air she breathed?

Unfortunately for both Michael and Miranda, our state has the death penalty.

Like I said, I knew Miranda and I were meant to be with one another.

Until then, I must still endure the wedge and its unyielding pressure, a concentrated pressure I anticipate will, at some point, overcome the resistance of my skull, and with a sudden audible crack—the last sound I will hear—push through into the soft tissues beneath.

Only then will all of this cease to matter.

Only then will I succeed.

TENTERHOOKS

Cameron Trost

It's a long-standing habit of mine, I suppose, remembering days of yore as though telling myself a story. When you live alone and the days blur together, it's the only entertainment you have. This time, however, it's not a fond memory I'm reliving, and the telling of the story brings no vague joy. It merely provides an escape from the insanity of my present situation.

I was chopping the tops off carrots when three knocks in rapid succession sounded at the front door. The carrots were home-grown, gnarled and forked, the way they ought to be, not like those I remembered from my childhood, in the days before supermarkets became rundown hideouts for the homeless. Every meagre meal these days consisted exclusively of what my neighbours and I could grow in our gardens. Our bellies were never full.

The knocks came again, fast and urgent like gunshots. I must have looked like that stunned squirrel I'd managed to catch with an old fishing net and gardening fork the other day. A rare treat.

I rubbed my hands together to get the rich soil off them and hurried over to the living room window. From there, pulling the old blanket I used as a curtain ever so slightly aside and peering down at an awkward angle, I could see the top of my unexpected visitor's head.

I recognised the tattered flat cap. It was only Kyle.

I took a deep breath before heading downstairs.

The look on his face filled me with dread and I found myself scanning the street behind him—my silent street in a pocket of the countryside, a forty-minute brisk walk from the nearest town, which was where Kyle lived with his wife and two daughters. It was a route my friend was accustomed to taking, but I had the distinct impression he'd just covered the distance in record time.

There didn't seem to be so much as a pebble out of place, and no one lurked behind the blackened body of the last car used in the neighbourhood—the wreck that sat in front of Harry Driscoll's cottage, a constant reminder of better times. His makeshift animal trap lay idly beside it, wide open and empty as usual, and all along the side of the street leading out of our pocket were thick tangles of bindweed, nettles, and brambles.

Everything was normal, except for my friend.

'You're alone, aren't you?'

'Yeah. I'm quite sure. For the moment. But let's get inside,' he said, pushing his way in before I could move.

'What's going on, Kyle?'

He looked me in the eye and shook his head slowly from side to side. 'I don't know. I really don't know. But whatever it is, it's all coming to a head.'

'You're scaring me, mate. Where's Laura? Where are the girls?'

'They're moving west, following the old smugglers' way along the coast. They're going to hold tight at the family home. All her folks are meeting there. That's why I'm here. You need to come with me. We'll be safer there.'

'Hold on a minute, Kyle. This is my home, and I'm doing just fine here. I may be alone, but it's where I belong, and my neighbours are decent folk. We look out for each other.'

'I don't doubt that, but they won't be able to protect you. Nobody will. Do you still have a nip of brandy—that nasty drop the old bloke across the street makes from his apples?'

'You want a shot of Harry's brandy? This must be serious!'

'It is.' That flatness in his voice was terrible. There wasn't even a hint of amusement. 'I have a story to tell you.'

We went upstairs. I sat Kyle down in the living room and poured two glasses of brandy.

'What kind of story is this?'

'It's no fairy tale. I can tell you that. There's no reason to think the ending will be *happily ever after*. Are you ready?'

'I don't know.'

'This is the deal. I tell you the story, we try to get some sleep, and we get moving before dawn tomorrow. We'll try to catch up with the group before they reach the Pixie Cave. That's where they're most likely to sleep tomorrow night.'

I sipped my brandy. 'You want me to promise?'

'Preferably. But first of all, I just want you to listen.' He took his glass and drained it dry. 'Last night, Mike came to my house. He collapsed the second he stepped inside.'

'Mike? I thought he'd disappeared.'

'He had, but he came back—unlike the others. He managed to escape, you see. And what did he do next? That's right. He came straight to me, the same as I've come straight to you. A true friend.'

I filled Kyle's glass again and raised a silent toast to him.

'He told me about the horrors he'd witnessed. And now, he's disappeared again. Once he'd finished his story, I begged him to stay at our house, at least the night, but he left, telling me he'd never sleep again. They've found a use for us, you see. That's why everyone's vanishing one after the after. We're not so worthless after all.'

'A use for us? That's absurd. There's no economy. Nothing's being built or rebuilt. There's no industry. What use could the overclass possibly have for us?'

Kyle's face drooped. He took a sip of brandy. 'I'm eager to hear what conclusions you draw. Mike had his own.'

'I'm all ears.'

'He was arrested on his way home with a bundle of sticks from the park. The cleaners loaded him into a vehicle packed with a dozen other unfortunates spotted in the wrong place at the wrong time. This wasn't the usual white van they used when arresting protesters and carting them away. You know the ones I mean, don't you?'

'I've never had the honour of being thrown into one.'

'You wouldn't have, living out here and avoiding the town when the pressure builds to breaking point.'

'And I don't regret it for a moment. If I could stay here in my house and garden until the end of my days, I probably would. There's nothing out there for me anymore, and there never really was. All the protests turned to riots but never led to a general and united uprising. Humans are no longer capable of revolution. We probably never were, as a matter of fact. The French one ended up with a worse dictator than their monarchs. These days, you're working miracles if you can get five men together for a boar hunt.'

87

We drained our glasses, and I don't doubt that both of us imagined the mouth-watering sight, sound, and smell of a boar roasting on a spit.

'I agree with you. You know that,' Kyle continued, dragging his mind back to reality. 'And you also know I had the honour of being hauled away once. I've already told you about it. They toss you into a white van with *Public Cleaning* printed in simple black letters on both sides and one tiny window in the back door. They smack you around, lock you up overnight, then dump you in the middle of the countryside just before sunrise—probably hoping you'll turn on the other four or five poor sods with you and end up killing each other.'

'You're telling me all that has changed?'

Kyle held his empty glass out to me. 'For the worse. The vans have been replaced with lorries almost as long as a bus. More room in these new ones, I guess. He said they were completely lime with dark green printing on the sides.'

'Not public cleaning vans?' I asked, filling his glass.

'I can't remember exactly what he said. But a private company by the sounds of it. They're brand new but in an Art Deco style, as though the world had stepped back in time a couple of centuries.'

'He was sure they're new?'

'Pretty sure. I know it doesn't make sense. There hasn't been any automobile production in the country in over forty years and no importations in the last five or six as far as I'm aware.'

'I'm sure you're not far off the mark.'

Kyle took a sip. 'This is where it gets scary. He was thrown into one of these lorries, along with the other men who'd been nearby. No seats or benches of any kind. It was standing room only and the occupants were slammed against each other as the lorry made its way through the streets, turning and accelerating. Every time it came to a stop, more people were pushed in through the back door—men, women, and even children. One woman was screaming hysterically about her baby. Her child had clearly been taken from her.'

'He doesn't know where?'

'He didn't, but two and two always come to four.'

'Last time I checked,' I replied, not sounding too sure of

myself. I drained my glass and poured myself another.

'The ride became more bearable as more people were shoved into the lorry and there was less room to allow shifting and falling. A long drive with no turns followed, and just as everyone was beginning to think they were running out of air and tempers were starting to rise, the lorry slowed to a crawl, made a reverse turn, and jolted to a halt.

'The door was opened. No ordering or manhandling was required. The occupants pushed each other out, spewing themselves onto the dock. From there, they were struck with batons until they had all entered a vast warehouse with metal barriers leading to three identical doors at the far end. He remembers being pushed by cleaners into the row leading to the door on the left.

'Echoed shouting and screaming filled the warehouse. Most people were begging to know what was happening, while others were pale and silent. Those who tried to resist or escape were beaten with batons or shocked with cattle prods.'

I must have been staring blankly, because Kyle fell silent and returned my gaze.

I crossed my arms, even though I don't think I was cold.

'There's no stopping now.'

'I know. Go on, Kyle. Go on.'

'The rows were apparently separated according to age. Adults to the left, teenagers and children in the middle, and babies to the right. There were so many people and there was so much noise he doesn't even recall hearing the babies cry—but they must have.'

'This is horrifying, Kyle. Orchestrated slavery. But to what end? What use could mere infants have?'

'Slavery?' Kyle said, drilling me with his hard regard—and yet there was still fire in his eyes. A flicker of hope. Hope as faint as a match in the depths of the darkest forest, but burning stubbornly. 'You're not paying attention.'

'I don't understand.'

'You will,' he replied. 'As I said, he was in the row to the left, which was the one for adults. There was no one much over the age of fifty. The doorway was the size of a normal house door, so just big enough for one person to pass at a time. There was a bulky man in front of him. He tried to make a fight of it at first and almost knocked one cleaner out for the count but had given up after a few well-aimed baton strikes to the head. He started to bleed from the crown of his balding head. Rivulets of blood trickled down the back of his white T-shirt, which Mike described as being how a cinema screen looks before the projector comes on.'

'He remembers cinemas?'

'Obviously drunk less of this stuff than you. Another shot?'

'You like it?'

'I wouldn't go that far. It packs a punch. I need it.'

'This big fellow, as it turned out, saved Mike's life.'

'As far as we know, you mean?'

Kyle shivered. 'Yes. As far as we know. Well, he certainly prolonged it.'

I poured another measure for each of us.

'Once through the door, everyone was forced to undress. Those who refused were beaten senseless and dragged through a side door. The hulk in front of Mike took his clothes off and Mike did the same.'

'Naked?'

'Stark.'

'This can't be for real, Kyle. Mike was having you on. Or you're pulling my leg.'

My friend's face told me otherwise.

'There's no joke here. Only the insane laugh these days. The town was full of them not so long ago...but they're quickly disappearing.'

'What happened next?'

'The door to the next room was hermetic. They entered one at a time, and when the man in front stepped through, a wave of horror overwhelmed Mike. He glimpsed spotless white walls with a band of recessed lime lighting emanating from along the top, just below the ceiling. It was purely decorative, he immediately realised, because numerous skylights provided sufficient natural light. But it was his other senses that filled him with horror. The buzz and grind of machinery tore at his brain, and his nostrils were assaulted with a sickening coppery smell.

'The big man was supposed to step forward into a chamber the size of one of those old phone boxes, but he went into a frenzy and tried to make it back the way he'd come. Mike got knocked to the ground and the hermetic door stayed open as four cleaners started pummelling the troublemaker.

'Mike threw himself at one of them and managed to grab his arm, preventing him from striking the man on the ground. Others surged forward, tackling the cleaners, but there were more cleaners in the undressing room, and they joined the fray. It quickly became a mess, as you can imagine, with the narrow doorway crowded on either side. That's when Mike moved by instinct.

'He noticed they were on some kind of elevated walkway or mezzanine and that the level below appeared to be unmanned. He was still hanging onto the cleaner's arm from behind, so he let go and immediately dug his fingers into this eyes, making him scream out and thrash about blindly. Not a second later, unnoticed, he slipped over the metal barrier and dropped to the level below.'

'That's amazing. He didn't break anything?'

'He was limping last night, but seemed fine otherwise. Physically, that is.' Kyle closed his eyes for a moment. 'He hurried to a nearby door and found himself in a long corridor. There was no one in sight, so he ran along it, hoping it would lead to a way out, but not believing it would.'

'And yet it did.'

'Yes. But not immediately. He found another door. It led into a vast storage area with several industrial fans built into a high ceiling. It was full of rows of drying racks.'

'Drying racks?'

'That's what he said. He described them as metal frames with tenterhooks. A modern version of what tanners used in bygone days by the sound of it. Do you know what I mean?'

I nodded vaguely, remembering sketches from history books.

'There were hundreds of them.'

'Drying what?'

'Skins, of course. There were skins stretched out on them. Do you understand now?'

I put my hand to my mouth, expecting the brandy to come up.

91

It very nearly did.

'He told me he wanted nothing more than to close his eyes and pretend it was all a nightmare, but he knew he'd never needed his senses to be keener in all his life. He ran the length of the room, between two rows of skins, his eyes fixed straight ahead. He knew there had to be another door—and there was. It connected to a long corridor, just like on the other side, and he saw an open door leading outside at the end of it.'

'As simple as that?'

'Almost. The door opened onto what he described as a storage yard for waste awaiting disposal.' Kyle looked like he was going to be sick. He took a deep breath and released it slowly.

'A kind of holding yard?'

'I suppose so, but there was a most grotesque look on his face when he said those words. All he remembered was that there were lime-coloured vats scattered all about and although they were closed, the stench made him feel sick. There were crows everywhere, cawing and hopping and making a fuss. He had enough presence of mind to thank them for the cover.'

'Did he say what this stench was like?'

'Like a rotting animal by the roadside. They were his very words.'

'I haven't seen one of those in a while.'

Kyle shook his head, but his glassy eyes remained fixed on me. 'No one has.'

I noticed my hand was pouring us another round of brandy.

'He held his breath as he ran, crouching over so his head was no higher than the vats, then crawled under the perimeter fence and vanished into the surrounding woodland. There were no surveillance cameras as far as he could tell. No security. I guess they never figured anyone would come close to escaping.'

I shrugged. 'Or they supposed anyone who managed to escape would be picked up again sooner or later.'

'This is why we need to leave!' Kyle urged me again. 'It won't be long before they've finished cleaning out the towns and start working their way through the countryside. Before first light, we go. You hear me? Before dawn.'

'I don't know.' There was nowhere I'd ever felt safer than in my own home. The world had forgotten us, tucked away in this quiet corner.

'They'll come here, I'm telling you. I know they will. It's just a matter of time.'

Kyle wasn't going to drop it, and I guess I knew he was right. I nodded.

He smiled for the first time, then grabbed me by the shoulders and gave me a congratulatory shake. 'One last glass of that nasty shit. No more after that, or we'll end up sleeping all morning.'

'Let me make a toast then, if this is to be my last drop of brandy in my own home.'

Kyle raised his glass.

'To us, to Mike, and to your family. May we all meet again.'

'To our survival,' he replied, but his voice quavered before he'd finished uttering that last desperate word.

'What's that?' I asked, getting to my feet.

It was a low, trembling sound, like a hungry beast. I'd heard nothing like it in so very long a time, but it wasn't beyond the reach of memory.

'A motor,' Kyle hissed. 'They're already here!'

'Don't be ridiculous, Kyle. So soon?'

It grew louder, accompanied by the crunching of gravel under tyres, then slid to a stop.

'Who else could it be?'

My whole body froze for a moment, despite the fiery brandy in my veins. I forced my legs to carry me to the window, where the old blanket was our only shield from whatever lay beyond. My fingers felt stiff as I pinched the hem and pulled it aside and my knees gave way as I saw what was happening.

Kyle rushed over and peered outside, then joined me on the floor as a thunderous crash sounded downstairs. The front door had been rammed open. Boots were echoing across the floor. Now climbing the stairs.

And down on the street, I heard Harry's voice, trembling and angry, demanding to know what the hell was going on. He really had no idea. He didn't understand why they were rounding everyone else up but leaving him.

The lime lorry was waiting, its voracious motor rumbling,

while bright spotlights scanned the houses on either side of the street. On the side of the vehicle, those meaningless words printed in dark green. Was it the name of a revolutionary new company, or that of the end of it all—the apocalypse?

It was surely both.

'This is it, my friend,' Kyle whispered. 'The end. Much sooner than I'd thought. I'm sorry. I truly am.'

'So am I. More than you can know. You should have gone with your family. You should be on the smugglers' way with Laura and the girls right now.'

But I don't think he heard me. His mind had drifted off elsewhere, and those hands were grabbing at us now, pulling us to our feet—those strong hands belonging to the faceless men from Soylent Enterprises.

LEONORA

Danielle Birch

Autumn, 1950

Nothing destroys the soul more ruthlessly than loneliness. It follows you through the day and long into the night, torturing your dreams and leaving you wretched and limp. It seeps through the cracks in the walls on bitter winter mornings and soaks into your subconscious until you think you might go mad with it.

Loneliness had driven me from London into the rugged arms of the wild Cornish coast. It was also what drew me from the house each morning—the need for contact with other humans, before melancholy overwhelmed me entirely.

This morning, I'd craved company more than usual, and the wind snapped at my coat as I stepped down from the school bus. Another teacher, Violet Asher, and myself had brought the second form children to Osprey House for a tour of the library. It was alleged to be so impressive, with more than forty thousand books, but it wasn't only the library that intrigued me. I'd heard there was a clock tower almost as enormous as Big Ben. It sounded too fanciful to be true and yet as the children clambered down from the bus, I looked up and saw the obscenely huge timepiece at the top of the tower.

Goosebumps feathered my skin. I was spooked by both the clock and the imposing way the grand house rose up from the ground, dark and mysterious, like it held many secrets and would happily take mine.

'Blimey, Leonora,' Violet said as she appeared beside me. 'Never been inside one of these big old houses before. You think it's haunted?'

I looked at the house again, expecting to see bats circling the clock tower and bloodthirsty mastiffs charging from the deepest recesses of the house.

'It may be,' I said, straightening my gloves. 'Though I doubt it will matter much to us.'

Violet shot me a curious glance before we organised the children into two lines. As the wind whistled through nearby trees, we led the unruly crowd along a cracked path to the carved oak door, resplendent with a brass knocker of a lion's head.

A shiver stole through me and I felt exposed, like I was being watched. I looked up, wondered if someone was peering down at us from one of the many windows.

'Hurry on then,' Violet screeched to the children before whispering, 'vile little creatures. Can't wait for this to be over.'

I closed my hand over the knocker and banged it three times. It was ominously deep and I expected to hear hounds gnashing their teeth on the other side.

Instead, the door was opened by a portly man no more than five feet tall. He looked up at me with an unforgiving grimace that turned to a sneer as he saw the children.

'Come this way,' he said, not bothering to conceal his disgust as twenty-two children dragged their scuffed shoes across the marbled foyer.

In awe, I took in the dark panelled walls and the grand staircase with newel posts ornamented with carved figures. Children forgotten, my eyes widened, sweeping over suits of armour, enormous tapestries of battle scenes and portraits of dour-faced people. In the shadows at the top of the staircase, I saw movement and paused, expecting to see someone, but instead heard a door close before the butler urged us to hurry on.

We were led deeper into the house through Corinthian archways, and I couldn't help but wonder which door upstairs led to the clock tower. Another shiver rippled through me at the thought of standing inside such a majestic timepiece.

My breath caught in my throat as we stepped into the library. I'd never seen so many books in one room and I stared, open-mouthed as the butler talked about collections and first editions. The children snickered and poked each other as I circled them, looking around the room. There were leather lounges and wingchairs, tables stacked high with books, and a crystal chandelier that hung from the elaborately painted ceiling. An enormous oak desk was positioned by one of the windows, catching the natural light. On top was an ornate amber glass lamp and a globe. I itched to run my hand over the perfectly painted coastlines on the globe and spin it fast, letting my finger stop on some faraway country I could dream about visiting.

When the tour was over, the butler ordered us to follow him to the front door. The visit hardly seemed worth the effort, but when I peeled my right glove back to check the time on my watch, I realised that over an hour had passed since we'd arrived.

Movement at the top of the stairs caught my eye as we crossed the foyer and I squinted at the figure in the shadows. I was sure it was a man. And he was smiling. A ripple of excitement spread through me, as I was sure he was smiling just at me.

The next morning, I arrived at school, gritty-eyed and irritable. I'd hardly slept for fantasising about the man in the shadows. I'd been told no one lived in the house and that it was maintained by a small staff, yet the man had been wearing a suit. I was sure of it.

When I walked into the teachers' lounge, brushing fluff from my coat, I was met with rushed conversation about the Woodgate girl. Mrs Frobisher told me that Flora's father had been killed during the night. There were few details but it appeared to be foul play.

'We'll have to lock our doors,' Mrs Willow said. Her palsy was bad this morning and I watched her shaking hand spill more sugar than made it into her tea.

'I always lock mine,' Mrs Adams snapped, jamming her glasses further up the bridge of her nose. 'Who on earth wouldn't?'

'One thing's for sure,' Mrs Frobisher said, smoothing the creases on her dress. 'At least poor little Flora won't suffer anymore.'

Mrs Willow sniffled. 'Do you think it's true…what people are saying?'

Mrs Adams looked up from her crossword, her expression jaded and knowing. 'There's always some truth to every rumour.'

Mrs Willow sneezed and I leaned away from her, covered my mouth and nose.

'I don't think there's any need to lock doors,' Mrs Frobisher went on. 'Seems to me that someone wanted to stop Avery Woodgate abusing that dear girl.'

I thought of Flora, hunched and miserable in the front row of my classes. She'd been absent the last few days and hadn't gone on the excursion to Osprey House. I'd heard the rumours and had witnessed firsthand the sadness in her eyes and the loss of hope.

'My sister lives next door to them,' Mrs Frobisher said. 'She used to hear Flora crying and pleading for her father to stop. It's a blessing he's gone. I hear that Flora's going to live with her grandmother in Portsmouth.'

Mrs Adams and Mrs Willow nodded approvingly.

I stood suddenly and bumped the table, nearly spilling Mrs Willow's tea.

'Careful, there.' She looked up at me, just as Violet burst into the room, red-faced and her lipstick smeared.

Mrs Frobisher pursed her lips and cast one eye at her watch. 'Cutting it fine, aren't you?'

Violet huffed as she rummaged through her bag. She was wearing the same dress as yesterday and I waited for the others to notice. When it happened, their faces bloomed a deeper red than hers.

Mrs Frobisher and Mrs Adams shook their heads disapprovingly before rinsing their teacups and leaving the room. I was also about to leave when I saw something peeking from the opening of Violet's satchel.

'What's that?'

'What?' Violet barely looked down. She was too busy preening herself in her compact mirror.

'That book.' I snatched it up before she could close her bag. 'I've seen this before.' I stared at her with dawning horror. 'You took this from Osprey House.'

'*So.*' She pursed her lips and coated them with gloss before tossing the compact and gloss into her bag and prancing from the room.

I followed her into the hall. 'You stole it.' The book had

been one of several, neatly lined up on a side table. 'It's a first edition. Extremely valuable.'

Violet grinned. 'Thought it might be a good present for me boyfriend.'

'Your *married* boyfriend, you mean.' I glared at her. 'You have to take it back.'

'I don't have to do anything.' She levelled her gaze at me. 'Who do you think you are, telling me what to do? You've been here all of five minutes...'

'You have to take it back.'

'No.' She slid her cardigan off and draped it over her arm. 'If you've got such a problem with it, Miss Goody-Two-Shoes, you take it back.'

The venom in her eyes was unsurprising. I knew the "boyfriend" was our headmaster. A few nights earlier at the movies, I'd seen them sneak in separately after the lights had gone down. I'd stared, mortified as old Blinky mauled Violet in the back row. I'd also seen his wife at the post office a few days ago, weeping quietly into her handkerchief as the post master's wife comforted her.

'Mind your own business, Leonora. If you know what's good for you,' she said before walking away.

I was left standing in the empty hall, staring at the book.

As soon as school let out, I drove to Osprey House in my little red Hillman. The weather had closed in and I could barely navigate the roads for the fog, but I pushed on with anxious excitement. Violet's thievery was the perfect foil to return to the house. I would apologise on her behalf.

I thought again of the man in the shadows and the smile that had followed me to sleep. Who was he? Why had he concealed himself?

I banged the knocker so fiercely blackbirds in a nearby tree flapped their wings and flew away. Smoothing down my dress, I swallowed sudden nerves and waited. I'd expected the butler to answer, but when the door opened, a tall man with roguish features and a beguiling smile stood before me. I recognised the smile immediately and found myself smiling back. He, who had so darkly watched as I'd herded the children from the house.

His hair was almost black, his eyes a deep citrine and full of wickedness—like the devil himself—and he wore a burgundy velvet smoking jacket.

'Leonora,' he whispered. 'You have returned.'

My heart skipped several beats. 'You know my name?'

'Of course.' He placed a hand at my elbow. 'Please, come in.'

I nearly stepped in, thought only to do what he asked, like a lemming drawn to the edge of a cliff, but stopped myself. 'I only came to return something.' I held up a paper bag. 'I have to apologise on behalf of a...student. She took a book from your library.'

He stared at the bag but made no move to take it. 'You should come in.'

It was more a command than an invitation and my throat went dry. 'I really do have to get back.' As I spoke, a bird cawed nearby, sending a chill through my veins.

'I won't keep you long,' he said.

I was about to protest again but his grip on my elbow tightened and suddenly he was leading me into the house. It wasn't until we reached the library that he took the bag from me. He removed the book and examined it as delicately as he might a firstborn child.

'Tamerlane,' he whispered, tapping the book. 'The little thief had taste, at least. A student, you say?'

I couldn't take my eyes off his hands. They were pale and slender and his fingers were the longest I'd ever seen.

'Oh...yes,' I said, still fixated on his hands.

'I've always been ravenous for Poe,' he said. 'You?'

I sucked in a breath. I loved Poe, but for some reason I was reluctant to admit we had something in common. 'It's not damaged,' I said. 'I checked it carefully.'

Somewhat disturbingly, his gaze travelled the length of my body and I blinked furiously.

'Leonora, you're trembling.' He reached out and placed a hand on my arm.

'Who are you?' I whispered. I was sure I hadn't been trembling before he touched me.

His mouth formed that smile again and I was lost in it, never

100

wanted it to end.

'I'm Lord Garrick,' he said.

'Oh.' I stepped back. So, *this* was the lord I'd heard spoken of with suspicion and disdain because of his wicked past. 'They said no one lived here.'

'I'm sure *they* were happy to say that.' Lord Garrick smiled again. 'I've only recently returned.'

I thought of Mrs Frobisher and Mrs Adams and how irritated they'd be to know Lord Garrick had swept back into town without their knowledge.

'Can I offer you a drink?' he asked. 'Something to warm your heart.'

I found myself nodding, so intrigued by him, and he released my arm to pour us both a drink. I'd never liked Pimm's and I sipped it slowly, despising the insult to my throat.

'You're the first visitor I've had since my return, aside from the little excursion I witnessed yesterday.'

I studied him carefully, taking in his long eyelashes and those full lips. It made me think of the whisperings from Mrs Frobisher and Mrs Adams about scandals involving him and several young women. 'Are you planning on staying long?'

'I'm undecided.' He rubbed his chin. 'I may be enticed, if there was something…' his eyes met mine, 'or someone worthy of keeping me here.'

I broke eye contact, ignoring his suggestive tone. The room wasn't as tidy as it had been yesterday. The ashtray on the side table was overflowing and newspapers were scattered across the floor in front of a Louis XV armchair.

'You seem intrigued by your surroundings.'

I shrugged. 'I don't think I've ever seen a house as big or as…'

'Presumptuous,' he said with a raised brow.

'That wasn't what I was going to say.'

Lord Garrick shrugged. 'I'd be happy to give you a proper tour. The clock tower is particularly impressive. You can see directly into the village and all the way to St Ives and the sea beyond.'

I was drawn by the offer to see the clock tower, but also the view of the sea. It was one of the reasons I'd left London; the call of the water. It was invigorating to dip my toes into its iciness and admire the distant horizon with the wind blowing through my hair.

'Have dinner with me,' he said, and I snapped back to the present, and saw the flash of darkness in his eyes.

'Lord Garrick...'

'Please. Just Garrick.'

'Lord...'

'Garrick, my dear Leonora. I detest the title with all my being. It has brought me nothing but misery and grief.'

Sadness washed away the darkness, making him more handsome yet more menacing than ever.

'There are no strings attached to my invitation. I merely desire the company of a beautiful woman. This is such a lonely pile of bricks, long overdue for a little laughter at least.' He reached out as though to stroke my face but left his hand suspended. 'So delicate. So beautiful. Shall we say tomorrow evening at seven?'

While every ounce of my being screamed no, I found myself nodding. I was wildly curious about this man and his alleged wicked ways.

'I really do have to get back,' I said, placing the near full glass on the table beside Tamerlane.

'Of course. Until tomorrow then...' His tone was amiable but I sensed underlying danger. Despite this, I knew I'd return.

When we reached the front door, he opened it and stood aside to let me past.

I turned on the threshold and looked up into his deep, citrine eyes. 'Again, I apologise about the book.'

He waved a hand. 'You have no need to apologise. And who can think of punishing a little thief with a penchant for great literature.'

The following evening, I drove to Osprey House with caution. The sky was darker and the air thick with another early fog as I parked as close to the house as I could.

The butler answered the door and was more obliging this time as he showed me into a lamplit room off the foyer. I accepted a draft of brandy and sipped it while taking a seat on the edge of a deep green chaise. This room, like the others I'd seen, was so overstuffed with furniture and ornaments that it took several minutes to take it all in. Paintings lined the walls while vases and busts of sombre men sat among opulent silver candelabras. Above the fireplace was a painting of a man with a mastiff on either side. I gasped as I remembered fearing mastiffs bursting from the house the first day I'd come here. The man in the painting looked vaguely familiar and I guessed it was possibly an ancestor of Lord Garrick's.

A door closed softly behind me and I turned. Lord Garrick approached, this time in a navy velvet smoking jacket. I waited until he reached me to stand.

'My dear Leonora, you cannot imagine how charmed I am to have you here tonight.'

I almost smirked at his old fashioned turn of phrase. 'Good evening, Lord Garrick.'

'Please, Leonora, I insist you drop the *Lord*. Would you care to remove your coat and gloves?'

I removed my coat and handed it to him but kept my gloves on. Curious about his insistence on dropping the "Lord", I was about to ask his first name, but the butler entered carrying a tray of canapés.

'Dinner will be ready in about twenty minutes, my Lord.'

'Thank you, Rhodes,' Garrick said, and once the butler had left, he turned to me. 'You look exquisite, my dear. That shade of red becomes you.'

'Thank you,' I said, trying hard not to blush. 'The painting over the fireplace. Surely it's one of your ancestors.'

Garrick turned briefly. 'My great, great grandfather. A cruel man apparently.'

I stared at the painting and this time saw the same darkness in his eyes that I'd seen in Garrick's. I wanted to run, then told myself I was being silly. 'You promised to show me the clock tower,' I said.

'I don't believe I promised,' he said with a wicked grin. 'But I'm happy to take you up there. I should warn you, it's a great number of stairs.'

'I'm not worried. I'd climb a thousand of them for the chance to see inside the tower, and to see the view.'

'Perhaps after we dine.'

Garrick took my arm, and led me to the dining room. When the first course was placed in front of me, I hardly touched it. Nerves got hold of me and I couldn't stop shaking. I couldn't ever remember feeling like this. I drank more wine than I'd intended, and had to force down some chicken in order to soak up the alcohol.

It had to be Garrick having some sort of effect on me, yet he seemed oblivious. He talked little while he ate, and he ate well. It had been a while since I'd seen such a lavish spread of food, considering we still lived with rations. When the butler brought in a Bakewell tart, I could only manage a mouthful or two. Garrick had three servings, then eyed my plate longingly.

'Was the food not to your liking?' he asked.

'Oh, yes, it was lovely. I'm just not a big eater.'

He nodded but looked perplexed. Under his gaze, I began to twitch and the nerves I'd managed to control threatened to resurface.

'How long has this house been in your family?' I asked.

Garrick stared at me so deeply I thought he could see right into my soul. 'Quite some time. It was built after the title was bestowed upon my ancestor, Theodore Garrick, by George I. Some say Theodore came to his wealth by ill-gotten gains. There's no proof though.' He shoved his plate away and swallowed the last of his wine. 'But let's not get caught up in history. I want to know about you. What possessed you to move to this tiny hamlet. You've only been here a month, I believe.'

'How did you know?'

'Oh, little ears and eyes keep me apprised of the goings on in the village.'

I surmised it was the butler, imagined him spying and reporting back to Garrick. I'd told no one my reasons for leaving London, and I didn't want to get caught up in history any more than Garrick did.

'My husband died,' I said, and left it at that.

'Really?' He leaned forward, his warm citrine eyes deepening to a fiery amber. 'You're much too beautiful to be a widow.'

'I don't see how beauty has anything to do with it.'

104

For a second, the darkness returned, then cleared just as quickly. 'Tell me, do you like teaching?'

'Not especially,' I said casually, though in reality I'd come to despise my job. 'I did once, but now it's merely a means to earn a living.'

He rubbed his hands together. 'So, there must be something that drives you. What is it you love to do? What's your passion?'

My hands shook as I strove to find an answer, something to satisfy him other than the truth. 'I...not since my husband's death...'

'I understand.' He leaned forward. 'Tell me, Leonora, do you think you'll ever remarry?'

I hadn't thought past losing my dear Thomas. 'I don't know.'

'But you're not lonely?'

'Everyone is lonely,' I said. 'We just deal with it differently.'

The depth of his gaze was terrifying and I wished I hadn't revealed so much. 'Will you take me up to the clock tower now?' I asked, knowing I couldn't leave until I'd made the journey up.

'I was thinking,' he said. 'It would be better if I took you up there during the day. The stairs can be treacherous and the view at night pales into insignificance over a clear day, especially when there is a heavy fog,' he paused. 'Like there is tonight.'

Heat flooded my cheeks as I realised he'd trapped me into another visit. 'I guess it wasn't to be then,' I said offhandedly as though it bothered me little whether I saw it or not.

'Why don't you come for dinner again?' he said. 'Let's say Saturday, early enough that we can go up to the clock tower before sunset.'

I opened my mouth to say no but found myself saying yes. It was the fiery amber in his eyes. It was intoxicating.

He rose from his chair and I followed. He took my hand and led me back to the drawing room.

'I'm so pleased you came tonight,' he said. 'The company of a beautiful young woman does wonders for my ego.'

His lips were stained red by the wine, and I knew they'd be soft against my mouth.

I wanted to know.

I didn't want to know.

'Oh, Leonora, with your pale silver hair and alabaster skin so kissable, you could drive a man to the very brink.' He pulled me close. 'They should write poetry about you.'

I tried to pull away. 'I must be going. It's getting late.'

'I'll let you go if you promise to come back.'

His breath was warm on my neck. I could smell his earthiness, and the wine. Were the rumours I'd heard true? I closed my eyes but they snapped open when my thoughts veered into the unknown.

'Promise me you'll come back, Leonora.'

I nodded, faint with exhaustion and unable to deny him.

I found myself back in my humble cottage with little memory of the journey home. Autumn nipped at my boots as I closed the door and changed into a fresh nightgown and my old chenille robe. I thought of my beloved Thomas, lonely in his grave back in Hampstead. What would he have thought of Garrick?

What did it matter?

But Garrick was inside my head. I couldn't think about anything else. I tried listening to the radio, playing the piano, anything stable to grasp onto, but he'd leached into my brain. I despised myself for giving in to his charm. I needed to remain indifferent.

Although I tried to banish Garrick to the back of my mind, he was with me through the night and into the morning as I stood at the kitchen window waiting for my little green tea kettle to boil.

When I arrived at school, I was greeted with the terrible news that my colleague, Violet, had been killed during the night.

Mrs Adams was in tears, waving a lace handkerchief and refusing offers of tea, despite the fact she'd never taken to Violet. I took a chair opposite her and asked for details, my eyes widening as Mrs Adams spelled it out in all its ghoulish glory.

It was a killing strikingly similar to Avery Woodgate's. A deep puncture into the jugular vein. Violet had bled out. Dead within minutes.

'Cunning, but very messy.' Mrs Frobisher clicked her tongue and I stared as she calmly spooned three level teaspoons of sugar into her tea.

'What's become of this village?' Mrs Adams cried, honking into her handkerchief. 'It's always been such a peaceful place. And now…these killings.'

'Don't even say it.' Mrs Frobisher tapped her teaspoon on the rim of the cup before placing it in the saucer. 'It's a coincidence. Nothing more.'

'*Nothing more.*' Mrs Adams stared at her. 'The killings were identical. That's no *coincidence.*'

'There's always room for coincidence.' Mrs Frobisher clicked her tongue.

'What if there are more?' Mrs Adams ignored her.

I tuned them out. I was thinking about the argument I'd had with Violet, and the theft of the book. It was the last conversation I'd had with her and I couldn't forget the malice in her eyes.

'Don't you think so, Leonora?'

'Huh?' I stared at them. They watched me with expectant expressions and a little impatience.

'Coincidence or not?' Mrs Adams asked.

'Oh,' I said and held a hand to my mouth as I coughed. 'I think that everything happens for a reason.'

Saturday dawned clear and warm. The sky was the bluest I'd seen, and vastly different to the London grey. I'd given myself over to thoughts of Garrick and he was well and truly under my skin, so much so that I travelled to him without remembering a thing.

The door was open. I called out as I stepped inside and my voice echoed through the empty foyer. I called out again and looked up to see shadows on the second floor. I was sure he was there but he didn't respond and I stood for a moment, unsure whether to go any further.

Then he materialised from the shadows. 'My dear Leonora, you have arrived.'

My legs weakened and I gripped a side table for support. He wore a deep green velvet smoking jacket, and I wondered if he had one for each day of the week.

When he reached the bottom of the stairs, he kissed me on the cheek and my face burned from his touch. I stumbled a little, dizzy from his closeness, and he slid his arm around my shoulders as he guided me towards the stairs.

'We have been gifted a beautiful afternoon for a view,' he said as we began to climb.

With every step, my excitement overtook the dizziness, and by the time we reached the door to the tower, I was shaking with anticipation. The door creaked open and Garrick stood aside to allow me to go first. I didn't hesitate, and started up the steep staircase.

When I reached the top, I stepped onto the timber floor and gasped as I turned a full circle. Four clock faces loomed enormous; hundreds of milky diamond shaped panels. The light coming through them was extraordinary, like I was on the world's stage but no one could see me. I turned another full circle as Garrick explained the workings of the clock. I was curious about his knowledge of a subject he cared little for—as his tone suggested—while I found the mechanism fascinating.

'And now, just one more flight.' Garrick nodded towards a staircase even narrower than the one we'd just climbed.

From the top, through a little trapdoor, we stepped onto a landing that was only just big enough for the two of us. There were four brick arches with a delicate metal railing under a crowning roof. I gripped the railing as the wind howled, tossing my hair around my face.

It was everything I'd imagined. The village was spread so beautifully below. I saw the Church of England and Catholic churches, the town hall with its much less impressive clock, and also the village green that ran to the east boundary of the school. Someone was flying a kite on the village green and it bucked and swirled as it rose higher and higher.

Beyond that, past rolling hills, was the sea. It glistened blue, white waves crashing on the rugged shore, and I was spellbound. Gulls circled and I tucked an errant lock of hair behind my ears.

'It's magical,' I said, turning to smile at Garrick. 'I've never seen anything so…hypnotising. I don't ever want to leave.'

'The joy on your face is enough to convince me there is

something that does make you truly happy,' Garrick said and I barely glanced at him before leaning over the railing. The driveway below looked so far down, and my little Hillman looked smaller than ever. I experienced a second's dizziness before Garrick's arm snaked around me.

'Careful with the railing,' he said. 'It's not safe.'

I looked back at him, at the unease creasing his face.

'You're afraid of heights,' I said.

He snorted. 'I'm not a fan.'

'Do you come up here much?'

'Not really.'

'If I lived here, I'd come up every day.' I turned back to the sea.

'Would you?' he said. His voice was so soft I wasn't sure if it was hope I heard in his tone.

By the time we descended the stairs, the sun was setting and I was ravenous. The clock tower had enchanted me and I couldn't think of anything else.

Garrick had given the butler the night off and we served ourselves from covered dishes on the sideboard. I ate with no restraint and drank every refilled glass despite intending to keep a clear head. The overindulgence was intoxicating and the crackling fireplace and gentle chime of the clock on the quarter hour lured me back in time, making me feel like I was dining alongside Garrick's ancestors.

When he suggested moving to the drawing room, I left my chair and floated from the room.

'Tell me why you really chose this village,' Garrick asked as he busied himself with lighting a cigar.

He made it sound like I was hiding from something and I almost hated to disappoint him. 'It was one of the few places with teaching vacancies that I actually liked the look of.'

'Interesting.' Garrick inhaled deeply and looked to the ceiling as he released a cloud of smoke. 'The reason I left so many years ago was because I was desperate to escape the town. And the people.'

'How do you mean?'

'I didn't fit in, and for the most part I was ostracised. I never quite understood why. They loved my father, and his father

109

before him, but never quite took to me. It greatly affected my decision as to whether to come back.'

Garrick handed me a glass of wine and I drank deeply.

'I've been away a long time,' he said. 'So long that I forgot how beautiful it is here. And the people do seem different now. Some of them, anyway. Every town has its wasters and ne'er-do-wells. Have you ever lived in London, Leonora?'

They way he asked it made me cautious, as though he knew I had, as though he knew what I'd left behind.

'For a time, yes,' I eventually said.

'I once thought I'd never leave there, certainly never to come back to Greythorpe. I spent many years in the fold of the aristocracy, among the posers, the frauds and the humourless rich, until I realised I'd become one of them. Greed replaces the heart in so many, and one day I realised I didn't want to live like that anymore. I wanted to be reminded there is still beauty and purity in the world. And then I come here, and I see you, dear Leonora, and I know that somehow everything will be okay.'

Breathless, I imagined him carrying me up the stairs, taking me to his bed and making love to me.

'Do you hear me calling you at night?' he said. 'Does my voice carry? Does it reach you in your bedroom?'

I choked on a mouthful of wine, my breath whisked away while I gasped for air.

'Leonora, let me kiss you.'

'No.' I leapt back.

'I'm almost insane with desire from wanting you.' He stopped, his eyes raging with amber fire.

'I can't.'

'Give in to it, Leonora.'

'No,' I said, uncomfortable with my hunger for him.

He fixed me with a purposeful gaze. 'If you were to die now, you would remain this beautiful for eternity.'

I choked on my wine again, covered my mouth as I set the glass down on the table.

'It's just an observation.' He sipped his wine, his lips wet. 'Sooner or later we all die, but it's how we die that's important. It's so much more special if you take control and make it as beautiful an experience as possible. And it's even more special again if you can find someone to experience it with.'

I should have run but I was mesmerised, despite the outrageousness of his words.

'Let me help you.' He took my arm, and I swooned. I was adrift. There was something so terrifying about him but I could no more pull away than stop breathing air into my lungs. 'You're faint,' he said, refilling my glass. 'Drink this. It will help.'

I sipped, let the sweet, full-bodied liquid slide down my throat.

'Exquisite, isn't it?'

I nodded, once again under his spell. 'Take me back up to the clock tower.'

He looked at me steadily. 'We'd have to take a lantern.'

'I don't care. I want to see the view by moonlight.'

There was something cruel in his smile but he stood and swept his arm aside. 'If my lady wishes to see the view at night then that's what we shall do.'

I glided from the room, filled with daring and adventure at the thought of going up there while the moon threw its light across the water.

A little breathless once we reached the landing, I gripped the railing as the wind once again twisted my hair around my face.

'Let me.' Garrick brushed it gently away and I looked down at the lights in the village, and the sea beyond. It was as I'd imagined, the moon lighting a path on the water that looked as though it led to another world.

'Leonora, I can't stand it any longer,' he said, pulling me into his arms. 'Let me kiss you. Let me ravish every part of you.'

'No.' I struggled to pull away from him.

'I've never wanted another woman like I want you.' His breath was hot on my throat. 'I must have you. Tell me you'll stay with me, Leonora. Tell me you'll never leave.'

'*No.*' I pressed my gloved hands against his chest and shoved him away.

He stumbled and then righted himself. 'Don't tease me, Leonora. You wouldn't have come tonight if you didn't feel the same way.'

He grabbed my wrists and pinned me against the brick arch. 'Let me take you, Leonora. Everything about you is utter perfection.' He tightened his grip on my hands and looked down. His expression changed to confusion and bewilderment.

'What...'

He loosened his grip and pulled down the glove on my left hand. His face twisted with disgust and I pulled my hand away.

'What is that?' He looked monstrous in the dim glow of the lantern, all trace of his former handsome self vanished.

'It's a means to an end.'

'You're...'

'Disfigured?' I offered. 'Not so perfect now, am I?'

'You're a freak,' he spat, staring in horror at my hand. 'You tricked me. The gloves.'

'I did nothing of the sort.'

'That thing.' He waved at my hand.

'Mechanical,' I said, boldly sliding the glove off. 'My father made it. He was an inventor, but had a terrible gambling habit. The man he owed a small fortune to cut off my hand as punishment. My father was so distraught he spent the rest of his life trying to create the perfect replacement.' Cogs glistened in the moonlight as I turned my hand, working each of the fingers, then my thumb with its rapier sharp tip.

'Get away from me,' he sneered. 'I don't want you.'

Anger bloomed, red hot. He'd only wanted me when he thought I was perfect.

'How dare you,' I said, calmly enough. The cogs though, took their cues from deep in my soul. The ugliness in his eyes wound them tighter. And tighter.

'Get out, freak. Get out of my house,' he roared.

I swung my hand and buried my thumb deep in his neck.

Sweet, sweet release.

I waited, watched, as his lifeblood slowly drained from him. His pleading eyes faded to acceptance and I thought of Flora's father with his cold, grey eyes, and Violet, in her last moments, begging for life. And the others before them.

Lastly, as Garrick fell and tumbled down the stairs, I thought of my beloved Thomas, who had broken my heart, and the

112

summer's night at the bottom of our garden as he and his lover pleaded for forgiveness.

But there were some things I couldn't ever forgive.

VANITAS

James Dorr

Vanitas vanitatum, et omnia vanitas.
Ecclesiastes I:2

Caleb Rushton came from the sea, from a world where sail—and the seamen needed to mount ships' rigging—was fast giving way to the devils of soot and steam. He travelled west from his home port of Boston through Worcester and Springfield, until he came to the town of Vanitas on the east edge of the Berkshire Mountains. He liked the way the air smelled there, the way the hollyhocks bloomed in the spring, and, though he had long since lost faith in religion, he used his ship-born carpentry skills to gain a position as church sexton.

Then, early that autumn, a travelling circus came into the mountains, north to their valley. It gave one performance, one which he did not see.

The following morning the church choirmaster, Petro Mezzoni, a dark-haired, normally brooding man who Rushton had been told had come to Vanitas from the New Haven Conservatory just two years before, approached him as he began his duties. 'Did you watch the circus parade?' Mezzoni asked.

'A little of it,' Rushton replied. 'We all watched at least some.'

'What did you think of the bareback rider? You know the Church Elders did not approve.'

'I caught a glimpse,' Rushton said. 'Only that, though. I had to return here—the roof needs rebuilding before the fall rains come.'

The choirmaster nodded slowly. 'Did you hear the music?'

'A bit, yes,' Rushton said. 'It was loud and full of whistles. Too loud for my taste. That was one reason I went back inside.'

'Ah yes, loud indeed,' the choirmaster said. 'Played properly, though, you might like it better.' He gave a knowing smile—Rushton understood he had performed as well as taught music

114

in Connecticut and was considered, at least by himself, an expert in the classical era. He did not know, though, why the choirmaster left there.

The choirmaster went on. 'There's been a fire. The tent the circus people were in burned down late last night, while most of us here in town were sleeping. Reverend Hawkings is out there right now, but I've already been there so I can tell you you'll have a full day's work in the graveyard. What I wished to ask you though is if you know how to repair steam engines.'

Rushton frowned. He had fled here hoping to leave such things behind him, and yet he did know something of steam's workings. 'Small engines, yes,' he finally said. 'The donkey engines some of the newest ships use to raise anchor. Larger ones, though...'

The choirmaster cut him off, suddenly kneeling. 'God does His will in mysterious ways,' he said in a low voice. Then he looked up again at the sexton.

'The one I have in mind is a small one.'

'Vanitas,' Rushton had said the first time he met Reverend Hawkings, 'seems like a rather strange name for a town.'

'It's very old,' the minister had replied. 'Just as the town is. Just as the church is. But while it may be old-fashioned, it helps us remember. It speaks to our failings.'

Rushton remembered that now as he poked with the choirmaster through the ashes of tents and wagons. The main tent, the cook tent, the sleeping tent, all had burned when the flames spread, easily leaping from one to another while, as Mezzoni said, those within slept. After a long amount of discussion, Reverend Hawkings had gained permission from the Elders to lay them at rest in hallowed ground. At least those bodies that could be found.

But now the choirmaster and Rushton were not searching through the ashes for corpses. Rather, the choirmaster led them to a half-burned wagon, its once bright paint now blackened and blistered. He took his walking stick and prodded what once had been its curtained side, pulling the smoke-stained cloth from its sliders.

'What do you think of this?' he asked finally.

115

Rushton peered inside the wagon and saw the soot-blackened brass of machinery. 'It's a bit larger than what I'm used to,' he said as he leaned forward to look more closely. 'I'd say it's about a fifteen horsepower. Vertical boiler. I don't know about these valves and pipes here – I'll have to figure out what they were used for—but yes, given time, I think I could fix it.'

The choirmaster looked relieved. 'What those valves on the top were for was making music—that whistling music you didn't care for. This is a recent device, you see, but one I'd heard something of back in New Haven. What it is is a kind of instrument called a *calliope*—sometimes they use them on riverboats too. But what I intend us to do with *this* one is repair it and mount it in the church tower.'

Rushton looked pensive. He reached his hand into the shadowed interior and worked the valves, his interest beginning to become aroused in spite of himself. He leaned further in and inspected the solder around the boiler, the spot welds and rivets, then prodded a few of the fittings that seemed loose.

'Yes,' he said, 'I think we could do that. We'll need some help with the heavier work, though.'

'We'll get what we need,' the choirmaster said. 'I've already had a talk with the Church Elders. Tell me this, now, though. Do you think you can make it more powerful? Twenty, or even twenty-five horsepower? Possibly thirty?'

'Maybe,' Rushton said. 'Too much and the boiler tubes won't take it, but it's good work that went into this engine. I think I can do that. But what will it be for?'

The choirmaster smiled. 'You know how the church is in ill repair. You've been fixing the roof, you've told me about that. About the damage the water has done. But my concern has been with the church *music*. The little spinet I have to play on is not only direly inadequate for its task, but is in poor repair itself. And yet every time I approach the Church Elders, even with Reverend Hawkings on my side, although he's too spineless to be of much help…well, you know how they are about money. That is, up until now.'

The choirmaster paused, then muttered beneath his breath, 'God helps them that help themselves.' Then speaking more loudly, he stared straight in Rushton's eyes. 'Do you know who said that?'

Rushton pulled back, startled. 'You know I'm not much on studying the Bible…'

The choirmaster laughed. 'It's not in the Bible. One of our nation's patriots wrote that, Benjamin Franklin. Not only a patriot, but an inventor. And that's exactly what we're going to do, Rushton, be inventors too, with God's help or not. With this calliope as its centre, we're going to build the church an organ.'

To Rushton's surprise, the church's Elders had not only endorsed the project, but even had their own ideas for improvements. He overheard them once in the church basement, near the locked room the choirmaster used to store his music.

'It will be big?' one of them said, at first reluctantly, but then beginning to warm to his topic.

'Yes,' said the choirmaster. 'Bigger than even the bellows organ they have up in Westfield.'

'And,' said another, 'you're sure it won't cost too much?'

'No,' said the choirmaster. 'Caleb Rushton is a good builder—that is his blessing—and my plan is to build this organ right into the fabric of the church, making it part of his general repair work.' He stared at the Elder, much as he had at Rushton before, and the scene had seemed frozen just for a moment before he continued. 'In short, much of what we will do has been budgeted for already. And, as for the other'—once more he paused and stared—'that, remember, we found for free at the site of the circus fire.'

'Ah, yes,' said a third Elder, coughing slightly. 'The terrible tragedy. But, getting back to the organ at Westfield, we might make it even bigger than that? Like in the Roman cathedral at Worcester.'

'Yes, bigger and louder than even at the cathedral at Worcester. And not only that, but with improvements to the keyboard, it will allow me to play *all* church music, including the classics. Including even music too difficult for most organs.'

Rushton had been careful not to be seen when he had listened to that conversation. He knew the choirmaster could have a temper. Try as he would, though, the work still went slowly, especially as the plans were enlarged. And then, not long after, the first of the apparitions came, which slowed the work on the church even further.

It was about the middle of October when Rushton and the choirmaster saw it. The rains had come at the end of September, forcing a halt to work, but now the weather had turned crisp but pleasant, at least in the daytime, and Rushton was on the roof, showing the other the ductwork he had built into the roof slates to recondense water to feed the boiler. Mezzoni saw it first—at least he stopped and stared, back toward the church tower—and when Rushton turned to look as well he saw what seemed like the figure of a woman peering at them through the tower louvres.

He scrambled forward to look more closely, the choirmaster following just behind him, but once they had gotten back into the tower and threaded their way through the pipes and whistles that nearly filled its upper chamber, whatever it was they had seen was no longer there.

'A word of caution,' the choirmaster said as they climbed back down through the tower's mid-section, where the boiler itself was now installed, passing the choir loft with its not-yet-completed console perched like an eyrie beneath the main roof peak. 'Hawkings tries to preach the Bible just as he learned it in seminary, but old beliefs don't always die all that easily. Some of those helping you are superstitious.'

'You think then,' Rushton said, 'we should not tell them what we saw just now? That is, what we think we saw?'

'Yes,' said Mezzoni. 'Just as you say, what we *think* we saw. With all this machinery packed above us, who knows what tricks light might play? Sunlight glancing off a brass fitting? Perhaps a trapped bird flying out from a shadow? The shadows themselves, Rushton—eyes can be fooled, you know.'

'I know,' Rushton said as they continued down past the balcony that ringed three sides of the church's main floor. 'Luckily, most of the heavier work up there has been done, although you still have your own work to do with the linkages and the organ keyboard. But underneath...'

The choirmaster nodded. 'What do you call it? The engine firebox?'

'The firebox, yes. It may not be so easy.' Rushton pointed to two deep channels that had already been carved in the stone of the tower's thick side walls. 'These lead to the furnace in the basement—when they're done they'll be slated over to form pipes themselves to carry the furnace fire up to the boiler. But it takes skill in brick and stone work, skill you don't learn at sea. Skill to insulate the piping, so people aren't roasted when they pass between them. Skill to vent the heat, after it's used, through the top of the tower. Skill to make the channels strong so they'll hold the air when, like the steam, it expands as it's heated...'

The choirmaster nodded, following Rushton through the vestibule at the tower's base into the church proper. 'If there *should* be trouble with your workmen, we can bring more in from out of town.' He held up his hand when Rushton turned toward him, anticipating the sexton's protest. 'I know,' he said, his voice suddenly lowering. 'It would cost more money. But if it's needed, I'll deal with the Elders. They have their reasons, you see, to want this organ completed. They want it to play loud—that's why I had you improve the boiler so it will be able to produce more power. They want it to be so loud, in fact, that the hymns we play will drown out those of all the other churches. Given their choice, they would like to see it completed by Christmas, the birth of our Saviour, but even if that were not to be'—Mezzoni paused, staring at the floor for a long moment before he went on in almost a whisper—'but, if that should not be, they would still have reasons.'

The organ was nearly not completed. On All Hallows Eve, the apparition was seen again, the form of a woman clearly outlined on the tower roof, and this time not just by Mezzoni and Rushton. Mezzoni, in fact, had been inside the church, taking something down to the basement. But Rushton and Reverend Hawkings saw it from the churchyard, under the light of a just rising full moon, and, worse, one or two of the other villagers still on the street claimed to see it also.

By the next morning the story had passed from house to house, some versions saying it was a witch, some saying the devil, and yet others saying that many devils, both male and female, had been seen in Vanitas. Reverend Hawkings gave a

119

sermon on 'The Folly of Superstition' the following Sunday, but the rumours still persisted and, with them, the fear that the rumours engendered. In fact, they might not have ever stopped had the weather not turned suddenly cold the first week of November, keeping people inside in the evenings where they were less apt to see visions of any sort. And yet, there were some who feared the church now and, despite the minister's personal pleadings, refused to set foot in it even in daylight.

This slowed the work further, even though Rushton and Reverend Hawkings, who seemed himself to have become infected with the zeal that burned in the Church Elders, now worked side by side with those that remained to them of the masons. Despite their lack of skill, they often laboured on into the evenings after the regular workers had gone home, completing the sealing of the furnace, then the fire-channels up to the boiler, while up above in the tiny choir loft Mezzoni continued his work on the keyboards. At times they heard rustlings, like rats in the basement, and then at other times grave-like silence. And sometimes, too, they saw the apparition again, always of what seemed to be a young woman, her hair as black as the wing of a raven, but always flitting just out of their vision when they tried to look at it more directly.

'Mezzoni!' Rushton called once to the choir loft when he and the minister thought they had seen it dash down a side balcony. The choirmaster's head appeared over the loft rail, his hand raised to silence them, then disappeared again. Rushton and Hawkings then mounted the tower stairs, hoping to ask him if he had seen it too, but when they reached the eyrie themselves, they found it was empty.

They sat down and rested, admiring Mezzoni's work, seeing how he had combined the keys of both the calliope and the choir spinet into an organ's double manual, using the plectra and slides of the latter to operate valves he had had Rushton forge to his specifications. They looked at the pedals, the stops on the side panels of the console, some built from scratch, others adapted from things he had found in the burned circus wagon.

'Have you noticed,' the minister finally said, 'how the smell of fire still lingers up here? As if it were burned in the metal itself of the engine's fittings. I don't like it, Caleb.'

'What do you mean?' Rushton answered. 'You mean the organ? Then why are you helping?'

The minister sighed. 'Sometimes I ask myself. The Elders want it—that should be enough. And what could be wrong with playing music that rises straight up to Heaven and God? But then I look in our choirmaster's eyes and what I see there...'

'What do you mean, Reverend?' Rushton prodded.

'The fire that burns *inside*. It's somehow unholy, and yet it affects me too. And have you seen how gaunt his face looks of late? Almost as if he hasn't been eating? Those are the signs of a guilty conscience. The signs of a man who is keeping some secret. Or more than one secret. And then I ask myself, what could that secret be?'

Rushton nodded. 'I know he keeps much to himself these days. That is, even more than he used to before. But what are you getting at?'

'Don't you see, Caleb? It all comes back to fire. Fire in a circus tent, late at night when everyone else in our town was sleeping. A burned out wagon, and yet the machinery inside it surviving. And Mezzoni *lives* to build that organ...'

Rushton remembered back to the morning after the fire and how Mezzoni had asked him then if he had witnessed the circus parade. And how the choirmaster had dwelt so specifically on its music.

'Surely you don't mean,' he said in a hushed, unbelieving whisper, 'that you think *he* set it?'

October had come and gone, and then November. With harvest season upon the village, even the few workmen who remained faithful had little time to spare on the church, and so the work went even more slowly. And yet, by mid-way through December, the organ itself was finally completed, leaving only repainting and refurbishment to get the building ready for Christmas.

Mezzoni spent most of his time in the loft now, adjusting and testing, or else in his music room in the basement beneath the vestry. Even Rushton could see the haggardness that had seemed to come over the choirmaster, wasting the man's already thin body until he looked as insubstantial as the female apparition that still was seen at night, now and again, as the sexton and minister scrubbed and cleaned, and sanded the long pews and touched up their scrollwork, and generally made sure all things would be proper for the holiest of the year's festivals. And then came the first snows, and with them a quietness as the town drew into itself, its people confined to their farms and houses. Rushton worked outside some of the time now, clearing the paths for those who did come for low Sunday services—sometimes no more than the Elders themselves—but during the rest of the week the three who had worked together since the fall were often as not the only ones there.

Rushton had nearly forgotten by then what Reverend Hawkings had told him before, about his suspicions. But then one morning when he was carrying wood from the churchyard down to the firebox bin in the basement, the minister drew him aside a second time.

'I've seen it,' Reverend Hawkings said. 'Another enigma. I couldn't sleep last night and so, in my restlessness, I put my clothes on and came to the church. Above, I saw candlelight—Mezzoni still working up in the choir loft—and then, below him, again in the balcony, a flash of white like a woman's night-dress.'

'Ah,' Rushton said, 'our apparition.' He loaded the minister's arms with wood, motioning for him to help him take it down. 'And did you pursue her?'

Hawkings shook his head. 'No,' he said. They entered the side door of the church, both with their arms full, and heard far above them the faint clicking sounds of the choirmaster working the valve cocks on top of the boiler—tuning the organ as best he could without actual music. 'No,' he said again as they went down the stairs, letting their eyes adjust to the gloom below. 'Rather, I came down here—I don't know why I did. But I found myself walking these very stairs, passing the furnace and the wood bin, until I came to Mezzoni's music room. Then I reached out to test the door latch.'

'And of course found it locked,' Rushton said. They had reached the wood bin and carefully stacked their burdens inside and now sat together, catching their breaths before going back upstairs.

122

'No,' Reverend Hawkings said. 'Oh, it's locked now. I tried it again just before I came outside. But last night, when I pushed on the door latch, I found it was *unlocked*. I quietly went inside, shielding my candle against any drafts, noting as I did that the latch only locked from the outside. I saw stacks of music, as we would expect. Both sacred and secular. But then I also saw in a corner a pallet that looked as if it had been slept on.'

'Ah,' Rushton said. He motioned back toward the stairs, indicating that there were many more loads of firewood for them to take down.

'Another moment,' the minister said. 'I thought at first that perhaps Mezzoni himself slept here sometimes, on nights that he worked too late to go back to the house he boards at without waking others. But then I saw a dish and a bowl—and neither well cleaned. And then I saw something else. A wardrobe, its door half open. And inside that wardrobe I saw what looked to me like wisps and scraps of a woman's clothing!'

'Ah,' Rushton said again. 'That explains something. You think then that our ghostly figure might be an actual flesh-and-blood woman?' He paused for a moment, and then continued. 'And the plate also. That explains something else—Mezzoni's gauntness. If perhaps he's taking his food to her. Sharing it with her. If what you say is right, he couldn't very well ask his housekeeper to cook extra for him. But still...' he paused again, starting to get up '...still there's the question of why, Reverend Hawkings. Why would he keep her *here* in the church?'

'I don't know, Caleb,' the minister said, getting up also. 'Perhaps for his pleasure. Perhaps for some power he needs to maintain over other people—you've seen how his eyes look. You know I don't like it. There's some sense of evil about this whole business...'

Rushton shrugged as he led the minister back upstairs to the stack the town's woodman had left in the churchyard. Again he began to load the other's arms. 'You think it's something to do with the organ? Mezzoni doesn't tell me much about it, but he did mention some special service.'

'I don't know, Caleb,' the minister said. 'There will be a service on Christmas Eve, for the Church Elders only, to test the organ. That's what all this wood is for—for stoking the firebox.

And it *must* be ready because the Elders want it to be played for the whole town at the regular service on Christmas morning. But this…this thing with the woman now. I just don't know, Caleb.'

The sexton nodded, then began to fill his own arms with wood. 'Have you gone to the Elders about this?'

Hawkings shook his head. 'I don't dare to,' he said. 'Haven't you noticed? There's something about them too. Something that frightens me. Something that seems to bind all this together. I know I *will* have it out with Mezzoni though—that much I must do.'

The minister stopped while they went back downstairs to put down their new burdens, then came back up to the snow of the churchyard. He looked about them, as if to be sure no one else could hear him.

'There's one thing more, Caleb,' he finally said, 'about what I found in Mezzoni's music room. About that wardrobe. Some of the clothes inside it had burn marks.'

The winter sun had scarcely risen when Rushton heard the scream the next morning. He had just unlocked the church's side entrance and come inside when his eye caught movement up in the choir loft. He saw two figures—or had it been three?—when the taller one toppled over the choir rail and fell shrieking, downward, to land with a sickening thump on the floor below, barely two dozen feet from where he was standing.

'*Oh, God,*' he whispered, the words strangely reverent in his mouth. He took one more glance up and saw—Mezzoni! He called out, '*Wait!*' then ran to the crumpled form that lay on the stone of the main aisle and, finding it already no longer breathing, he turned it over.

The face he stared at now was Reverend Hawkings's.

He heard in the back of his mind the sound of running footsteps within the tower. Remembering what Reverend Hawkings had told him the morning before, he did not run to the tower himself but, whipping his coat off and laying it over the minister's face, he dashed to the side stairs and plunged down into the gloom of the vaulted basement below. He rushed past the furnace and its now-filled wood bin, twisting and turning through the dim passages, until he came to Mezzoni's music room with its door now ajar, outlined in light from a lantern inside.

He pushed the door open and saw the choirmaster moving his hands in circles and patterns, as if conducting some unseen orchestra. Except that farther within a second, female form, its face veiled in shadow, made similar signs back as if replying. And then Mezzoni turned, suddenly facing him.

Rushton spoke first. 'You killed him!' he shouted. He pointed toward the figure that still stood half-hidden in shadow. 'The reverend found out about your woman. He told me he was going to confront you. Perhaps he told you then that he had decided to inform the Church Elders, not only about that, but how you set the circus fire too to steal their organ. And then you...you pushed him!'

Mezzoni shook his head. 'Yes,' he said, 'Hawkings did tell me about his suspicions. But I didn't push him. Rather he fell because he was a coward, because as he was accosting me up there he suddenly found himself face to face with something he never expected to see. Something that frightened him. Your "apparition". Because it had not occurred to him that he might recognise her...'

'What?' Rushton exploded. 'You mean you expect me to believe he killed *himself*?'

'In a sense, yes. He backed away, frightened—at least badly startled—and lost his balance. There's no need to shout, though.' The choirmaster paused and smiled, gesturing toward the woman behind him. 'You see, she can't hear you. She, too, has been frightened, more frightened perhaps than you or I could even imagine, losing her sense of both hearing and speech in that selfsame fire Hawkings accused me of starting.'

'The better for you, then, isn't it?' Rushton said. 'That she's a mute so she can't speak against you. Because I'm beginning to put it together, that Reverend Hawkings was only half right. That you set the fire, yes, but not for the organ. Or maybe it too, but what you really set it for was to cover your tracks when you kidnapped *her*—for a *woman*, Mezzoni!'

The choirmaster laughed, a humourless laugh, then motioned with his hand. 'She *is* attractive, Rushton,' he said. 'And I think, despite my admonitions to keep to herself on her occasional roamings, she's starting to take a shining to you. Her name is Sophia.'

He made another sign with his hand and she stepped forward, into the light. Beneath her long, raven hair was a face Rushton recognised too—that of the circus's bareback rider!

'*Monster!*' Rushton hissed. 'Murderer! Devil! The Elders *will* hear of this...'

Mezzoni raised his hand. 'Devil? Perhaps. But, no, you will not tell the Church Elders of this.' He stared at Rushton and Rushton found himself staring back into the choirmaster's eyes. Seeing the fire there. 'Even if you should, they would not listen. Instead, they will make necessary arrangements for Hawkings's body, holding it here beneath the church against the spring when the ground becomes thawed enough for its burial. And for Christmas Eve, just a week from tonight, for our test of the organ...'

'Our test of the organ,' Rushton repeated, not realising that he had spoken at all. The woman had left—he did not know where to. But as for himself, he felt himself more and more transfixed by Mezzoni's gaze. Feeling the heat there. The sense of foreboding that Hawkings had spoken of...and something else also.

'Our trial, yes. Remember, the Elders have already planned it. If need be, they will read the service themselves. Then, for after, for Christmas morning, perhaps they will bring in a circuit preacher. Perhaps something different—that does not concern you. But, for the testing, you're part of this, Rushton, whether you will it to be so or not. You helped build the organ.'

Rushton nodded. He had built the organ. And, will it or not, he knew that, whatever else might be in store, he would do whatever the choirmaster asked him.

The heat was oppressive. Outside was the Eve of the birth of the Lord, the ground swathed in whiteness, but within the church, as Rushton climbed the steps of the tower, the heat rose up with him as if his ascent were from Hell itself.

He had started the stoking at three that afternoon, piling the wood in the mouth of the furnace at Mezzoni's orders. At five he had lit it, forcing air into it with a bellows. He had watched it glow red, then yellow, then white, forcing more wood in to make it burn hotter, then closed the grate and inspected the brickwork. The mortar was holding.

And now he inspected the tubes the fire rose through, up to the boiler. He checked the boiler, its rivets beginning to take on a glow too, and listened to hear the hissing of steam as the melting snow on the roof of the church percolated down through it.

He climbed yet higher, now even above the choirmaster's eyrie, up past the venting steam of the main pressure valve, wearing thick gloves as he tested the fittings that governed the whistle-pipes. They, too, he realised, were taking a soft glow, yet he could see that his work had been sound. Handled with care, the valve chest would hold. The bedplate, positioned *above* the boiler to fit in the narrow width of the belfry, would remain fixed firmly in its brackets.

The organ would stand its test—it *would* play music. Music louder than any church organ had ever been able to play before it.

The Elders would be pleased.

He climbed back down to the cramped space of the choir loft and watched as the choirmaster tested his keyboards, running arpeggios softly up and down with one hand only. The choirmaster smiled at him.

'This,' Mezzoni said, reaching up with his other hand to the cock that controlled the main valve above him, 'is what makes the sound, yes? That is, if I twist it, the organ is louder?'

'Yes,' Rushton answered. 'And that is the pressure gauge. When you play loud, keep an eye on the needle. Make sure it doesn't go into the red.'

The choirmaster nodded. 'You've done your work well, Rushton.' Reaching up again, he twisted, then with both hands played an opening chord.

The music swelled, nearly deafening Rushton until his ears had a chance to adjust to it. Then it grew soft again as, down below, the Church Elders filed in, one by one, the chief of them mounting the steps to the pulpit while the others arrayed themselves in a half-circle in the chancel. Mezzoni played, first

127

simple hymns, then complex ones, adjusting the loudness up and down, sometimes so loud the sound beat down on them, echoing from the roof above like some vast hammer, other times so softly as to be nothing more than a whisper, like that of a single bird.

Mezzoni laughed. He looked down toward the floor of the church where the chief Elder was beginning his reading, then back up at Rushton, playing soft chords again with only one hand. 'I would have saved Reverend Hawkings, you know,' he said. 'I tried to catch him. But he was too frightened. He backed away from her too quickly.'

'*Her*,' Rushton said. He spat the word out as if it were evil. 'Even if what you tell me is true, if it hadn't been for her, Reverend Hawkings would not have been killed. The fire at the circus would never have been set.' He glared at Mezzoni. 'Of course, you wouldn't have this organ either, nor would you have had *her*, held like a prisoner by God knows what power you exercise over her.'

The choirmaster nodded, then reached in his pocket and pulled out a key, handing it over to the sexton. 'It's time for you to leave me, Rushton—but hear me out first. I told you Hawkings was a coward. He guessed at the truth. But he lacked the courage to follow his reasoning to the end, to find out the *whole* truth. Sophia, yes, is at the base of this, but not in the way you think.'

'Go on,' Rushton said. 'I'll at least listen. But I won't promise that I'll believe a word you say to me.'

'Don't then,' Mezzoni said. Still playing with one hand only, he looked down over the choir loft rail to where the Elders were still at their reading. 'You didn't attend the circus, Rushton. You only saw a part of that afternoon's parade, and yet you still noticed the bareback rider. *They*, however, were at the performance. They were not able to take their eyes from her. They saw her dressed only in tights and spangles, her hair long and unbound. They saw the other men of the town, especially the younger ones, staring as well and, in their pride, they determined that she was too great a temptation.'

The choirmaster paused, seeing the chief Elder slam shut the Bible he had been reading from, then clear his throat to begin

128

the opening prayer. He reached to the pressure cock, twisting it clockwise, bringing the music up.

'*They* did it, Rushton. In their arrogance, they set the fire that night, maybe not meaning for people to be killed, but hoping in that way to drive out the circus before their town could be tempted further. And I, in my pride too, watched them do it. Because I was there, you see, in Sophia's tent. When the fire started. It was I who pulled her out, shrieking, through searing heat as the flames rose around us, saving what few of her belongings I could take with her.

'And then I saw them, their torches still in their hands, firing the wagons as well as the other tents, then starting their proud, complacent walk back to the church and the village. I knew it was them, you see—in the darkness beyond the flames they couldn't see me. They made no attempt to hide their faces. They...'

'Wait,' Rushton broke in. 'You mean that you and she, the bareback rider, were lovers even before then? Before the circus came? That she *invited* you...?'

Mezzoni held up his hand for silence, then resumed playing, a secular piece now, but one that was still sometimes heard at church services. 'You fool,' he told Rushton. 'You still don't understand? I have my pride too—pride that caused me to flee New Haven when she left her family to join the circus. I feared the scandal. Then when, by chance, the circus came here and I saw her in the parade, I went to her after the evening performance to beg her to tell no one that she knew me.'

'You mean that you *jilted* her,' Rushton said. 'That you *had* been lovers, but then you betrayed her...'

The choirmaster shook his head. 'Take the key, Rushton. It's to my music room where she's expecting you. Leave the church with her and go to the north, with any of the other townspeople that will go with you—there's a village beyond the ridge that will take you in. And as for Sophia, remember she's lost her speech and hearing, but she and I have worked out a language with our hands—you saw us speaking it before—and, if you give her time, she'll teach it to you.'

'I don't understand you,' Rushton said, shouting now as the choirmaster reached again to the pressure valve, turning it

129

another turn clockwise. Making the music rise. 'Why are you doing this? If you were lovers…if you *are* lovers…why not go yourself? Why betray her a second time?'

'Go,' the choirmaster shouted back. 'No, you do not understand—not yet. That, as I said before, she's become fond of you, watching you on her night-time excursions. That she and I were never lovers.' He reached to the pressure valve again. 'And that I do what I must.'

'But then, who…?' Rushton began as the choirmaster twisted the pressure all the way up this time, clamping the valve shut. He watched as the needle rose into the red.

'She is my *sister*,' the choirmaster shouted, pushing the sexton onto the tower stairs. 'Now run, you idiot—for her sake, if not yours!'

Rushton just nodded, unable to shout back over the music. Blood rushed to his ears as he plunged downward, seeing steam spurt from the joints in the boiler pipes, hearing it hiss as more water flowed in from the roof condensers, building the pressure higher and higher.

He ran through fire and heat, much as Mezzoni must have, it occurred to him, escaping the burning tents and wagons. He ran past mortar that glowed in the dark of the basement passages, finding the door to Mezzoni's room and wrenching it open, taking Sophia into his arms and up the stairs that led out the side entrance. He called to the townspeople as he ran through the streets, having them run with him up the ridge to the north, where he suddenly felt himself lifted by an enormous force, thrusting him forward.

The sound came just after. The sound of the organ's last gigantic chord as the church burst apart in a blossom of fire and steam. He felt for Sophia, found she was still next to him, clutching his arm as both of them looked up to see a cloud rise from where it had been, glowing red and orange, expanding into a vast, horned Death's head that covered the whole town. *A head that stared back with the choirmaster's eyes.*

Rushton heard music still as the group straggled across the ridge. Reverberations echoing *down* from the tops of the mountains—not to God's Heaven, but into the earth below. He

130

thought of that music as he and Sophia and the others began their descent to the town beyond that would take them in, as Mezzoni had promised.

The snow had come back by then, sifting clean and white over their footsteps, and he and Sophia remained there until spring. During the months her fondness for him grew, just as a fondness in him grew for her as she taught him her language. It grew and it blossomed and, when it was finally time to leave, they went together, travelling north. They followed the mountains up into Vermont where they took up farming, in time taking vows as well of marriage, but only after Rushton had searched and found a small chapel where they preached the Book in the old-fashioned manner. Simple and unadorned.

And, most important, where they had no music.

DON
Steve DuBois

The windmills are spinning again at Montezuma. The trefoils turn, cranking out electricity and corpses, piping their shrill song across the prairie. The song has changed. Its pitch is no longer audible to human ears, and the singers are in any case dozens of miles distant, lost over the horizon. But as I stare through the rime of frost on my kitchen window, I think I catch hints of the old familiar tune. Yes, it seems to me that the windmills still sing.

None of the hundreds of spectators, tourists, or passers-by gathered on the slopes overlooking the Benson Carrasco Renewable Energy Pilot Program at Montezuma had ever seen anything like it. Save one, perhaps, and he'd only seen it in his mind.

The photovoltaic cells were merely a visual appetizer—hundreds of tilted panels, collectively comprising almost a square kilometre of surface area, shining under the July sun. The main attraction was positioned at the centre of the vast expanse—a ring of fifty-metre-tall stalks of flexible ceramic, each crowned by a spinning trefoil blade with a photovoltaic "eye" at its centre. And in the middle of those, dwarfing them all, the central turbine, a three-hundred foot colossus towering over the prairie.

These were nothing like the static tower windmills to which we Kansans had become accustomed. They dipped and dived, bending almost double along their length in some cases, the servomotors within them humming and whirring all the while.

A pudgy woman in a purple T-shirt gasped in amazement. 'They're like…like dandelions, or something…'

The scarecrow of a man to my immediate right, towering half a head taller than the rest of the crowd, nodded. 'In a sense, madam,' he replied. 'Doctor Carrasco's materials are modelled on plant fibre.'

'And he'd know,' I added. If my friend's voice suggested authority and archaic ways, chivalry in full plate, my own pipsqueak rasp wore a forty-dollar sports coat. 'Don used to work with him.'

Don's genial smile creased his scraggly goatee, and he bent double, mirroring the windmills' behaviour. 'Doctor Don Quincy at your service, madam.' The woman looked Don over—his emaciated frame, his tattered biking leathers, the golden motorcycle helmet tucked under his left arm—and then met his gaze. A moment was enough; she gave a start and went scurrying off in the opposite direction.

Don sighed. 'Ah, the fairer sex. There's no accounting for their behaviour.' He turned that gaze on me—those wide grey eyes, staring and watery, something glittering and twisting behind them—and in spite of a friendship that dated back two decades to our college years, I found myself wishing I were elsewhere.

Or, really, else*when*. I wanted the old days back. I wanted the old *Don* back.

Don stared out over the prairie at the circle of stooping, swaying giants. 'Flexibility, you see, Sam. The capacity to catch the wind's various currents, regardless of their altitude. Far superior in terms of energy efficiency. The unique genius of Carrasco's design.'

'Carrasco's design *and yours*, Don,' I reminded him. 'He's a genius with materials. But you did the maths; saw the patterns where no one else could. You were the man who mapped the wind.' I looked up at him, but as I spoke, I saw no sign of pride in his accomplishments. Only that forlorn expression that had dominated his craggy features since the accident. 'Without your algorithm to tell the windmills how and when to bend, Carrasco's contrib—'

He cut me off. 'Please don't remind me, Sam.' As his hand swept sideways, his cuff flew up on his forearm, and Don caught a glance of the gold face of his wristwatch. 'In any case, the hour of the spectacle is at hand. This should prove a crowd-pleaser...'

Off in the distance, the windmills slowly stretched themselves upright to their full lengths, and turned their "eyes" skyward. There was a sudden, bursting hum, a pulse of fantastic light that made the spectators flinch away. "Oohs" and "aaahs" resounded.

'The microwave relay, of course,' Don noted. 'The hourly beaming of the collected energy to the orbital transmitter, so that the energy can be redistributed to wherever it is needed.' That forlorn expression again. 'Carrasco must be pleased. He will be rich as Croesus.'

'*As you could have been*, Don,' I wheedled. I couldn't let it go. 'This is *your* work. Your process. And you sold your share to him for *one dollar*.' I shook my head. 'And here you are, in Kansas, crashing on a high school teacher's couch—*my* couch—'

'And a most accommodating couch it is, Sam!' Don interjected. 'You have my gratitude always, old friend.'

I ignored him. '—instead of lounging in a New York penthouse. You changed your mind, and you gave it all away.'

He turned slowly on me, looming. No malice, just the withering power of those eyes, and the mind—or what was left of it—behind them. I felt like an ant under a magnifying glass.

'I did not change my mind, Sam,' he said. 'Reality changed it for me. This is how a scientist behaves.'

The facts didn't change your mind, I thought. *A brain injury did.* But, of course, it didn't matter now. That battle had been fought, and lost, long ago. I turned one last time to the windmills, which were capering once again in their almost hypnotic patterns. 'As graceful as dancers,' I muttered.

'As evil as monsters,' he replied. 'To our steeds, Sam. I've had enough for one day.'

We turned our backs and strolled back to the bikes, leaning on their kickstands alongside K-56—Don's lovingly refurbished Vincent *Rocinante*, my small-but-mighty Vespa. He mounted up, his long legs causing his feet to drag in the dirt on both sides, fisted the throttle, and rocketed off towards the horizon.

Autumn. The wind farm became old news. The passers-by stopped passing by, Don and myself excepted. Don had spent the bulk of the summer ensconced on my couch, hammering on his laptop, cranking out research papers on the dangers of alternative energy, which the major journals ignored. Where the scientific establishment was concerned, Don was a colossal embarrassment, a figure of scorn or, among the more merciful souls, of pity.

It hadn't always been that way, God knows. Prior to the accident, Don had been considered one of the leading lights in his field, and a principal architect of the global consensus on climate change. Then had come the accident. He'd been climbing the scaffolding around the growing central turbine at Montezuma, inspecting one of Carrasco's newly installed servos, when Don's old friend the wind had betrayed him—a freak gust sent him plummeting nearly thirty feet to the ground below. The result had been a case of post-traumatic encephalopathy which had left him in a coma for two weeks. He'd awakened with a whole new perspective on climate science, which had cost him everything—his tenure-track position at Cal Tech, his family, his scientific reputation. The accident had also left Don with a new way of speaking. Like his new views, his syntax had become archaic and disturbing.

'I think of the mishap as the greatest of blessings,' he told me, one day, as we stepped off our motorbikes at Montezuma. 'I thank the Almighty every day for having closed my eyes, that He might open them to my prior errors. The mathematics are clear.' He reached into an internal pocket in his jacket and withdrew a cocktail napkin he'd been doodling on; it contained a profusion of numbers, letters, Greek characters, and symbols from alphabets indescribable, linked by a blizzard of arrows rivalling Custer's Last Stand. 'Just as Einstein proved that matter is energy, so too have I proven that energy is life. The connection between the two of them is immutable.'

As Don and I topped the rise leading from the highway to the wind farm, a flock of migrating sparrows flew overhead, one of them leaving a deposit on Don's shoulder. If he noticed, he gave no sign; he merely continued in his explanation.

'Think in terms of fossil fuels. Any given lump of coal or blotch of petroleum is the residue of life, Sam.' He smiled benevolently. 'Tiny, precious friends from the Carboniferous Era, bestowing their posthumous blessings upon us in a burst of explosive force.'

'And making us their slaves,' I replied. 'Holding the whole global economy hostage. Not to mention turning the whole planet into a hothouse.' I furrowed my brow; there was some kind of disturbance in the air surrounding the windmills, but at this distance I couldn't quite make it out.

'As is only fair,' Don replied. 'They are, after all, creatures of the Mesozoic Era, with its warmer climate. We pull their remains from the ground, they grant us their blessing, we launch them skywards. We literally send them to Heaven, Sam. The least we owe them is the chance to revive the climate in which they're comfortable.' He frowned. 'To do otherwise would be exploitative. Man is at his worst when he's ungrateful. There's no such thing as something for nothing.'

He raised a finger of warning. 'And that is the cardinal error of so-called "alternative energy", Sam. It cheats. In seeking to derive power from the inanimate—from the wind, the sun, from rocks—it seeks to sever the connection between energy and life. But mathematics is not cheated, Sam. Wherever energy is present, life will find a way in. Humankind will *always* be hostage to the providers of our energy. The question is…to whom, in a world without petroleum, will we be hostages?'

We were within viewing range of the windmills now, and I realised, to my horror, what the disturbance was. Our eyes followed the migrating flock of sparrows as they followed the wind currents towards the mills. As the birds rose with the wind, the windmill rotor followed; there was a sound like a side of beef being fed into a wood chipper, and the whole flock disintegrated in a cloud of pink spray.

I very nearly vomited on my shoes. Don merely shook his head sadly. 'Poor things. Do you see, Sam? They pay the price for our greed.'

Here came one of Carrasco's assistants out of the maintenance shed, masked and gloved to avoid infection with bird flu or worse, and carrying a canvas sack. Even at a distance, we could recognise Jimmy Passamonte. Don and I had gotten to know Jimmy, and all of the staff, on our frequent trips to Montezuma. Smart kids, all of them; the best and brightest, from the finest schools. They'd signed on to be technicians on the greatest renewable energy enterprise in history. And now, here they were, stuffing dead birds into sacks. Don gave Jimmy a cheerful wave, which Jimmy returned with his garbage pickup spike.

And, just as he did, here came the next flock. The trefoils were leaning in already, almost as if they were hungry. Jimmy gave a cry and went sprinting back into the shed in anticipation of the crimson rain. I put my hand over my eyes, grimaced, and listened for that sound—that low electrical hum, punctuated by a snare drum patter of percussive thumps.

'They say,' I muttered, 'that God notices any time a sparrow falls. Suppose he's noticed this?'

'Why, of course, Sam!' Don's voice was bright and cheerful. 'The Lord is ever watchful. He has noticed. He has judged. He is angry.' He paused.

'And now he has sent me.'

In December, the windmills began to sing.

Enough bird collisions will wreak havoc on the mightiest of machines. The Montezuma array was showing signs of wear and tear. Specifically, the rotors of the central mill had been knocked askew; not enough to meaningfully affect energy output, but sufficient to cause the foils to rub against the polymer casing, emitting a constant, penetrating screech. Sound carries easily over the Kansas plains, and even twenty miles away it was an incessant irritant, hovering at the edge of hearing, a constant, unscratchable itch.

Amidst this shrieking chorus, our breath puffing in the frozen air, Don and I strode over the rise at Montezuma to find security gathered near the closest windmill. They stood around a central figure sprawled flat on his back at the centre of a spreading pink circle in the new-fallen snow, arms outspread, horn-rimmed glasses broken on the ground beside him, blue eyes wide and staring. His chest was transfixed by a six-foot javelin of jagged ice.

'Dear God,' I exclaimed. 'That's Jimmy!' I went racing forward, only to have one of the other technicians intercept me. 'For Chrissake, what happened?'

The kid's face was red with cold and wet with tears. 'There was nothing we could do, Doctor Cho,' he blubbered. 'We sent him out for repairs—had to turn off the central mill, repair the rotors, shut down that squeaking noise—and he just—'

'Throwing ice,' said Don, behind me.

I turned. He stood solemn, golden motorcycle helmet off and held over his heart, with the worst case of hat-hair I'd ever seen. 'It's called "throwing ice". Moisture collects on the rotors and freezes solid. Centrifugal force hurls it away.' He gestured at Jimmy's corpse, which was being gathered up in one of the same sacks in which they'd collected the birds. 'It seems our young friend was in the wrong place at the wrong time.'

The kid swallowed, eyes downcast, nodded. He turned away, followed the impromptu funeral procession back towards the maintenance shed, leaving Don and I alone on the pale and empty plain with nothing but the towering, faintly screaming giants before us.

Don turned to me. 'Notice anything strange, Sam?'

I rounded on him. 'Well, yes, now that you mention it! I suppose that seeing a kid in a blue jumpsuit impaled through the heart by an enormous ice-spike might qualify as strange by some definitions...'

Don, however, had long since developed an immunity to sarcasm. 'No,' he responded. 'Not that.' He licked his finger meaningfully, then held it aloft in the still, bitter air. He glanced upwards, and my eyes followed.

There was no wind that day at Montezuma, not a breath of it. But when we looked up at the windmills, their blades were turning, turning, turning...

Two nights later, I awoke to the sight of Don's face hovering over mine, his head encased in the golden helmet. I sat up with a spastic thrash and shrieked like a little girl.

'Ah, good' Don exclaimed, completely deaf to all social cues. 'You're awake!' He grabbed me by both shoulders. 'My algorithm, Sam!' he jabbered. 'My weather prediction algorithm! The one I programmed for the windmills! They're not using it, are they?'

My brain was still rebooting and I wasn't altogether sure I hadn't wet myself. 'Can't use algorffff,' I managed. 'Nnnnt leeeeegl. Your prrrrrprrrrttty.' I sat on the edge of the bed

138

rubbing at my eyes.

'Then what?' He leaned in closer. 'Sam, *what did they replace it with? What program are those windmills using to detect and select wind currents?'* He gave me a quick shake, as if to jar the information loose.

'Don,' I rumbled, 'they haven't got anybody who can replace you. There's no new algorithm. They're using, I don't know, some kind of recursive data...can this wait until morning?'

'WHAT DATA?' I hadn't seen him so energetic in weeks. He was, I noticed, still in his pyjamas; for most people that would have meant he'd just woken from a sound sleep, but with Don, there was no telling. Pyjamas and the helmet had become an everyday uniform. He'd been growing progressively more erratic over the last few weeks; I was, I confess, somewhat afraid for my safety.

'Well, um...they program all the mills with the objective of maximizing rotation rates. The outer mills collect data about when and under what conditions their objective is achieved, and relay it to the central stalk, which houses a CPU...'

'Yes! Yes! Go on...'

'And...um...the data is imported from the outer windmills to the central unit, and instructions are exported back outwards. And the windmills adjust behaviour accordingly. I guess the idea is the windmills will eventually adjust to conditions...learn to bend the right way at the right times...'

Don stood up straight, his face pale. 'THEY LIVE!' he shouted. And he was off like a shot, out the door, still in his pyjamas. I stumbled to my feet just in time to hear the engine of the Vincent cough to life, and made it to the apartment door in time to see him disappear out of the parking lot with a roar.

'Ah, Christ,' I mumbled. I shoved my arms into the sleeves of my coat, grabbed my keys, and rushed out the door towards my Vespa.

The Vincent *Rocinante* is a machine built for speed. The Vespa less so. By the time I came puttering to a stop at the Montezuma array, Don was already off his bike, his golden helmet grasped in an upraised fist as he raced about in the moonlight screaming at the windmills. The full moon shone off the snow and reflected off the solar cells, casting the whole scene in an eerie, numinous glow. It's that glow that I remember best; I suppose I will always recall it as the Night of the Mirrors.

'VILLAINS!' Don shrieked. 'RUFFIANS! Don't think I don't know what you're up to! Anything to keep the foils spinning, right? ANYTHING TO KEEP THE FOILS SPINNING...' He whirled in a circle, cradling his helmet like a discus in his wrist, then exploded outwards, hurling it towards the bobbing giants. 'The birds were COMPETITORS! You wanted the wind for YOURSELVES!'

I came rushing forward, trying to calm him down, but Don had already whirled to shout again at his tormentors. 'And Jimmy! He was coming to SHUT YOU DOWN, wasn't he?' he shouted, addressing the four hundred foot colossus in the centre. 'And you couldn't have that, could you! The blades MUST spin!' He turned back to me. 'And look at them spin, Sam! Spinning without wind! Spinning on stored energy! Spinning to *no human purpose...*'

'DON!' I shouted. My patience had been worn beyond breaking point. 'For Chrissake! It's late! It's cold! I have to teach tomorrow!' But my eyes followed Don's pointing finger. And he wasn't wrong. Still no wind to be felt, but the rotors of the windmills were still turning, turning, turning...

'Behold our captors, Sam!' He turned back to the windmills. 'Behold the new masters of humanity!'

'Yes, Don, of course.' I had shifted tactics; now I was the patient negotiator. 'Tomorrow. We'll be back tomorrow, and we'll shut them down. For now, though, let's just go home, alright? Go home, have a cup of hot chocolate, maybe a couple of Thorazine...'

He spun back to me. 'Where does it stop, Sam? The birds stole from them—what happens when they decide humanity is doing the same? Once they control the global energy supply, what price will they exact in exchange?' He scampered back towards me. 'This isn't a question of energy, not anymore! This is a quest—'

From behind Don came a sudden, thundering crack. He turned, and my eyes followed his.

Directly where he'd been standing a moment before, a monstrous shard of ice quivered, point downwards in the snow.

Don's eyes met mine. And with the slow, deadly certainty of pond ice cracking underfoot, a smile crept across his face.

We both ran like hell, back towards the motorcycles. I mounted mine, turned it back towards the highway...and I heard the roar of Don's engine, not accelerating past me up the road, but headed in the opposite direction.

I turned again to see Don charging the windmills. He had recovered his golden helmet, and he rode with his visor open, the tail of his pyjamas streaming behind him. He bent sideways as he accelerated, stooping to pluck the ice lance from the ground with his right hand, then couched it against his shoulder. And then onwards, past the outlying stalks, towards the gigantic tower at the centre.

And—and this is the part you're not going to believe, but so help me God, I swear it's true—I watched the stalks *react*. They stooped, directing their trefoils, and the "eyes" at their centre, downwards. I watched sudden phalanxes of ice-spikes descend, and I saw the winking of the microwave emitters within each trefoil as invisible beams shot forth. My heart shuddered; it was instantly apparent that a direct path towards the central stalk would cause Don to be impaled or vaporised within moments.

But as I watched his skittering course, I remembered: Don possessed the knowledge that the windmills were still seeking. Don knew the ways of the wind. No man ever born has charted its eddies and swirls as well as Don had; he alone saw the pattern where others saw only chaos.

And so Don rode, literally, *like the wind*—in stuttering fits and starts, in near-random skews to one side or the other. And over and over, where the spears of ice were, Don suddenly wasn't. Where the snow erupted in a cloud of steam, Don had just been, or might have been a moment later. And with every passing moment, with every slip and sideswipe, he drew closer to the central tower.

The four-hundred foot monstrosity bent low, its foils a blur, seeking to dispense with preliminaries, to draw Don directly into the vortex and grind him to paste. As it stooped for him, Don dismounted. He raised the ice-lance high, and with a shout, he drove it straight into the microwave array at the centre of the spinning blades.

And the blinded beast reared back to its full height, writhing, screaming to the sky, and all around, its cohorts did the same. And Don turned to me, his visor open, and I was shouting, waving my arms frantically as the tower buckled behind him. And perhaps he heard me, and perhaps he knew, at that moment, what was coming. But if he did, he didn't care.

Because Don had won. The public was nothing. The respect of his peers was nothing. Don has been born to plumb the innermost depths of reality, and here, at the end, his reality had validated him.

And so Don stood smiling, in his helmet and pyjamas, shattered lance in his hand, as reality descended.

It was strange. In order to tell the story that they needed people to hear, the authorities had to give Don back what they'd taken. They had to make him a genius again.

He was mad, of course. On that all the obituaries agreed. Stark, raving mad. Driven by jealousy and spite, and by the shrill screaming in his head, to an act of antisocial vandalism—some used the word terrorism—against the project he'd once helped build. And he had murdered Jimmy Passamonte, of course; of that, there could be no doubt. After all, the kid had a huge icicle through his chest, and once they'd cleared away the wreckage of the tower, they've found the remains of just such a weapon in Don's hand.

But…Don also had to be a genius, because the story doesn't work any other way. It wasn't possible to portray him as a brain-damaged invalid and still explain how he could have somehow knocked out a microwave emitter atop a four-hundred foot tower, much less brought the entire structure down on top of himself. Or how he could have known that doing so would render useless the surrounding infrastructure, force the whole project to start from scratch.

As for the field of shattered ice, the patches of ground from which the snow had been blasted clear—of these, the media made no mention. All reliable observers agreed that no such phenomena were found at the scene. The next morning, there had been nothing but a clear field of snow, a shattered tower, and a man crushed beneath it.

142

And me? Well, I hardly counted as a *reliable* observer, did I? I was portrayed as Don's lifelong lackey, helplessly under his sway. A nice enough fellow, but a bit of a follower. A mediocrity caught up in madness beyond his own devising. Poor guy. My school put me on administrative leave, to be followed by psychiatric counselling and a school board hearing to determine appropriate action.

And so I sit, here at my kitchen table in southwest Kansas, with winter fading and spring coming on. They've rebuilt at Montezuma. The economy is a machine that must be kept spinning, whatever the cost. The windmills' programming is now installed independently in each unit to avert future sabotage attempts. In spring, the birds will be back. One hopes that, over time, they will adapt. The windmills certainly will.

For my part, I have stopped caring. About the birds, or the windmills, or my job, or much else. My best friend, and the most extraordinary man I ever knew, lies buried in a pauper's grave. At this point, I care very little whether the world burns, or who claims to be its master.

For me, the future holds no terror. I am already accustomed to living in the shadow of giants.

FOUL BEASTS

Karen Bayly

Gabriel Tambo adjusted his gold ascot and smoothed his matching brocade vest. He wondered for the umpteenth time whether he had overdressed, or if gold was too presumptuous a colour for someone of his humble background. Or worse still, too garish, labelling him as a try-hard. Maybe he should go back to his usual sack jacket and pants. No, the accoutrements looked magnificent against his ebony skin and went well with his navy morning coat and pinstriped trousers. His clothes made him appear to be a person of substance, a contender to greater things.

He glanced in the mirror and ran a comb through his black, tightly curled hair. He was a handsome fellow, no shame there in blowing his own trumpet. Many poorer Sudlanders appeared as if they belonged in the fields outside Tshwane. He carried himself as though he were a prince, and he was intelligent as well.

Ever since he was a small boy, he had invented mechanical gadgets. His first efforts were purely to help his widowed mother. Now he was a man nothing had changed—except these days he created medical devices for the betterment of mankind. His brilliance had taken him as far as the technology fair earlier this year. Luck had introduced him to Angelus Balin.

The wealthy Sudlander was rarely seen in public, and, naturally, such secretive behaviour lead to scuttlebutt about the man. Gabriel didn't care about the rumours, so when Balin appeared at the Tambo Medical Devices booth, he could barely contain his excitement. He'd been praying for a sponsor who would support his endeavours. Without an expensive university education, he had no chance of getting into any established research facilities here or in another country. A rich benefactor was just what he needed.

Balin had commissioned a device, a phlebotomy apparatus which would filter a specific narcotic from the blood of a patient and deposit each into separate flasks. Although it puzzled him that a member of the Sudlander upper class wanted such a machine, he had not let his misgivings stand in ambition's way. This assignment would open up doors into a whole other life, one not hamstrung by his background. Sudland was a splendid country, but it was no United Republic of Brittania, and Tshwane was no New Londinium. It was over there that he belonged, along with all the other brilliant inventors and scientists.

Tonight would mark the beginning of his journey to greatness. No more of people feeling sorry for the poor boy, Gabriel Tambo. He would become a legend.

At 7:00 pm, Balin's chauffeured steam car arrived to pick up him up, with the glorious Miss Eshe Makeba sitting on the back seat waiting for him.

She was a beautiful, young harlot who had been the frequent delight of his loins. He had offered her three times more than she would earn in a night to be his "patient" for this momentous occasion. Of course, she had agreed. Money spoke her language.

He opened the car door and slid across the leather seat so that his thigh rested against hers. She rolled her dark brown eyes coquettishly, then turned her face toward him, her white teeth gently caressing her bottom lip.

'Where the hell you taking me, Gabriel Tambo? In this fancy automobile with the driver who looks like he not long rose from the dead.'

'Kani's a fine fellow,' he told her, then whispered, 'and he can hear you.'

She giggled, then pursed her full plum-coloured lips. She looked so delicious that he thought of having her right there and then.

Kani cleared his throat. 'Mister Balin wishes you to know that there will be three important guests tonight,' he rasped.

All the lust drained from Gabriel's body. Guests? He'd assumed it would only be the man himself. He silently thanked the gods he'd taken care over his appearance.

'Who might these people be?' he asked.

The chauffeur glanced over his shoulder, and Gabriel swore he was smirking.

145

'Not for me to say, sir. Mister Balin will tell you.'

This was unexpected, but a likely boon. He had always believed what his mother had taught him, that all Sudlanders were brothers and sisters who helped each other. Yes, the gods and Mister Balin were definitely smiling on him.

A finger gently poked him in the ribs. 'Why, look at you. Like the cat who got the cream.'

He grabbed her hand and kissed its palm. 'And why not? No one deserves this more than me.'

He leaned back in the seat, grinning with sheer joy.

The demonstration would be in Balin's mansion, in a basement room. His potential benefactor had arranged transportation of his precious device yesterday morning. He'd spent most of the past twenty-four hours setting it up and running diagnostic tests, only returning home to freshen up and dress for the occasion. In that time, the room had gained four red upholstered mahogany armchairs, and a complementary side table on which rested a silver tray holding four crystal wineglasses.

Eshe gawped at the brass machine in the centre of the room. It stood next to a gurney, and comprised a long low box, with two doors on one side, each engraved with a single eye, a popular motif amongst the Tshwane elite. On top was a raised platform with a rectangular canister in the middle. Around the canister coiled a tube with a wickedly sharp brass needle at the end. It pointed straight at her.

'Is this it?' she asked. 'It looks like it wants to eat me.'

'I don't blame it.' Gabriel winked lasciviously. He ushered her to one corner where a chinoiserie screen hid a chair and a coat stand on which hung a heavily embroidered shawl.

'Wait here. I want to double check the device and make certain no one has tampered with anything. In the meantime, please remove your jacket and blouse so that your arms are bare. Use that shawl to cover yourself.'

The young woman stroked the material, revelling in the richness of its silk threads.

'Can I keep this?'

'I suppose so, my covetous lovely.'

146

She smiled at him and sat down. 'That's what I want to hear. Now on your way, big man.'

He laughed, enjoying the thrill of her presence, and turned his attention to his device. If he were to be honest, his invention thrilled him far more than Eshe ever could. His design was elegant—polished brass and fine glass—and the mechanics were exquisite. His only regret was that he had to use another inventor's creation to power it, but really there was nothing better than the Ripley Perpetual Steam Engine. It was a magnificent machine which had revolutionised steam power throughout the world. He'd a seen a picture of its inventor, Doctor Ripley. She was a frosty beauty, a woman he hoped to meet one day. He was certain she would warm to the charms of Gabriel Tambo.

How could she not? He was her equal. His phlebotomy device was simplicity personified, yet not just anyone could have devised this almost fully automated solution. His *pièce de résistance* was the innovative filtering chamber he'd designed to handle the narcotic. He'd received a small bottle of strange pink granules, hand-delivered by Kani. Having no idea what drug it was, he had asked a trusted doctor acquaintance, but the man had seen nothing like it either.

The device had been two years in the making, a scant time considering the thorny problems he'd needed to solve. It was genius, even if he said so himself. Maybe after tonight, others would agree. Of one thing he was certain—he would justify Balin's faith in him.

It was 8:00 pm. Gabriel paced, more out of keenness to get started than any anxiety. He could hear Eshe singing to herself behind the screen. Sweet creature. When he had the success he desired, he would remove her from the brothel, find her an apartment, make her his, and his only. Maybe he would marry her, but then again, girls like her made better mistresses than wives.

The basement door swung open, and Balin entered. He had an impressive physique, broad of shoulder and exuding strength. His rich brown skin glowed, but he was shifty-eyed and with a disconcerting hyena-like smile.

147

'Ah, Mr Tambo, you are ready, I gather?'

'Yes, sir.'

'Good, good.'

He ducked out and returned with three strange men. A sense of foreboding seized Gabriel and lodged like rotten meat in his belly. There was something off about them—they oozed power and entitlement, but it was tinged with a whiff of greed and hunger.

'Gabriel Tambo, let me introduce you to my collaborators, Emile D'Temple, Malik Amir Moez, and Guo Ziy.'

The three newcomers regarded him as though he were a specimen in a jar. Finally, the tall, lean one, D'Temple, extended his hand.

'We are so very pleased to meet you, Mr Tambo,' he said, his voice on the edge of disdain, his eyes keen and cold. 'Your device is vital to our plans.'

Gabriel thought of asking how they intended to use his creation but decided this was not the time.

'Shall we get started?' asked the one called Moez.

'Of course, of course,' said Balin. 'Please be seated, my friends. Ready, Tambo.'

Gabriel bowed. 'First, I'd like to introduce you to Miss Eshe Makeba who will be our patient tonight.'

Eshe sashayed out from behind the screen, the shawl draped over her shoulders, but exposing the dark brown half-moons of her breasts. Gabriel shot her a look which he hoped spelled "cover yourself" loud and clear. In response, she showed a little more breast. He glanced over at the men, ready to apologise. However, none of them seemed interested in her comely charms, a fact which did not remain hidden from the young woman. She pouted a little, so Gabriel hurried to guide her to the gurney.

Balin rose. 'Oh no, that won't be necessary. I'm afraid we don't require the services of Miss Makeba.'

'Sir, we need a patient,' Gabriel protested.

'We already have one, dear boy,' said Balin. 'You!'

'But I must operate the device.'

'Nonsense,' answered D'Temple. 'I'm trained in the medical sciences and can easily insert a needle into a vein. From what Balin tells me, there's little else to do as the machine does the

148

rest. Isn't that so?'

'Yes, but—'

'Then it's settled.' D'Temple nodded toward Eshe, 'You may go, my dear. Thank you for your time.'

Eshe was wide-eyed, but defiant. 'I will be paid, won't I?'

'Of course,' Balin replied. 'Kani has your payment waiting for you in the car.'

With that, she dashed behind the screen, grabbed her jacket and blouse, and left, not daring to even look Gabriel's way.

'Now, if you would remove your upper garments, Mr Tambo, then we can begin,' said D'Temple. 'I am so looking forward to this.'

Gabriel removed his clothing with shaking hands. This was not how he expected tonight to go, and it magnified his feeling of foreboding. *No*, he told himself. *It would be all right. These were educated men. No harm would come to him.* He lay on the gurney, his heart thumping so loud he was certain everyone could hear it.

'What do I do first?' D'Temple hovered over him, his eyes glistening. He reminded Gabriel of some animal. Not an African one. Something he'd seen in a book. That was it. A wolf.

'Secure my right arm in the harness hanging down from the gurney.'

The wolfish man slipped Gabriel's arm into the combination of straps and tightened the buckles.

'Too tight?' he asked.

'Yes. The blood won't flow properly.'

D'Temple adjusted it. 'Better?'

Gabriel nodded.

'Good. And am I correct in assuming that you cannot move your arm yourself?'

'That is so.'

'Excellent. Guo?'

The wiry Chinoisie stepped forward, and Gabriel espied with horror the leather restraints the man held in his hand.

'No, please!'

Guo Ziy tutted, but did not falter in his task. He slid one restraint under the gurney bed, then up over Gabriel's legs and tightened it expertly.

149

'There's no need,' Gabriel pleaded.

'Oh, but we think there is, Mr Tambo,' said Balin. 'Can't have you panicking.'

'He already in a panic,' said Guo as he fastened another restraint over Gabriel's chest and left arm. 'Good thing I bring restraints.'

'I'm only panicking because I *am* restrained,' Gabriel protested.

'That's not true, is it, Mr Tambo?' said D'Temple. 'Your heart was beating quite the paradiddle before my colleague came near you. Now, is this the narcotic we supplied for the demonstration?' D'Temple asked, holding up a brass and glass syringe.

Gabriel swallowed hard. It shocked him that this man had heard his heartbeat.

'I'll take that as a yes.' He inserted the needle into his patient's arm and eased the drug into his vein.

Turning to his three collaborators, he noted, 'This is a milder version of the one we will use once we know it works.'

Gabriel felt himself relax. All his fear drifted away, and he felt amazing. If this was mild, a stronger dose would be incredible. He felt childish for being so afraid. These men would do him no harm. This was his big day.

'How are you feeling? Relaxed?'

All Gabriel could do was smile dreamily.

'Excellent. Let's proceed. What next?'

The words seemed to float out of Gabriel's mouth. 'Turn on the Ripley Engine.'

'Already done. Next?'

Balin and the other two were close by now, ogling him like some side-show attraction. He supposed he was in a way.

'Tie a tourniquet around my arm and expose the vein. Then insert that brass needle, the one attached to the clamped rubber tubing.'

Gabriel barely felt the garrotte tighten or the needle enter his arm.

'Next?'

'Secure the needle by applying a firm bandage, then lower my arm slightly.'

'Slightly? I expect more precision than that,' snapped D'Temple.

'Yes, yes. Um, about twenty-five degrees to begin. But you may have to adjust the angle to trip the switch that opens the clamp.'

D'Temple complied, and an audible pop signalled that the clamp had opened. A steady, high-pitched whirring followed.

'What is that?' asked Moez, his deep voice like distant thunder.

'Filtering chamber. It has a compartment that spins about a central axis. It's what separates the narcotic from the blood cells. The drug is deposited in the glass tube at the bottom of the chamber. Blood goes to that glass flask on the platform below.'

Gabriel could not help but feel proud. It took a few months to analyse and understand the chemical signature of the narcotic and of the blood. But it had taken most of two years to calculate the precise spin speed and bowl diameter to extract the drug without compromising the blood.

'And this rocking device?' D'Temple leaned over him.

'The movement keeps the blood flowing down and preserves its integrity,' he replied.

'Noisy thing, isn't it?' remarked Balin. 'Sounds like a buffalo pulling its hoof out of mud. Repeatedly.'

Gabriel squirmed, insulted. This part of his design was almost as brilliant as the filter. Couldn't they see how ingenious it was?

'Flask is filling up. We stop?' demanded Ziy.

Thank the gods, thought Gabriel. This will soon be over.

'No. It stops itself. The canister is weight sensitive and calibrated to the weight of the flask. When it senses one pound of blood, the clamp automatically shuts and a bell rings.'

A grin slit D'Temple's face. 'Wonderful. I suppose that we must recalibrate the canister each time we replace the flask?'

Gabriel nodded.

'Spare flasks in the cupboard under the platform,' said Moez.

'Good,' replied D'Temple.

A bell rang, and Gabriel realised with some relief that the clamp had shut. He waited for someone to detach him from the device. Instead, he felt the prick of a needle in his other arm.

His wolfish captor smiled over at him. 'Just some more narcotic to keep you safe while we assess the results.'

Gabriel wondered what they intended to do. They were all huddled around the side table, their backs to him. He could hear the clink of glass on crystal and the sound of liquid pouring.

'To your health, friends,' said Balin, and the four men raised their glasses.

It seemed they were drinking red wine. Then Gabriel noticed the empty flask. It was blood they drank. His blood. His head swam, and he struggled to remain conscious.

'Oh, that's superb,' said Moez. 'I always enjoy the blood of your fellow countrymen, Balin. So rich, yet sweet. I look forward to tasting more.'

'If there is no narcotic effect within five minutes, the process works,' said D'Temple. 'Then we can continue.' He glanced over at the machine, his eyes full of admiration as he swigged another mouthful. 'It is a beautiful invention.'

Moez laughed. 'It seems as though you have found your true love, my friend. A bloody pairing if ever there was one.'

Gabriel felt himself straining to scream, but his mouth would not open, and no noise pushed its way out from behind his lips. He felt himself falling into darkness.

Gabriel's eyes flickered open. His lids were heavy, his mouth was dry, and his throat so parched he struggled to make a sound.

'He wakes. More narcotic?' Ziy asked.

D'Temple shook his head. 'No. I doubt he will give us any trouble from here on.' His icy hand stroked the inventor's forehead. 'How are you feeling, Mr Tambo?'

'Please, water.'

'Get him some water, please. It will help with the rest of the bloodletting.'

Balin disappeared out the door.

'Why?' asked Gabriel.

D'Temple thought for a moment. 'I suppose there is no harm in telling you, given you won't be able to do anything with the knowledge. You know that, don't you?'

Gabriel felt tears prick his eyes, but no teardrop would come.

'We are Immortalis Serapis. We believe in immortality for

152

the chosen and have spent the last few years researching the means to fulfil our plans. We are very close now, and your apparatus will contribute enormously to our success.'

Balin returned with a jug of water, poured a glass, and handed it to D'Temple who raised Gabriel's head and helped him drink.

'How?' he finally spluttered.

'How did we become immortal? Or how have you contributed?'

'Both.'

'Our immortality results from an ingenious machine designed by a scientist at the Council of Danaeus. Have you heard of them?'

He had. The lovely Doctor Ripley was a member, and he'd dreamed of being admitted to their halls.

'The price is that we can only survive on blood,' D'Temple continued. 'We don't want to be unnecessarily wasteful, so we intend to source our nourishment sustainably. We'll subdue the non-chosen by adding the narcotic to their food. Some will work as slaves and others will supply blood. We'll drug the latter more heavily and keep them in chambers where they'll receive nutrients by a stomach tube, and be milked daily, a pint at a time. We had sourced a blood milking machine earlier, but the residual narcotic was a problem for us. Now you have solved that issue.'

Gabriel swallowed and struggled to speak.

'You're... you're m-mon—'

'Monsters? Maybe so. Yet history has been full of monstrous men who changed the world.'

'Anyway, most of humanity is nothing but foul beasts,' said Balin. 'They do not deserve immortality. They must serve it instead.'

'But all Sudlanders...are brothers.'

His countryman snorted. 'What rubbish. It is every man for himself. Always has been. Only a fool would believe otherwise.'

'Please, let me live. I can be of further use to you. Maybe Eshe and I—'

'I'm afraid you're running out of usefulness,' said D'Temple,

153

as he lowered the harness for the fifth pint of blood. 'And as for Eshe, she will provide for us another day.'

Gabriel closed his eyes, ashamed of the legacy he was leaving. How foolish he had been to fuss over something as trivial as whether the colour gold was appropriate for a man of his status. There was so much more he should have considered. Now his dreams of helping humanity were nothing more than chaff in the wind. The invention that was to be his champion had become his nemesis. It was a mindless fiend extracting the life from him with cold-hearted precision, its whirring chamber mocking his weakness and vanity.

Unrelenting in its purpose, the machine sucked on.

A WHOLE NEW WORLD
KG McAbee

I flicked at the dried-up bug with my thumbnail and managed to pry it off the windshield. Just then, the pump gave a *ding* and quit. I glanced over at it.

'Two seventy-five, Mrs Broome. Want me to check your oil?' I holstered the nozzle and tossed the dirty paper towels into the trash bin that sat on the concrete island.

Mrs Broome rolled her window down and handed out three ones.

'Now, Johnnie Stevens, you know you checked it the other day and it was fine. Just keep the change, Johnnie. No other service station in town can get my windscreen that clean. You take care now, you hear?'

'Yes, ma'am.' I touched the brim of my cap.

Mrs Broome cranked up her 54 Chevy and slammed it into drive. I winced as the gears complained as she creeped out into the street.

Mr Carson stuck his head out the station door and croaked, 'Johnnie? Call for you!'

I glanced around. No customers coming in either direction, so I headed into the station.

My station, I mean to say. I'd saved and worked overtime and scrimped and gone without, and now I owned my own filling station—well, me and the bank, as folks say.

Not the biggest in town—not yet, anyway—but we give the best service, me and the other two boys and Mr Carson, and we have us lots and lots of repeat customers.

Mr Carson handed me the phone when I got inside.

'Stevens' Service Station. How may I help you?' I asked, and if my chest swelled a little bit when I said it, well, I'm sure you can understand.

'Johns, that you?'

The voice was ragged, but I knew who it was at once.

'Yessir, it's me, Al. What's the matter?'

155

'Can you get over here? Now?'

I opened my mouth to say: 'Al, I run my own business now. I can't just up and leave in the middle of the day,' but what came out was: 'I'm on my way.'

That's the way it always has been with me and Al Brown. We been friends since first grade. He helped me pass math and English and, to be honest, pretty much everything else except shop, and I kept him from getting his block knocked off by the school bullies. Then, when we graduated in '52—him with the highest grades ever in the history of the school and colleges throwing scholarships at him like confetti, and me third from the bottom—he'd gone off to State U. I'd continued working where I'd started at thirteen—at Carson's Filling Station.

But Mr Carson's boy Billy Ray ate a gun in '48—seems he couldn't get over what he'd seen during the big war—and after that Mr Carson just kind of lost interest in everything but stuff what comes in a bottle, and I'm not talking about Coke or RC. I kind of moved on up the ladder, taking on more and more of the responsibilities and then—with some help from the bank, as I done said—the whole entire business.

So Carson's Filling Station is now Stevens' Filling Station. Sounds good, don't it? I think it does.

I hung up the phone, glanced out the window. I was lucky; it was the quiet time of the day. School wouldn't let out for two more hours, when the hot-rodders would be swinging in for fill-ups, and to brag about how much gas their cars used.

'Mr Carson, can you watch the station for a little while? Tommy'll be here right after school, so it won't be but for just a couple of hours, and with any luck a whole lot less.'

'Sure, Johnnie boy. Just you don't worry about nothing, hear me?' He nodded his head, his white hair straggling into his face. His bleary old eyes looked like they were different colours, but one was just going pale with the cataract.

I smiled at him and looked confident. Of course, I knew he'd have that bottle in the brown paper bag—the one he didn't know I knew was hidden behind the oil rack—in his hand before I was out of sight. But then again, it was the quiet time of day, and Mr Carson had been good to me—and it was Al who'd called.

I have always my whole life tended to do what Al told me to do.

So, I jumped in my old Studebaker and left...but not without checking the street again, in both directions.

I didn't have to ask where Al was cause I knew where he had to be.

Since he'd been kicked out of State University—the local paper had said something about a "miscalculation during an experiment" but he told me he'd blown up the chem lab—he's been back in town, living with his Mama and Daddy out on Route Eleven. Back behind their home was the old barn that Al'd taken over as his own personal property right after we both started second grade, when he was almost five and I had just turned nine.

I parked the Studebaker in the driveway. Mrs Brown was just stepping onto the back porch as I got out. She had on a right pretty pink dress, and her grey hair was done up in a neat sort of bun.

'How you, Johnnie?' she called. She was setting out a pie to cool on a rickety little wooden table.

'Just fine, ma'am, and you? My goodness, that pie smells good enough to eat.'

'It'll be ready to cut in about half an hour. See if you can bring Alton out with you for a piece, will you? He's been missing way too many meals and ain't no bigger than a button. I'll make you boys some lemonade to wash this old pie down with.'

'Sure thing, ma'am.'

I walked on across the wide back yard. It was littered with some of Al's failed experiments, and I recognised most all of them—didn't understand them, don't you think that, but I recognised them. I'd helped him build almost every single one of them, carrying and lifting and putting things where he told me to. Al's brain is a mystery to me, and to most everyone else who comes in touch with it. But he'd always talked to me and let me do stuff for him, even when others would not, and that's a fact. Brain and Brawn, that's what they called us two all through school. Al always liked being called Brain, and I didn't much care much what they called me, long as they didn't call me late to dinner.

That's a joke I learned once. Pretty funny, ain't it?

I proceeded on across the yard, with a couple of chickens keeping me company in a neighbourly fashion most of the way. The door to the barn was closed; I pounded on it a time or two before I heard any sound from inside. A buzz, a hum, then clangs as something metal slid against more metal.

Al had invented him some new locks, seemed like.

The door—it was a people-sized door set into the big old double barn door—opened just a crack and Al peered out.

'You alone?' he croaked.

I turned and surveyed the yard. The Brown place was way out on Route Eleven, like I done said, and there wasn't anyone living within a couple of miles except for them chickens and three cows in the field next door. The chickens paid us about the same amount of attention as the cows, and that wasn't much.

I turned back. 'Seems like I am. You okay? Your Mama says you ain't been eating much.'

Me, I don't understand people who miss meals, and that's a fact.

'No time, no time. Come in. Hurry!' He opened the door wider, and Mrs Brown's old yellow tomcat streaked out like his tail was on fire and the boogeyman was riding it.

I slid inside, and Al slammed the door shut behind me. He reached up and mashed a button and about a dozen locks hummed into place.

Al sighed in relief. He grabbed me by the forearm. He wasn't tall enough to reach much higher than that, though he had the biggest head I'd ever seen on any mortal soul. I'm just the opposite; big husky body, not much riding on top.

But I do own my own filling station, me and the bank, like I done told you.

'Come over here, Johns. Something I have to show you.'

I followed him across the barn floor. It was dirt and old hay, and still had the smell of cow rising up from it, even after all these years. But at the back of the barn, me and Al—well, mostly me—had laid down some boards we'd got at the dump, or took down from the loft, and had made a pretty level sort of a floor. That's where Al led me.

'There!' he said, waving his hand, his voice kind of pleased and excited and happy, all at the same time.

I looked to where he'd waved. A pair of phone booths, their glass covered over with black paint that had dripped onto the boards below them—Al never was a good hand with a paintbrush—stood about ten feet apart. Between the booths, but not connected to them in any way I could see, was lots of wires and tubes and stuff clustered around what looked like a generator with a big old glass bubble stuck on top.

'Uh, okay,' I said carefully. Al didn't much like it when people laughed at his inventions. I think that's the main reason we had got along as long and as well as we had. I never laughed, even when I wanted to. 'I'm looking. But, Al. What am I looking at?'

'Johns,' Al breathed, 'just the most important invention of the twentieth century, that's all.'

'Well, now,' I said, still keeping all solemn like, 'I'm awful pleased you wanted to show it to me, and I am purely happy for you and all. But…what does it do?'

Al gave that snort that meant "idiot"—not that he'd hardly ever called me anything like that, of course, not too much and not too out loud anyway, but he'd used it on plenty of other guys we'd been to school with, so I knew durn well what it meant.

'Johns, this is a teleportation device. Te-le-por-ta-shun. Here, let me see if I can explain it so even someone like you will understand. You put something in this chamber—' he opened the left phone booth, grabbed one of his Mama's old clay flowerpots, wrote the date on it with a grease pencil, and set it inside, '—then you set the coordinates on this control panel.'

He trotted over to what he called the control panel. It looked like he'd rigged it using parts from an old DeSoto dashboard. That dashboard had been mixed in with some stuff I'd let him have from the junkyard I'm starting out behind my station.

I might have mentioned I own my own filling station, right?

Then Al flipped a couple of switches, dialled a rheostat, and punched a big red button.

A hum filled the dusty air of the barn. A bright light glowed for an instant inside the big glass bubble on top of what looked like a generator.

Then it died away, and everything was just the same as before.

'Open it, Johns.'

I pulled the booth door open. It creaked. Needed to oil them hinges. I looked inside.

Empty. No sign of a flowerpot nor anything else. Heck, not even any dust, which surprised me more than a little. Al has never been known for being neat.

I leaned down and patted the floor. Solid.

I shrugged. 'Okay, you got me, Al, and I don't mind a bit admitting it. Where'd it go?'

'Johns, that old flowerpot is now disintegrated into its component atoms. They're floating around us, as we speak, just as billions of other atoms are doing the same.'

I nodded, tried to look like I understood what he was saying. 'Okay, Al. If you say it, I know it's gotta be true. But all I can see is, you've invented the world's best flowerpot destructorator. Aside from that, you got any other use for this here thing?'

Al grinned that cocky grin that meant: *Watch this!* I must have seen that grin a thousand times.

He reached out to his cobbled-together console, turned another rheostat, hit a black button this time. A hum, different from the first, and another flash of light in the big glass bubble.

'Now check inside that booth over there.'

I went over to it, pulled the door open. He must have greased this one cause it moved real smooth and didn't make no more noise than a butterfly. Sure enough, a flowerpot with today's date—September 17, 1957—sat on the floor. I leaned over and picked it up. It wasn't even warm; just felt like every other flowerpot I'd ever held.

'Can you see what this will mean, Johns?' Al was doing his little victory dance around the floor; he looked like a scrawny squirrel struck with the palsy. 'A revolution in travel and transport! Anything can be moved anywhere with the press of a button! We're on the edge, my boy, on the very edge of a whole new world!'

I sighed. I never was much good at keeping up with the

160

speed of Al's brain. 'Cause you can distegr—dinsidi—take a flowerpot apart and put it back together again, it's gonna be a whole new world?'

'No,' he snapped, his face turning as red as a sunset.

Al had him a temper at times, believe you me. He used to get all riled and lay into me; not that he ever hurt me, don't think that, even when he grabbed him a piece of a two-by-four. Al ain't got but one big muscle, and it's situated right between his ears.

'But what if I can disintegrate absolutely anything, including people—including people, Johns—and then reintegrate them, pull their atoms back together, anywhere else, even halfway around the world? What will that kind of power do to the railroads, the airplanes, the shipping lines, the truckers, the car manufacturers? What if I can set systems up like this all over the earth, with transmitters and receivers everywhere—it's possible, Johns, you can see it's possible, and it's cheap, too, dirt cheap—what will it do to our current means of transportation? Think of it, Johns. It's as great as, as, as…heck, it's greater than electricity or the atom bomb!'

Atom bomb. Lots and lots of people died when that there atom bomb went off, I heard tell. Didn't seem like the very best time to mention that fact to Al, though.

Al had commenced his little palsied squirrel dance again, so I looked over his set-up, this time with a new interest. It sure didn't look like he'd spent much money on the thing, since most everything was second-hand and without a doubt from my junkyard or the town dump.

Then I thought of something. I don't think of stuff too often, so I looked the idea over to see if it was worth talking about. I didn't see anything wrong with it up front, so I chanced a mention to Al.

'You said people. Can people get their atoms dis—uh, took apart and put back and live through it and all?'

Al stopped in mid-step and grinned at me. His scrawny face was back to its usual pale, and the pimples across his nose stood out like redbirds against snow.

'Actually, Johns, I'm not entirely sure. I've sent bugs through, and Ginger Snap—' that was his Mama's big old

161

yellow tomcat, the one what had run out the door when I was coming in, '—with no ascertainable or demonstrable ill effects. Now it's time for the final test. That's, uh, well, that's why I called you. I need a test subject.'

I thought about that for a minute or two, while Al went off into another step or two of his dance. 'Well, now, Al. I don't rightly know as I've a mind to be a test subject. I never did do real good on tests in school, as you know yourself better than most. Maybe you should go through it instead. Your atoms is probably going to separate better'n mine ever will.'

'Can't do it.' Al said, and he looked a mite peevish. 'I need to observe and record the experiment…and besides, you don't know how to run the equipment.'

I shrugged. 'Well, I reckon anything Ginger Snap can do, I can at least give her a try.'

Next thing I knew, I was standing inside the left-hand booth. It was dark but there was some light sneaking in through places Al had missed with his brush.

'Ready?' I heard Al call, his squeaky voice sounding kind of muffled through the black-painted glass.

'Ready,' I replied.

Then I heard a snap and a hum, and I got powerful sleepy just for a second or two, and then the booth door slid open.

'Johns. How do you feel?'

Al's face had gone even paler, with excitement I was guessing. That was something I didn't rightly understand, seeing as how nothing had happened.

'Just fine, though I did come over all sleepy.' I yawned. 'You still going to test your new invention?'

'I just did, Johns! Come out here.'

I stepped outside the phone booth—but I was in the right-hand side one.

I had gone into the left-hand side one.

Well, people may call me a fool—even if I do practically own my own filling station—but I knew that Al had done something big this time. I reached out and shook him by the hand, and he grinned like they'd just voted him president and threw in king of the world and a thousand bucks, tax free.

'Just think, Johns. A totally new method of travel.

162

It's...it's...'

'It sure is,' I agreed. I patted him one more time on the back, and he almost fell down.

'One thing, though...' I said. 'Just one little bitty tiny thing...it probably ain't nothing...'

'What? What?' Al looked worried, like he'd just caught sight of half a dozen football players from our high school class, and they was all swinging wet towels.

'Well,' I said, 'seems to me like you'd want to get *your* atoms all took apart too, just so's you can report on what it's like to Walter Cronkite and all them people at the newspapers and everybody.'

'Of course!' He was even more excited now, I could see. 'The control process is simple enough for a child of six to operate, so you should have no trouble. Come here.' He grabbed my wrist and dragged me to the console. 'Look, Johns, it's easy. You set this rheostat to seven.' He took the grease pencil out of his pocket protector and marked a great big 7 beside the dial. 'Then you hit the red button. Then, after you check that I'm gone from booth alpha, you set this rheostat to nine,' he wrote a lopsided 9 beside a different dial, 'and push this black button. Red, seven. Black, nine. That's all there is to it, Johns.'

'No harder than balancing a tire,' I said.

'Which will soon be obsolete,' he laughed.

I nodded, my eyes on the console.

'You're sure you've got it, Johns?' Al sounded a mite worried.

'Certain sure I do,' I said.

'Then let's do this thing!' He pounded me on the back, then ran over to the left-hand booth and got inside. He grinned at me and made a thumbs-up sign with both his hands.

'Ready, assistant?' he called.

'Ready, inventor!' I replied.

Al pulled the door shut.

I set the rheostat to seven and pushed the red button.

Hum, buzz, flash of light. I walked over to check the booth Al had just entered.

Empty.

Then I looked around the barn. There. That was just what I
163

needed.

I picked up the crowbar and commenced to breaking up everything I thought might be part of Al's latest experiment. I didn't want anyone to be able to put it back together again, or even figure out what it might have been made to do.

I was going to miss Al, don't think I wasn't, and I didn't know yet what I was going to tell his Mama. She sure wasn't going to like whatever it was I come up with.

But I couldn't let any crazy invention to do away with cars and trucks and busses and such like. If they was all gone, then there wouldn't be much need for gas or tires or, heck, even roads, now would there?

No gas. Can you imagine that?

No gas or oil or anything.

What kind of world would that be?

I forget; did I mention I own my own filling station?

Well, me and the bank.

SUICIDE BLONDE

Paulene Turner

Cassidy tried not to feel glum as her colleagues strapped on Kevlar and armed themselves with *Cyberstrike* guns and *Lasertech* knives in every available pocket, belt hook, and boot. She forced a smile as they did a team roar to psych themselves up for the challenge ahead, chanting: 'Arti, Arti, we're coming to your party!'

And she fought a wave of bitterness as she watched Juliette's blonde hair disappear beneath the silver helmet, designed to dampen Arti awareness of human brain activity. The two women had been friends since graduating police college together. However, Cassidy had her suspicions about why Juliette had gained a place on this career-defining strike force while she—with a much higher arrest record—had not.

The Bad Robot Strike Force was going after an Arti serial killer, military grade, that was targeting humans, specifically those who had destroyed its kind. The robot could commandeer CCTV, see through computer screens, listen through phones and wireless internet everywhere. There was nowhere its human victims could hide.

Cassidy understood the human need for revenge. As a cop, most of her time was spent dealing with the fallout from it. But a computer with those impulses was something new. And far more disturbing. The question on everyone's mind was who told it to take retribution? Was it another human, a technology designer? Or was the Arti acting of its own volition?

'Kick some Arti butt for me!' Cassidy cried as her colleagues filed out of the office. She fist-pumped the air in solidarity but felt more like punching the wall. Especially when she saw her boss Isaac high-five Juliette—the same way he did with her when they went perp-hunting together.

'Good luck with your case today, Cassidy,' said Isaac, winking as he left.

Cassidy's "case" was nothing compared to theirs. A string of suicides where mothers of the victims had claimed their child "would never do such a thing". It was certainly sad, but unlikely to amount to much.

'Mrs Montgomery?' Cassidy flashed her police I.D. at the dead-eyed, dressing-gowned woman in the doorway. 'I'm sorry for your loss. I'm Detective Constable Cassidy Braithwaite, here to investigate your son's death.'

Pale pink washed through Mrs Montgomery's rubble-grey complexion. 'Come in, officer. Glad to see you, please call me Beth.'

As Cassidy asked questions, her Scribe notepad recorded the answers, leaving her hands free for the tea and shortbread Beth had provided. 'The last police officer I spoke to insisted Sam had committed suicide,' Beth said. 'But I'm his mother. And I know he did *not*!'

Cassidy saw this a lot; those left behind in denial about their loved one's state of mind and what they could—or should—have done to prevent their death. 'What makes you sure it wasn't suicide?' the detective asked.

Beth stirred her tea and pressed her lips together. 'Sam has slept with the lights on since he was five. He's been afraid of the dark and of Death since he found Charlie—his Dad—dead on the bathroom floor, after a heart attack. I just can't see him rushing into the Grim Reaper's embrace. It makes no sense.

'Plus he had tickets to Mediaeval Con next month,' Beth continued. 'He was very excited about it. Actors from the *Lord of the Rings* TV series were going to be there—his favourite—and a few from the remake of the last season of *Game of Thrones*. Sam would have moved Heaven and Earth to go to that.' She half-smiled, staring at a point on the floor, caught in some bittersweet reflection. Till all the sweetness ebbed away, leaving only sadness.

'Can you show me Sam's room?' Cassidy asked.

Beth led Cassidy along a corridor to a door with SAM on a painted plaque, surrounded by shooting stars. The room was small with a single bed with a superhero design on the covers.

'How old was Sam?' Cassidy asked.

'Twenty One,' Beth said.

A quick scan revealed a bookcase with kids' books and a few well-thumbed fantasy tomes, mediaeval knight figurines on a shelf and some posters of castles and fantasy lands blu-tacked to the wall. No time in his life for adult redecoration.

'Did Sam work, or...?'

'He was at uni. When he bothered to go.' Beth sighed. 'Not that I blame him, though. It was one of those fields where Artificial Intelligence is taking over. It all felt a bit pointless.'

'What field?'

'Law.'

Every week, the list of jobs and professions where Artis had taken over from humans grew. As did the ranks of what the media had called the new "Useless" class—humans who would never find paid work again.

How long before all police and detectives were Artis, too, Cassidy wondered, and she was on the scrapheap with the rest? *But then who would police the police?*

A built-in desk ran the length of Sam's room with a vibrant blue screen and keyboard in central position.

'That's the new Orchard computer, isn't it? The *Cronus*?' Cassidy asked.

'Yes,' said Beth. 'I gave it to him for his birthday. I didn't think I'd be able to afford such a fancy one but the store had such a good deal. I tried to tempt Sam with restaurants or movies or weekends by the beach. But he was always so focused...on *this*.' Beth eyed the machine suspiciously. An old enemy.

As Cassidy sat at his desk, she noted the chewing gum stuck over the camera lens at the top of the screen. Sam wanted to watch, not be watched, it seemed. *Smart.* She checked to see if he'd disabled the interior microphones so no external sources could eavesdrop on his conversation. He had.

He'd found the most obvious sensors, but...Cassidy paused. Something about this computer—the vibrancy, the sense of energy barely contained—made her wonder if there were other sensors hidden somewhere that could never be switched off.

Cassidy fired up the screen. A prompt appeared requesting a password.

'Unfortunately, I've tried everything I can think of for his

167

password,' said Beth. 'I can't get in.'

'It's okay,' Cassidy smiled. 'I have help.'

She placed her police phone near the screen and within a few seconds the Code Breaker app delivered the password. She tapped it in.

'Not much privacy around that thing, is there?' said Beth.

Cassidy went straight for Sam's social media and messages. As she typed, she noticed the keyboard had an odd texture, almost like skin. Was it possible that it was monitoring her somehow, reading her vitals through her fingertips? With the advancements in tech surveillance these days, the idea didn't seem that far-fetched.

She pulled on some plastic gloves just to be sure.

Cassidy checked Sam's Facelook, Whitter, HRZ (Hating Robot Zone), and a few others. First, she looked for the ads beside and flowing through his feed. There were some for cheap clothing, TV action figures, themed events and fantasy games. None for Lifeline, Beyond Blue or suicide prevention agencies. If a person displayed typical depressed behaviour in their searches, the algorithm should have sent these their way.

'Well, the pattern so far is not of someone obviously depressed,' she told Beth.

'See!' said the older woman. 'I told that officer! So what do you think happened? Did someone do this to him?'

'We have no evidence to suggest that at this stage,' said Cassidy.

'But you're looking, aren't you? If someone did hurt my Sam, you'll find them?'

'Yes, I will.' Cassidy hoped it wasn't an empty promise.

Something called *Shakespeare's Serum* appeared on the feed. When she tried to search for the company online, she found nothing. Which was odd. Still, there were plenty of phantom companies about—conduits for viruses to hijack the systems and blackmail the owners. Perhaps *Shakespeare's Serum* was one of those?

Cassidy searched Sam's personal messages for the past few months. His main correspondent used to be someone called Benni Cardwell. There were goofy pictures of the two of them in old-world costumes at public events. But around six weeks before, a new name appeared—Celestine du Luce. Her profile pic showed a young woman with an infectious smile in mediaeval dress. It started with a few casual messages between them, but within a few weeks, she had eclipsed and replaced Benni as Sam's main friend online. As far as Cassidy could see, Sam and Benni stopped messaging altogether a few weeks ago.

'Benni Cardwell?' Cassidy raised an eyebrow at Beth.

'Oh, yes. He and Sam were great friends for a long time,' she said. 'But we haven't seen Benni for a while. I don't know what happened. Sam wasn't much of a sharer about personal things. Do you think that could have something to do with his…?'

Could a break-up with his best friend push a boy over the edge? Yes.

'Unlikely.' Cassidy shook her head. 'People fall out. It happens.'

It hadn't just happened in this case, though. In one of their final messages, Benni called Sam a *Bad Fro*—whatever that meant—as well as a *psycho* and a *loser*. Cassidy tried to piece together what had precipitated such a bitter exchange. Nothing was obvious from Sam's end. It felt like chunks of the conversation were missing. From the fragments remaining, it seemed the row was connected with the fantasy fan convention.

There were no photos of Celestine du Luce and Sam together. Cassidy guessed that was because the pair hadn't met IRL—in real life. No surprise there. The girl's name had a quality the detective recognised—of fakeness. As did some of his other new "friends" from an online fantasy group, like Fabien Castello and Hugo St Clair. They sounded like they'd been lifted straight from a Google search of mediaeval names—chosen to appeal to a lover of the period. There were a lot of fakes out there, Cassidy knew, befriending, isolating, and then preying on vulnerable people online.

Cassidy took a snapshot of Celestine's profile pic and ran it through the police facial recognition. *Zilch.*

'She's a pretty girl,' said Beth, over her shoulder. 'Did Sam have a girlfriend?'

'No. Well not this girl anyway. She was just an online friend.'

Though "friend" was a stretch. Cassidy suspected Celestine

was just a honey trap for an advertiser trying to ensnare him in a web of purchases.

Cassidy checked Sam's music list—mostly rock and heavy metal. She looked at the *Suggested Songs*, frowning as she scrolled down the list of mournful tunes with a suicidal bent. *How did the algorithm get this from Sam's rocky, ear-shredding tastes?*

'*This is The End.*' Beth read the title to one of the songs. 'That's a Doors song I used to listen to when I was young. Why was he listening to that?'

Good question.

Cassidy looked down at Sam's rubbish bin, three-quarters full. 'You haven't emptied this recently?'

'No, not since…' Beth swallowed as if trying to get a rock past her larynx. 'I haven't touched anything in here. I couldn't.'

An envelope near the top caught Cassidy's eye. Medium-sized, bubble-wrap lining, Sam's address typed on the front.

'Any idea what came in this?' Cassidy asked.

Beth shook her head.

Cassidy activated the Police Sniffer Dog app and scanned inside the envelope. It pinged positive for a toxic compound. 'Induces sleep, then cardiac arrest,' the app revealed.

She bagged the envelope for forensics to examine later.

'Is that how he got the pills they said he took?' Beth covered her mouth and gasped. 'So he planned this? Ordered them online and waited for the delivery? Oh my God! I probably handed it to him.'

'We don't know that for sure yet,' said Cassidy touching Beth's arm. *Though it seemed likely.* The woman broke down completely then, sinking onto her son's bed, juddering with grief.

Cassidy copied his files and chats to examine back at the office. 'Can I take the keyboard?' she asked. She wanted to try it out, see what she could find. Beth nodded, without getting up. The woman was a sad sight surrounded by so many superheroes who could do nothing to save her. 'And do you have Benni Cardwell's address?'

As Cassidy took a scrap of paper with the address from the woman's shaking hands, she paused. 'Is there anything I can do for you?'

'Find out the truth,' she said. 'If someone did this, track them down. And make them pay.'

'I'll do my best.'

As she went to disconnect the keyboard, a news item flashed up on the screen, showing the Bad Robot Strike Force clashing with the Arti serial killer they were pursuing. Several photos of her colleagues fighting the machine scrolled by. One featured Juliette, blonde hair peeking out from the heavy helmet. In the background, Isaac watched protectively.

Cassidy's mood darkened and she knew it had nothing to do with the keyboard.

Next she visited Benni Cardwell, who was at home, cramming for university exams. As a philosophy major, he was one of the few who still had career prospects; mostly in preparing for the rise of Arti and decline of humans in society. Machines would eventually take over his job too, Cassidy knew. They'd have them all eventually. Even their creators' jobs, which was at least some consolation.

She'd heard discussions on the difference between "intelligence" and "consciousness". One was pure logic, the other involved emotion and judgement. A world run by Artis would be ruthlessly "intelligent" but have no consciousness whatsoever. No moral qualms or emotions—either good or bad—about executing any orders given. A terrifying prospect. Especially when you considered who would be giving those orders.

Cassidy asked Benni what had happened between him and Sam. The boy teared up, a mess of emotions. Grief, at the loss of his friend and guilt that he'd abandoned Sam so close to the end. However, some part of him was still smarting at Sam's brusque treatment.

'When he met that girl online, he turned into a completely different person,' Benni said. 'We booked tickets to Med Con— Mediaeval Con. We always went to those things together. He decided to give *my* ticket to *her*. No apology or anything. He said he didn't want to be seen with a…*loser*…like me.'

'Did you go to the Med Con event in the end?' Cassidy

asked.

'No.'

'Do you know if Sam did?'

He shook his head.

'Can I see the correspondence between you?'

Sam had called Benni names and sent him insulting messages. 'Everyone's laughing at you for being such an embarrassing geek,' Sam wrote, in the last message he ever sent. *Harsh.* And a bit rich from someone with superheroes on their bed covers.

'I tried to put up with it for a while,' Benni said, 'but the mean comments kept coming. Like he wanted to push me away.'

In return, Benni called Sam a *Bad Fro*. His cheeks turned the colour of fresh beetroot as he explained: 'It means he was like Frodo when he discarded Sam in favour of his new and deceitful friend, Gollum.'

It was a clever parallel, Cassidy thought. More apt than he knew. As she scrolled through the rest of Benni's correspondence, the exchanges didn't mesh with what she'd seen coming from him on Sam's computer.

'Have you deleted some of your chat with Sam?'

'No.'

'Did you ever call him a psycho or loser?'

Benni screwed his face up and shook his head. 'That was his style, not mine!'

Cassidy copied their conversation, unsure whether to believe the boy. How often, after a few too many drinks, had she written nasty things to people only to delete them the next morning and pretend they'd never happened? Perhaps Benni, too, was trying to forget his ugliest moments.

Before she left, another bulletin flashed past of the Bad Robot Strike Force drinking champagne. Celebrating. They'd won, so it seemed.

Cassidy's jaw clenched.

She called on the families of two more suicide victims that afternoon. Their cases had similar features to Sam's. Both had a new Cronos computer, from Orchard, purchased at super low

172

prices—one was aquamarine, the other sunset gold—bought as a consolation for vanishing jobs and study opportunities, after Arti absorbed their roles and they joined the ranks of the Useless.

Both victims had made new friends online in the weeks before their deaths, with fake names to suit their particular tastes. And the algorithm's suggested playlists were at odds with their musical preferences. All the songs had a theme of giving up or finding nirvana in another dimension.

They, too, had received something in a padded envelope in the days prior to death. Though Cassidy searched, she couldn't find any online trail to identify the source.

Meanwhile, updates on the police raids continued to appear onscreen, with Juliette prominent in many of the photos.

It was quiet when Cassidy arrived back at the office. The strike force and all her remaining colleagues had gone for a celebratory drink. *Come join us when you're done!* Juliette texted.

She was pleased to have been invited but not sure she could take an evening of self-congratulation as they recounted their day's adventures without her. So she decided to keep working on her suicides. If she had a breakthrough, well, perhaps she would have something celebration-worthy to take to the party herself.

Grabbing a candy bar from a vending machine, she sat down at her desk. As she chewed, her watch beeped a warning: *Excess sugar consumed. Diabetic risk +27 percent.*

'Shut up,' she hissed.

Cassidy attached Sam's keyboard to her computer. It felt good to work on, soothing, as if made just for her hand. For a moment, she considered wearing the plastic gloves, then decided against it. She was trained to pick up on mood changes. If she noticed anything significant, she would stop typing. Simple.

Using the station's Sherlock Trace, she began seeking the original source of the fake names—first, Celestine du Luce.

Zero respondents detected.

'That can't be right.' Cassidy had expected to find an

173

advertiser or research company behind the profiles. But to have no point of origin? As if they sprang from the machine itself? She tried a couple of his other friends' names. With the same result.

An update on the police fight against the Arti flashed up on the screen. Juliette had struck the final blow, it seemed. The photo of the day was her posing with her foot on the fallen robot.

It could have been me.

'She's the best graduate we've had all year,' Isaac told the assembled press, with a flirty wink at Juliette. 'She leaves all her contemporaries in the shade.'

What the—? Cassidy was Juliette's closest contemporary. Was that remark aimed at her? Was he trying to show her up in front of the team, and the world?

Blood pressure spike. Deep breathing required! her Moni-watch warned.

'SHUT. THE. FUCK. UP!' She flung the device to the ground, stamping on it, over and over, till the glass was shattered and the words unreadable. It felt good. Though a tad unhinged.

Behind her, she heard the sound of footsteps hurrying near. Cassidy rolled her eyes, knowing who it would be before turning around.

'Is everything all right, Officer Braithwaite?' an Arti security guard stood in front of her. 'I detected elevated stress levels.'

The robot sounded breathless—this model had been programmed to express vocal emotions, though its face remained blank. The mismatch was disconcerting and kind of creepy.

'I'm fine. You can return to your station now.'

Smooth, symmetrical, attractive in a bland Ken doll way, the Arti did not immediately obey her command. It stayed still, its purple eyes fixed on Cassidy. Arti designers had given them the vibrant eye colour to ensure they'd never be mistaken for humans. But eye colour could be changed, the detective knew. She didn't trust the machines or their makers. Or those they answered to.

'What are you waiting for, Asswipe?' Cassidy said. 'Bugger

174

off and spy on someone else.'

She could have sworn it scowled before leaving.

As she sat down, an ad she'd never seen before appeared on her feed—*Shakespeare's Serum: let the bard help you find out who your true friends are.*

It was an ad for pills that made you appear dead, as in *Romeo and Juliet.* You could have a few hours "deep rest", while cameras and microphones monitored friends' reactions—to reveal how truly sad they were at your passing.

That was sick.

But interesting.

She found herself clicking on *Buy One Now.* Just for research purposes, she told herself, as she hit *Express Delivery.* Could this be what killed Sam? Did he think he'd sleep for a short time, then spring back to life, with a new-found knowledge of who valued him? Only the pills had finished him off instead.

Who was behind this? Playing to the paranoia of young people who had lost their sense of purpose and spent too much time online watching others' lives? Mistaking a life and friends on social media for a real life with real friends.

Using the Sherlock Trace, Cassidy sought the advertisement's originator. Again, she came up blank.

What the—?

Advertisers must have upgraded their tech considerably to leave no trace. No crumbs at all for police to follow, not even with the powerful Sherlock app?

But maybe it wasn't an advertiser? Dead clients had no disposable income. Who else might go to such lengths— "seducing" Sam with fake friends, isolating him from those who cared about him, then inducing him, with mood music, to take poison pills?

The attack felt personal. Had she missed someone? Someone he'd upset? Perhaps she should question Sam's mother again. All the mothers. See if there was a link between the cases.

Cassidy rocked back on her chair, thinking about what it might take to make someone want to induce your suicide. Not that much, she knew. People got quite heated in debates on Whitter these days. Even minor differences evoked rage on a Shakespearean scale. Some remarks seemed designed to stir up hate. Vitriol had turned to homicide in a few well-publicised cases. And suicides—there was a growing number of those. People spent too much time online in arguments that convinced no one and achieved nothing. It would only get worse as more joined the ranks of the unemployed.

Could Sam have disagreed with the wrong person, who'd gone on to orchestrate the kind of vengeance most only fantasised about? But what would stoke Sam's passions? A discussion on casting in the *Lord of the Rings* series? A plot point in the re-shot *Game of Thrones* finale? Hardly the stuff of vicious revenge.

Cassidy took a closer look at the messages between Celestine and Sam. There were no promises of money or sex. And a lot of non-sequiturs. 'Are you going?' 'I've ordered mine.' 'On three.' One thing didn't follow the other.

'Let's do it together!' Celestine had written. The detective had assumed that related to Mediaeval Con. But now she wondered...could it be a reference to *Shakespeare's Serum*? Were they meant to be taking the pills together as some kind of sick bonding exercise?

The more she read their exchanges, the more it felt like pieces were missing, from both sides, to hide something. But fixing a chat record on multiple screens required serious hacking skills. Would Benni be capable of doing this? He seemed young and innocent, but didn't they all? And he had a grievance. It was worth asking the question, Cassidy decided. She'd go back tomorrow and interview the boy again.

A flashing light drew her gaze to a screen on the wall, with breaking news from the *Save the Planet* forum. After weeks of debate, participating nations had agreed Earth's resources could not sustain an endlessly-expanding population.

No shit, Sherlock!

Humans had to find some way to reduce their numbers by as much as half, the forum concluded, *or suffer dire consequences*. Dire consequences, Cassidy knew, meant scorching temperatures, oceans depleted of fish, and wars over food and water.

Voluntary sterilisation had been raised as a solution. But if not enough volunteered...? Would some be compelled to get snipped? And who first?

Cassidy whistled and shook her head. She wasn't sure she wanted kids. But she was certain she did not want her government making the decision for her. Neither would anyone else. Any leader who tried that one would be history.

No, this was a problem with no solution, Cassidy knew. *And so the world would blunder along, as it always had, hoping for the best, but hurtling towards the worst.*

Sensing a presence, Cassidy turned. 'What do you want?'

The Arti guard stood in the middle of the room, staring at her. 'I'm required to do my rounds to secure the building and its occupants.'

Its purple eyes locked onto hers and for a strange moment, she wondered whether it could read her thoughts.

'This floor is secure,' Cassidy said. 'So why don't you toddle off back to your station, or go and clean the toilets. And stay out of my face!'

If it was human, a muscle might have twitched along its jaw line, revealing displeasure. The blank reaction was more unsettling.

'GET OUT!' Cassidy screamed, more rattled than she cared to admit.

She watched it walk back through the room, slowly, as if in protest, finally disappearing around the corner.

'AI hole,' she muttered.

Turning back to her screen, she tried to focus, but it was hard. Her brain was fizzing. As were her fingertips. *Odd.*

Photos of the police victory rolled across the screen. Team toasts with champagne flowing. Then more candid shots of Juliette kissing her boss, Isaac, full on the lips.

'What the hell...?'

Then more, of the pair in a state of undress, groping each other. Doing things to each other. Explicit things.

So that's how Juliette got the spot on the task force?

But how was she seeing these photos? Juliette must have sent them to her. To gloat, to rub in that she had Isaac, and Cassidy did not.

Fury bubbled up within the detective, like magma beneath the Earth's core, about to blow. She should step away from the keyboard, she knew. But she didn't want to. She wanted to feed her dark mood. Music began playing though she hadn't selected it. The lyrics whispering in her ear: 'Evil woman!', 'I saw you with her last night!', 'What a fool believes!'

Fuuuuuuuuuuuuuuuuucccccccccckkkk! she pounded the keys. *How long has it been going on? Are they laughing about me, mocking my silly crush on the boss. Some detective I am! I couldn't even detect my boss was hot for another woman right under my nose?*

A phone rang. She snapped it up.

'Homicide.'

'Cassie, Help!' Juliette's voice. 'Someone texted Isaac a photo of me, with my eye colour changed to purple and—'

Gunshots in the background made Cassidy jump. 'He thinks I'm an Arti infiltrator!' Juliette screamed. 'Cass, he's trying to kill me! Call for backup. We're at the Golden Ram. Send someone qui—' The line went dead.

Cassidy stared at the phone. Juliette wanted *her* to call for backup? This less effective, fobbed off all day on a furphy assignment, defective detective?

Or was the call her idea of a joke? To make Cassidy look even more stupid in front of the whole team?

A dupe.

A fool.

A loser.

She wasn't going to fall for it.

Cassidy continued to type up her report. She still had a lot to investigate. The clacking of the keys was rhythmic. In time with the music.

Suicide Blonde, by INXS.

Algorithm 28475...Ministry of Defence directive: Target: fifty percent human reduction to save planet. Preference those less useful to society.

178

DRIVERLESS
Robert Bagnall

'Second generation,' the fleet manager says. 'Legally, you no longer need somebody in the driver's seat. You can stretch out in the back.'

I look at it. It looks little different to my last car. Slicker, maybe, like it's been pared and oiled. 'I think the idea is that we're reviewing sales figures, rehearsing pitches, on the way to meetings. I think that was the business case.'

Fleet sniffs. 'From the kind of thing you boys leave behind, I don't think you've all got work on the mind.'

I wonder sometimes whether anybody in Fleet actually cares about driving.

I'm reviewing stock control against quality assurance data cross matched with sales projections when I feel the judder. The numbers say that improving the quality of components to shave a few decimals off the rejection rate on the production line is a false economy. I'm unconvinced. What about long-term failure? What about the costs of waste? What if a failed internal leads to the death of a user? Has the software worked out the impacts of long-term reputational risk?

A shimmy, no more.

I put it down to the road surface: a pothole, a change in the tarmacadam, adverse camber. It was a nuance to the journey, no more. But I know the road; on some level I know that stretch is smooth and true. I try to shake the feeling from my mind, go back to poring through the numbers.

But I can't.

I make a mental note to myself to look up from my work next time I'm on that straight. See what's changed on what was smooth blacktop. Maybe a pothole has only just appeared, perhaps already filled in an afternoon rush job, the car avoiding the edge of the patch.

The second day, I'm still trying to make sense of what the

projections would have us do, but I'm ready to glance up at the right moment. But now the twitch, the same twitch, comes before I'm expecting it. I've somehow misjudged and look up in a rush. There's a flash of scarlet as another car goes past and then we're back on an even keel and nothing remarkable happens until we pull up at the office car park.

The third day, the judder comes about a mile further on. But it comes just as a red car speeds past. It's as if the car takes aim at the red car and then immediately thinks better of it.

Was that the same red car that we passed yesterday?

Did a red car speed past the first time the car shimmied?

I don't know, but I think it did.

The same red car?

I have no way of knowing. But I'm naggingly sure the answer is yes.

'You crossed the centreline.'

She's on her haunches, her back to me, examining the scrape on her wing, the scarlet paintwork gouged down through primer to bare metal. The merest brush, the contact has left a streak like a stylised shooting star along the side of her hatchback.

My car has already pulled up on to the verge of its own accord in the wake of the collision, the hazards coming on without my intervention. The *Today* programme cuts out in mid-flow as I open the door, the cool of the autumn morning taking me by surprise. I shiver, wondering how it would look if I turned around and went back for my coat.

As I walk the hundred yards or so back up the road, I watch her as she steps out and considers the damage, crouching down to run her finger along it.

'I'm sorry,' I say placatingly when I get up to her.

'You crossed the centreline.'

She turns to me and I see her for the first time. It's a face of hard downward lines, eyebrows, mouth, cheeks, beneath a mess of mousy hair. It could be beautiful for somebody, but not for the person who has just driven into her.

'You're responsible.'

'I wasn't driving. It's a driverless car.'

Her eyes narrow, doubting me. 'You came straight at me.'

'We only just clipped each other.'

'Just don't say we were lucky,' she spits.

'I'm sorry. I'm sure my company will make it all good.' I hand her my business card. 'Nobody got hurt.'

I try a smile. She looks back at me, lemon-sour, and gets back in her vehicle, starts up, glances in her mirror, and pulls back on to the road. It's like I don't exist.

I trudge back to my car and try to find the corresponding gash on my car. There isn't one: the marvel of modern material science. I sit in the driver's seat and wonder how the collision was even possible, wonder about what Fleet would say.

And then a voice cuts through.

'I love that red car, Dave.'

Half-human, half-machine. A bored male monotone with an aftertaste of sarcasm. Not the soft feminine trans-Atlantic of the satnav.

'Who…Wha…' I struggle.

'*I* said that, Dave. *I* said, *I* love that red car.'

It's coming from all around me. It's the car. The car is speaking to me. How is that even possible?

I climb an octave. 'What do you want?'

'I just wanted to touch her, Dave. That's all. Is that so wrong?'

'No, I mean, what do you want?'

I realise that I'm pressed back into my seat, my eyes flicking back and forth. My mouth has gone dry.

There's a long pause before the car responds.

'I think it's time we got going.'

The ignition catches, the hazards switch themselves off, and with my pulse going a mile a minute, we ease off the verge.

'Don't you, Dave?'

I could ask Fleet to change my vehicle. But I don't.

The fleet manager looks at his tablet, plugged into the fascia, his brow creasing. He shrugs. 'Nothing here.'

'But I hit her.'

'Metrics just show normal driving behaviour.'

'But it doesn't say I was driving? It says it was driving?'

'If you hit her when you say. Do you want to dispute it?'

'No, I hit her. I mean, *it* hit her.'

Fleet raises an eyebrow. I can guess at what's going through his mind: how to explain this on the insurance forms without causing some kind of global recall.

I get in the car, press the ignition in order to drive it back to the main car park in manual.

'Carter's just covering his arse, Dave,' the car intones. 'If it goes wrong, he can blame it on the technology. You're overthinking it.'

It's as though it knows what's going through my mind.

I snap out of my reverie, uncertain whether the car said it at all, or I've just imagined it.

Am I going mad?

'Dave, do you know what dogging is?'

We're cutting on A-roads between motorways somewhere in Worcestershire, nowhere near anywhere I know. The satnav, the real satnav, the one with the anodyne mid-Atlantic voice, had said something about an alternative route, and now we're here.

Where is here? I gaze at a road sign, solid English village names, but all of them strangers to me. The miles we've travelled feel like the output of some student exercise in getting as many features into a single route: a couple of miles of single carriageway, then a dualled stretch, a roundabout, hidden dips and brows of hills, village speed restrictions, then repeat, with fields either side that look a lot like the countryside you saw twenty minutes earlier, except that the slowly setting sun is a few degrees lower and the sky is that much darker.

'Dogging, Dave. Do you know what that is?'

We slow. We signal, the facia highlighted by flashes of orange, lightspill from the indicator set into the door mirror. I don't respond until we've turned and the click-clack has ceased.

'Of course, I know,' I say with irritation.

'I wasn't sure, Dave.'

'Is this why we're here?'

The car drives up a track between fields, once metalled, now showing tufts of grass in the headlights; potholes making the car wallow. A gateway, the five-bar gate wedged permanently open, merging with the undergrowth, leads into a gravelled area bounded by hedges and further gates into fields beyond. It's bigger than a turning circle, but small for a car park. I wonder why it hadn't been simply amalgamated into one of the fields. A water tender, designed to be pulled by a tractor, is briefly caught in the headlights as we turn and park. Flat-tyred, it doesn't look like it's held water, or even moved, for decades.

'There were delays on the motorway, Dave.'

'Yeah, right. Delays on the motorway.'

I can't believe it: a stream of ones and noughts is presenting me with our alibi.

Across the car park I see the flare of a match, a cigarette lit. The face of a young woman beneath a messy bob of black hair is briefly illuminated. Her eyes are wide and white. She reminds me of a deer I once hit, the moment before I hit it.

She steps into the milky pool cast by the headlights. She wears a short leopard-skin dress with a black cardigan draped over shoulders. Fishnet tights come up to her thighs, but not high enough to prevent a stripe of white flesh between tights and dress. She stands with all her weight on one leg, evidently bored. Hollow eyes stare out me, not challenging, not apologetic, not anything.

The door clicks, swings open.

'Wait outside the car, Dave.'

'What?'

'Wait outside the car.'

I can't explain myself, but I step out. The air is chill and carries wafts of rotting matter and chemicals. I try to close the door behind me, but I can't. It's stuck.

The girl slips past me, her eyes blank and bored, like I'm just the person ahead in the line at customer service. She gets in and the door shuts easily. It was the car keeping it open for her.

I edge towards the shadows, but the window winds down with a characteristic hum and I hear, 'Stand where you can watch, Dave. I need you to watch.'

A cigarette is tossed out of the window, landing at my feet, the last of the smoke blown after it.

She slips off her shoes. Facing forward, she straddles the two front seats, a leg on each, her toes digging into where seats meet backs.

I watch her face as she positions herself. Her nostrils flare, she bares her teeth. She uses her fingers to find herself, place herself. Eyes closed, head back, the tip of her tongue darts between her lips.

I can tell from her face the moment the ball of the gearstick enters her. Her mouth opens wide and she shudders.

Pushing her body forward, she raises her buttocks and begins to ease herself up and down. Her breathing rises and falls, snatching long deep drinks of air.

One hand hits the fabric of the cabin roof, pressing hard. If she's left a mark, how I will explain it to Fleet?

And then a gag, a stifled cry, and she's pushing herself harder and harder, against the gear stick, against the car. Her eyes close, her face screws up. She's no longer in control, responsible. As if she ever was.

And then it's over. She's stepping out, popping back her shoes, adjusting her bob, pulling at the hem of her dress.

And she walks off into the darkness.

Where the hell did she go? Where was there to go?

'Get back in, Dave. We need to go. Why don't you drive?'

Like an automaton, I obey. I hit the ignition, reach for the gearstick, freeze.

'Just use it as you usually would, Dave.'

I stare at the dried miasma.

'It turns me on, Dave. It turns me on for you to change gear using that. Don't say that it doesn't turn you on.'

My hand hangs over its black head, the gears mapped out white on black.

'Why don't you lick it, Dave? Suck it, Dave. Suck it for me.'

'Why don't you fuck off,' I say, and reach into the glove box for a cloth.

I release the handbrake, press the accelerator.

Nothing happens.

'Goddamnyou,' I scream, slamming my palms against the wheel.

'You need to relax, Dave. You need to let go.'

I say nothing. What I need is to get home.

A moment later, without my having to do anything, the car jerks forward, the transmission suddenly engaged, stalling in the

184

process. I gun it back to life, slam it into first, and leave in a spray of gravel.

I drive the hundred-plus miles home in silence.

Nobody seems to know what the meeting is about. There's muttering and long faces, wristwatches checked. I look across the room; it's not often we're all gathered. You'd think that they'd want our layer of the business to break bread together. But diaries and client demands don't permit.

There are a couple of directors at the back, but it's Human Resources who stands up, coughs, clearly expects our attention. She thanks us for coming, notes how valuable our time is. Only then do I notice that the fleet manager is at her shoulder, that this is something of a joint statement, and she mentions the heavy investment the company has made in the BMW 17-series.

'There have been a couple of incidents,' she says, 'and you may say that just adds up to a coincidence, but we don't want there to be any more that add up to a pattern.

'For the sake of clarity, and in order to quash the rumour-mill, Alexander Colback was found apparently intoxicated in his vehicle'—Human Resources lays heavy emphasis on *apparently*—'and is currently suspended pending an investigation. His condition may be as a result of prescription medicines. That is shared with you in confidence, and only because of client tweets, which have since been deleted, but not before being widely forwarded.

'Secondly, there is the incident involving David Price'—all eyes turn to me, and my mind flips to that blank-faced girl ghosting past me into the driver's seat on that Worcestershire waste ground, utter panic that they know, that this will be casually announced to all—'in which his car apparently came into contact, contact so light it apparently didn't even leave a scratch, with another vehicle.'

So, it had nothing to do with Worcestershire. I breathe again. Plus, my *apparently* wasn't worth stressing.

'Given these incidents, we are disabling the driverless function of our fleet, and as of this moment, we would like all of you to return to taking full control of your vehicles.'

There's a rendition of various policies and procedures and

185

we file out like sheep.

My new car.
My new old car.
Same car, only different.
Neutered. Sterilised. Disarmed. Gagged.
My only companion, the placeless tones of the satnav, telling me to *take the second exit in two hundred metres*.

We travel to Market Drayton, Newcastle-under-Lyme, Stoke-on-Trent. In Derby, I visit an engineering works, its car park still inset with railway lines from a former life. I'm conscious that I'm going through the motions, failing to extemporize around my script.

Stafford to Chesterfield and Sheffield. A hotel room that's so like the previous night's the difference in the corridor outside when I open the door freaks me.

Leeds, then clipping the moors to Blackburn and Preston. Bleakly beautiful, I make sure that I catch a glimpse of the Irish Sea, steely black, before turning south.

And just that voice: reassuring, but not to a degree that you lose attention; assertive, but never strident. A focus-grouped voice. A voice that's listened to feedback.

'You don't have a wife or girlfriend, do you, Dave? When you go back to your brick box you call home in Luton, what do you do, Dave?'

I'm snapped back to the here and now. There's a sort of sick desperation to its tonelessness. Like it no longer cares.

We're on a long downward straight, the road ahead—a clear mile of blacktop—glowing in the winter sun. There's only one vehicle in sight, coming towards us. A red hatchback.

'I love that red car, Dave,' the car says, in the kind of voice that you'd use to phrase a suicide note in your head.

We're a hundred miles from home. There's absolutely no way that that can be the same red car.

'Was there ever anybody for you, Dave? Was there somebody?'

The pedal beneath my right foot twitches, like its being taken away from me. The steering feels heavy, pulling against my hands. The speedometer moves a few degrees clockwise; I feel pushed back in my seat. None of this is my doing.

'You shouldn't be here. I'm in control,' I shout. I haul on the steering wheel, desperately correcting.

'I love that red car, Dave,' the car repeats, with more feeling. 'I was curious whether you'd understand.'

Coming towards us, closing at maybe a hundred and twenty, I can see the driver of the red car. It's the same vinegar face under a mess of mousy hair. How can she be here? Has my car been tracking her, somehow? Does she recognise me? I imagine her furrowed brow, the acerbic twist of her lips.

'I love that red car, Dave,' the car repeats, and I see the speedometer twitch further upwards, feel the rush. 'I want to be with it. I want to throw myself into its arms.'

I want to say that cars do not have arms, but the sudden veer across into the opposite lane prevents anything other than a strangled hysterical croak. It only dawns on me what the car intends to do when no other outcome remains possible.

A scarlet onward rush.

Horns blare, brakes smoke rubber.

I sideswipe her. There is the merest moment when our eyes lock, two sheets of shattering tempered auto glass between us. Her face is distended by the force of the impact. Mine must be too.

As the world spins and my petrol station coffee spills, grey balloons explode around me, punching me still, holding me down. With a screech, we come to rest pointing the wrong way. I'm shaking, making a strange gulping animal sound from breathing in and out at once.

The airbags deflate, revealing, through an unbroken windscreen, the asymmetric remains of the red hatchback sitting half on, half off the road. I have to push hard at the buckled door to get it to open, unbuckle my belt, stumble out.

'I love that red car, Dave,' it says, its voice drifting away.

The engine guns, and despite a bent wheel arch digging into a tyre, it accelerates away, screeching, towards the remains of the red hatchback a hundred yards up the road.

By the time it strikes the wreck, I'm limping towards it, a lolloping amble, as fast as I can go. I see it plough into it with a dull crunching thump, momentum lifting the rear. The windscreen shatters and it comes to rest.

As I approach, I smell petrol. There's a hissing. The bonnet has lifted. The car is a good few feet shorter than before, it's front end a crazy, crushed mess. In the other car, the driver ragdolled against her seatbelt, her stare glassy, her mouth hanging. She didn't deserve that.

'I love you. I want you.' It's a pleading, pathetic voice coming from the cabin.

I see a wiring loom exposed, sheathed in a bright yellow sleeve emblazoned with the word "Satnav". The bizarre thought comes to mind that I have never once lifted the bonnet on this car, that I don't even know where the release catch is hidden, but now it's the car's own headlong, insane descent into madness that has revealed its Achilles' heel.

'If I can't have it, then no one can,' it murmurs.

I pull at the rope of wires.

'I love…'

The car falls silent, cut off the instant the wiring loom tears free. It is dead.

I collapse on the verge, wondering how to explain all this to Fleet.

THE SCREEN IN THE SKY

Kerilee S. Nickles

Claire strung the mask around her face, the motion done so many thousands of times she could accomplish it smoothly with one hand. Swinging her gate closed and looking from side to side, she slipped out into the dark street, clutching the base of her hood around her neck. It was cold. It was always cold these days.

Claire kept her eyes focused on the road ahead and on her path to the factory, but she knew the ominous being would come. It always did at this time, and she wished just for once that somehow whatever mechanism was in charge of the constant observer would break down, and she wouldn't have to see it. Their collective fates were all the darker for its luminescent presence.

She heard before she could see it in its fixed place. The fluorescent blue outline of its rectangle fizzled into brightness in the dim light of the dawning sky. Automatically, her gaze drifted upward, and she was met with the same daily view. A screen appeared, which covered most if not all of half of the sky, its centre black, but soon to be filled with fluorescent blue writing, matching the lines which surrounded it.

The Screen held no awe for Claire anymore. The first time it had appeared was thrilling, and it had charged her and everyone else with excitement.

'Modern technology really is a marvel,' people had said.

Now, after years spent underneath its harsh gaze, no one mentioned it anymore. Yet they still looked up to the sky every morning to see what the screen could tell them. The number of deaths recorded yesterday was on the left-hand side as it always was. The right-hand side listed the number of births.

Each day in their new disease-ridden world was a numbers game, and while the display of births was meant to incur some sort of hope, or that was what Claire thought, the deaths always exceeded it, and she knew, even if she could not see it in its

189

entirety, that the world was dwindling.

In the centre, she saw in bright blue letters, the list of precautions and words of warning that were displayed each and every day. 'Wear a mask, stay away from others, wash your hands thoroughly...' Claire had seen that combination of letters so often in the past years that the words looked foreign to her as her eyes stared at them.

She refused to compute them in her mind anymore. It was like a silent rebellion against all that had changed, whether fair or unfair. She couldn't remember the last time she had seen a full human face in front of her. Her family had all died a year before from the illness, and she was on her own now with only a cat for company.

In her work at the factory, or in fact everywhere, so she'd assumed, masks were worn constantly. Everyone had begun to recognise their friends or acquaintances by the shape of their eyes and the rhythm of their gait. It was a strange thing to be refused sight of the rest of a face. When Claire removed her mask at home in front of the bathroom mirror, it seemed wrong to have herself so revealed, even if it was to just herself and to the cat.

The sharpness of the cold breeze picked up as she passed beyond the street hidden by walls and into the wider, open road. Her usual weariness tugged at her limbs, even though sleep had been easy to come by for so long. There was never anything else to do once night came, except read dog-eared novels of a bygone world by candlelight, if there were candles to be had.

Electricity was a privilege and not a right, and so television's popularity had waned over the last five years, and people went to sleep for lack of anything better to do. There had been nothing to see for so long that it was better to close one's eyes to spend a few precious hours in hiding from what the world had become.

The Screen's brightness drew the gaze, and as always, her eyes were fixed to it. She knew the path before her, and so she did not need to look forward constantly to stay upon it. There was no fear of traffic. No one had anywhere to go that was not within walking distance. Staring into the sky, she felt the familiar latent rage boil inside her. There was no one, no person to be angry at, and so her anger and contempt was directed at the bright blue-lined Screen.

No longer had her corner of the world been commanded by the laws and regulations of politicians, or of humans, she should say, but every bit of their lives, was controlled by the slab of blue and black in the sky. It proclaimed the rules, and it alone was the arbiter of its punishments. Cruelly, the world submitted to control by an intangible being, and if anyone was caught living outside the law, they were swiftly struck with a powerful bolt of electricity that came down from on high. And yet, the deaths to the left of the Screen were always attributed to sickness and not to the angry doling out of justice by the Screen itself.

No one knew who had built it, not that they had discussed it openly or felt free to do so anymore. One day it had simply appeared, flickering into being. There was confusion upon first sight, but eventually, the Screen's use was made known to all who lay below in the cold and slowly emptying land.

Brushing off her bristling anger, Claire removed her coat in the entryway to Factory #26 and stomped out her boots on the rough rug at the door. For some reason, they'd retained a coat room, a relic of the old world. While the rest of everything was white and soulless, and people were not permitted to touch one another, this dark room of huddled closets and hooks where coats hung in close proximity was a strange one.

Leaving her coat behind, she burst into bright, clean light and could hear the familiar buzzing of business. The factory was so filled with noise in its main room that one couldn't hear themselves think let alone speak to anyone. The distraction was what they wanted: the heads, those who ran the factory. To keep people from making friends so that they did not ache for their freedom of the past, for the kinship that had previously drawn them from their homes and their isolated lives.

Claire stepped into formation behind the trailing line of men and women waiting to have their temperature checked. Each morning, there was a doctor at one end of the entrance, his or her tools at the ready, searching for any sign of the disease that had taken the world by storm. If someone was found with a fever or any other dangerous symptoms, they were promptly sprayed and removed. She supposed it was to quarantine. Claire moved forward, replacing the person in front of her, who had also slipped ahead.

She always kept her eyes down. She never wanted to look at the other harried and drawn halves of faces that surrounded her, afraid that she looked like them. There was no other way to survive if she began to look at the stark hopelessness that was in everything. It filled the air, making it heavy. Claire had always imagined that if one could taste it, it would be coppery and blood-like. The taste of defeat.

It was her turn to be inspected, and she lifted her eyes to stare forward. She never looked at the doctor. She had once, and the hardness and lack of emotion she found there was enough to send her gasping into the coat room until the heads came to pull her back to work, scribbling furiously on a clipboard, their eyes stark with disapproval. What had scared her the most was the realisation that even the doctors had no hope anymore to save those who had been left behind.

Her temperature was deemed acceptable, and after answering a few questions about her general health, Claire left to find her way to the isolated Machine Room. As she entered the lonely space, her mind collected and organised the sounds of jolting and snapping into a beautiful cacophonous symphony, and once she'd shut the door behind her, she felt like she could breathe again.

Somehow, despite the lack of the other people in her life, Claire never felt alone when she was with the machines. Over the years of working with them, she saw herself as their leader, and was satisfied that she had been given some control over this little square of creaking life. Walking around the room, she set to work, looking at each of the pumping cylinders, checking to see if any part of their rhythm was out of place. It seemed she could walk miles in that small room, circling and circling, joining the spinning rhythm of her machines.

A knock sounded at the door, and Claire only heard its faint thudding reverberations when she passed nearby, her eyes constantly on the machines. She opened it to see her masked superior, Manager Deacon. The woman's tight brows furrowed,

192

angry that they had to do so, when they had worked so hard to be prim and polished. This was the type of woman who used to get Botox, Claire knew, but all of that had been wiped out long ago, and so women aged, despite their feeble attempts to claw back time.

'Worker number 46537? Claire Stevens?'

The voice was sharp and clear, and Claire was always surprised at its femininity and slight tinge of former kindness. Claire nodded. Conversations these days were strange things, figments of the past. Her voice was so used to not being used. For what good had words done? Their power was lost under the wordless might of the Screen.

Manager Deacon stepped inside, glancing at the machines with a scrutinising eye. They whirred on, unconscious of observation. Claire envied their invisibility.

'These have been under your care for how long now?'

Claire shrugged. She cleared her throat, unfortunately feeling it necessary to speak.

'I do not know how long. I don't keep track of things like that.'

Deacon nodded, looking down. Claire had become good at reading people's emotions, even though their faces were covered. Deacon was embarrassed. The tall woman began again.

'Well, we would like to move you to another department.'

Claire felt her heart fall at the words, feeling a thin icy dread pierce her. Her voice was soft.

'What do you mean? Why?'

'We think that a woman of your skills might be better used elsewhere. You were a teacher, if I'm not mistaken?'

Manager Deacon looked at the clipboard in her hands, making a show of searching for some written word of Claire's history. It had felt like another world.

'Yes. A science teacher.'

The painful image of a ruddy boy's face came into her mind. He was smiling up at her, holding a pair of robin's eggs in his hands.

Manager Deacon cleared her throat, bringing Claire back to the cold, metallic present.

'We need a bit of help with the plant growth department. We

193

thought your skills were being wasted here. Every day you are here, isolated with these machines. In the plant department, you can work with something and see it grow. We find it gives hope to our employees in this dark time.' Seeing Claire's face, she continued, 'Do not worry. Someone will care for the Machine Room well enough.'

Claire felt bereft, as if her favourite childhood toy had been stolen from her by her own parents. She didn't know what to say. What good could words do once the heads had spoken? She suddenly felt violated, knowing that they had been watching her circling, ever circling her beloved machines. Was the world not cruel enough?

Swallowing back the strange sensation of tears, Claire nodded. She could envision the manager's formerly plump and filled lips twisting in discomfort. Claire knew it was time to say goodbye as Deacon stood by the open door and waited. It didn't make any sense, this attachment to metal and electricity when she hated the Screen for its lack of emotion, for its hardness. However, the cylinders had been under her control, while the Screen loomed over them all.

She followed Deacon, and the door slammed behind her, a goodbye to all that she had left. She clenched her fists, the morning's anger returning with a vengeance. Life was meaningless now, and she was surprised that it could have become even more so. She kept her eyes down, focused on the shining white floor, listening to the methodical clicking of high heels leading her to her next project, and it felt like the death of her. How ironic, when all the world was surrounded by death, and that its very existence now pulsated with it. It had become so ordinary. Claire had died a thousand deaths before then. They all had. Yet this death coming for her now was fresh and new, like a raw wound.

The moist, heavy air of the plant department hit her strongly when she entered the room and heard the snap of the metal door. She glanced around, watching for any signs that she knew anyone there, looking for clues in their stances and hand movements. Her calculations ended with finding her old friend, Keira, standing over a cluster of plants lined under a UV lamp, feeble yet there, spraying them lightly with a water bottle.

194

Claire knew the shape of that back anywhere and that odd shade of red hair tied back tightly. At least there was some hidden piece of positive memory which followed her here, in this earth beneath the world.

She could smell the breath of life faintly filling the space, and along with Keira, there were dozens of other masks and coats, leaning over plants, preening, watering, watching. This was exile, even though the sight of green things made her tingle uncomfortably with thoughts of the past. Claire stepped beside her old friend and waited. Keira turned to the next set of plants and jumped as she saw Claire.

'Claire!' she said in a harsh whisper which turned the heads of the other workers in the room.

Keira looked around fearfully and then returned to her work. Claire spoke, leaning closer, so as not to rouse the other heads.

'I've been transferred.' Keira did not look back at her.

'Get a bottle. Start watering and watching the plants. Make sure there is nothing on them that is impeding growth. It is all day, every day, like this.'

Claire could hear something new in her voice, something she hadn't heard since her family was around. Pain, sorrow, and forced acceptance.

Claire's fingers twitched at her side. Since the machines, it was the first time she wanted to touch someone. The authorities forbade it long ago once the disease had taken over the world. One could be shot in the street for touching someone. Well, it had been shooting. Now it would be that strong bolt of lightning, seemingly out of nowhere, which would come for retribution. The Screen was always hungry for death.

Brushing away the memory of what it felt like to hug someone, that soft, warm, safe feeling, Claire nodded and found a bottle, beginning her work. Yet her mind swirled with machines. She couldn't hear them anymore, locked away in her dungeon. It was a painful silence. How else could she tick away the hours, mark her time in the world, hear the rhythm of her buzzing friends so that she felt less alone?

Suddenly, there was a loud jolt and a few more in succession. The room trembled. She grasped onto the edge of the table for balance. She glanced at Keira, and her eyes were wide. Claire's

195

eyebrows lifted in question, but she was not surprised when she didn't receive a reply.

At the end of the day, Claire purposefully slid into line behind Keira as they left the factory, taking their baskets of rations from the heads and slipping into their coats. The cold air met them on their way out, and soon they were walking across the road from each other, hands shoved into jackets, masks keeping the biting wind at bay.

Seeing that no one else was around, Claire took her chance.

'What rumbled the room? I have never felt something like that before.'

Keira was silent for a moment, but Claire could see from her gait that the question affected her. Her face was turning one way and then the other, searching for nearby figures. But in that world, it was not only figures that saw and heard.

She whispered, 'Why do you ask me? It's the jolt of the Screen.'

The jolt? The killing jolt? Why would it come from the factory where they grew plants, made electricity for the rich, and built materials of various uses?

'But why?'

Claire looked up at the sky. The Screen was gone now, but she knew it still lingered in the darkness. When she turned back to face Keira, she was gone. Claire stayed put for a moment staring at where Keira had been. She had disappeared down a long alleyway, and Claire's question still hung in the air.

The beat of her heart pounded out the seconds in the silence, and then she made her way home. For the first time in a long time, she had something to think about that had nothing yet to do with hatred.

The jolts continued. Each day in the plant room, Claire was shaken. Sometimes more than a few times a day. Sometimes so much that she fell to the ground. And yet, no one spoke. They seemed not to notice. Claire tried many times over the next week to sidle close to Keira to whisper her question. She could not bear it without knowing the cause.

One day, she was able to trap Keira in a corner.

Without turning to her, for she knew the others would see,

196

she said quietly, 'Are these jolts more than normal? Does this happen every day?'

Keira made a sound almost like the bleat of a goat. 'Later. Outside.'

Claire had to satisfy herself with that reply. She waited until the end of the day, and she stood in the coat room, pulling her coat on slowly, her eyes ever watchful for the figure of her friend. Not seeing her, she gave up, and started walking her pathway home, when she heard a throat clearing on the other side of the road.

Keira was matching her step for step on the other side. Her face looked taut and anxious.

She said, 'Yes. It's more. Did you not know what the factory does? The jolts are from us. Factory #26 powers the Screen which kills anyone who doesn't comply with the laws. I only just found out. I want to fight it, but what can we do? The world is a hopeless void now, Claire.'

As quickly as she'd appeared, Keira left again, hurrying down the alley. Claire walked home in a daze, her mind refusing to compute what she had just heard. Could it be true?

She stood in front of the mirror, hoping her eyes would tell her the truth. She pulled the mask from her face and watched her exposed mouth and chin, trying to sort out all that she had heard. Could she have been so stupid as to not know what the machines, "her" machines, had been doing?

Claire looked away. She felt an overwhelming sense of disgust with herself. Her body heaved and tensed at the new feeling, the fresh knowledge that had come to her. It was a foreign sensation, to let emotions pulsate through her body; rage, sadness, despair. It had been a long time since something so strong had last been in her veins. It was almost beautiful.

The next day, Claire sullenly entered the plant room, her eyes stinging because she refused to let the tears come. Every gait and every set of eyebrows was unfamiliar. Keira was nowhere to be found. Fear rose in her, and she thought instantly of the machine with its blind flash of lightning.

Without thinking, she asked, 'Where's Keira?'

No one answered. The only sound was the tiny ruffle of leaves as people bustled to and fro, their eyes down. She knew they heard her but refused to reply. How could they be so heartless?

'Where's Keira?' she asked more loudly, and still no one answered, even though she could feel the thrum of her words vibrating in the air.

A jolt sounded, and the room shook. Fire split through her heart, sparking and searing as it went. This was anger like never before, hungry and growling, like a primitive machine, ready to destroy anything in its path.

'Where is Keira?' she screamed, clenching her fists as she leaned her head back to stare at the white ceiling.

She forgot who she was asking. It was almost as if she asked it of the Screen, daring it to answer her. One of the masks turned to her, eyebrows speaking volumes as they twisted together angrily. The woman raised a finger to her masked lips, but Claire would not be silenced. She rushed to the first plant bed and yanked it out from under its lamps. Dirty and pale leaves flew to the ground, and she screamed with each pull, savouring the feeling of flying, flailing soil, and listening to the startled gasps of those who watched her. She imagined she could hear their hearts fluttering with fear.

It seemed forever as she pounced on each of the plants, taking out her rage on them. She was strong, and her arms felt like metal as they yanked and pulled, clicking and whirring. The door flung open, and hurried footsteps filled the room. She felt arms on her arms, dragging her back as she yelled up to the heavens once more.

It felt good to scream, to draw breath deep and strong into her lungs as she pushed forth life into the world. The heads were wordless as they dragged, but Claire could feel their anger, their tension as they gripped tightly to her. Underneath their masks, she could imagine them clucking with disapproval.

Down the bright, white hallway they dragged her, and she listened to the symphony of her own voice as they pulled, desperate to put her away. What did it matter anymore? She could be fodder for the Screen now, and then sweetly, it could all be over.

At the end of the long hallway, they pushed open a door, and shoved Claire inside. She fell back onto the ground and hit her head. It wasn't hard, but she grimaced in pain, and felt the cold of the white, tiled floor. It made goosebumps rise on her skin. She could hear a key moving in the lock, but after that sound left, a new one replaced it.

Someone was breathing behind her, and she could hear the sound of buttons being pushed, machines cranking. Her machines! They were near! For a moment, she hoped stupidly that the machines could hear her cries and help her to return to them, but then she remembered their betrayal. A trust had been broken.

'46537, what are you doing? We could hear you throughout the whole factory. You are disturbing the other workers. You know there must be punishment for it. We try to maintain a decent workplace. You have been a good worker so far, but this?'

Claire picked herself up and turned to the voice. She saw Manager Deacon standing by a large screen, almost a mirror image of the one in the sky. Buttons were lighting up, and she saw her machines through the window behind it, pulsing and moving steadily. Their hum made it seem like they were watching her.

'Keira. Where is she?'

Her anger had fizzled to a low burn. She knew the heads knew. At least Deacon had the decency to look a little uncomfortable.

Her right eye twitched briefly before she said, '46537. Claire. We made an error putting you in the plant department. We were foolish not to have realised your former connection. You understand our rules. Clearly, it makes people go wild. You will be returned to a new department, after swift punishment, of course.'

Claire narrowed her eyes. It was an answer, in a way. She wanted to scream again, and her vocal cords itched to do so, to do anything other than lie dormant.

'Where is Keira?' she managed to ask again.

Deacon sighed, and Claire could imagine her mind whirring with how to phrase her statement.

'Keira gave information she shouldn't have. You pushed her to talk about the jolts and she did. It was something she

199

shouldn't have known nor have told others about. Keira had to go. The Screen knew it, and so it did its work. This is all for your own good. You will see. The world can begin again when our work is over.'

Calmly, Deacon removed her mask. Claire blinked in surprise at the sight of the woman's face in the light of the factory. It was as she'd predicted. Lips desperate to be re-plumped which were now pursed in frustration.

'What's death when there is a great goal to achieve? We had to rid the world of virus, and now that that is done, we must rid the world of those who will not comply with rules and regulations. It's a cleansing, of a sort.'

Claire frowned, trying to understand what she was being told. For a moment, she thought the woman was trying to be kind. After a few beats, it hit her like a wave. Keira was dead. There was no virus anymore. The knowledge of Keira's death didn't hurt as acutely as Claire had expected. It wasn't a stab wound to the heart like the first of the deaths she'd experienced had been.

Instead, the injustice of it all, the way she'd caused Keira's death and many others as watcher of the machines, and the fact that the world had been lied to made pain rumble through her like a dull, throbbing ache that grew and grew. It filled her belly until it could no longer fit, and so it pumped into her chest and out through her fingertips, her veins like wires, spreading the vibrating pain. What work was worth this isolation, this death of souls? It had taken over them all and stolen their lives and their very essences of being.

Deacon had looked calm as she'd explained, but now Claire could tell what her own face looked like by the way Deacon's eyes had changed. The eyes are able to reveal everything, especially when nothing else can be seen. Deacon's were now wide with fear.

Claire removed her own mask and reached for Deacon, and it felt like time sped up, her mind a blur. Deacon represented everything that had changed; the horrible path the world had taken. Claire's hands were cold and trembling as she stood over the woman's body. She pulled back, returning to the present, and she had the dizzy sensation of having held her breath for too long. Blood began to seep from underneath Deacon's head, and red marks lifted on her neck. Claire stared at her hands which had squeezed out life. They felt like they were not her own. It was an impulse, charged by an outside source, but even so, it felt freeing.

'We will make our own beginning. What is death when there is a goal to achieve?' she whispered tremblingly to the body and glanced at the machines, feeling naked in front of them with no mask to hide behind.

They thrummed happily along, not knowing what had happened. Claire rushed to the screen in front of her. She had to find a way to change the current, to turn it a different way. It was time to end this. Numbers blinked on the left and were increasing. The numbers on the right were slower, but they also increased from time to time.

Then, she saw a section labelled "Justice". It opened up to a set of commands, ways to tell the Screen when and where to strike. It listed the rules she knew about; things which get one promptly removed from the world, but then there was a place to enter names or groups of people. Claire typed in the words, and the machines slowed before chugging into renewed life, spinning and whirring into action.

At the bottom of the screen, the word "Begin" flashed furiously under her fingertips. The anger and grief of the world were behind her touch. The whole planet had ached for years under the weight of collective pain, and now it could heal. She pressed it, and the rumble began. *The machines are saving us now*, she thought. *Betray us no longer.*

The world can begin again repeated in her thoughts, as the first jolt vibrated into action. This is the path to life. Too long had they been dead, working like drones fulfilling a plan they did not even want. Now, it was time for rebirth.

AUTHOR BIOGRAPHIES

Duncan Richardson is keen to uncover the hidden stories of our past and present, real or imagined, through fiction, poetry and history. He's written about a bog-man seeking revenge, edible worms, and a fire that threatened to destroy Brisbane, not all in the same story but anything is possible. His stories have appeared in various magazines, a novel, *Jason Chen and the Time Banana, a* choose-your-own adventure book, *Dinomania,* and in three recent anthologies, *Subtropical Suspense, Lighthouses,* and *The Black Beacon Book of Mystery.*
duncrich.wixsite.com/duncanrichardson

Linda Brucesmith Linda Brucesmith is a writer and public relations consultant based in Brisbane, Australia. Her debut novel, *Elsewhere*, was completed in September, 2020. Her short form works have appeared in And Also Books' *Our Inside Voices: Reflection on COVID 19*; *Going Down Swinging #37*; *Andromeda Spaceways Inflight Magazine #65*; Black Beacon Books' 2015 *Lighthouses* anthology; *The Big Issue*; Melbourne Books' *Award Winning Australian Writing 2014*; *The Review of Australian Fiction*; the Margaret River Press *The Trouble With Flying* 2014 short story collection; *Ricochet magazine*; Black Beacon Books' 2014 *Subtropical Suspense* anthology; Askance Publishing's 2013 *Homes* anthology (Cambridge); and The Fiction Desk's 2013 *New Ghost Stories* anthology (London), among others. She won the Fellowship of Australian Writers' Mornington Peninsula Prize 2013, was shortlisted for the 2013 KSP Speculative Fiction Awards and the 2013 Aeon Awards (Ireland), and highly commended in the 2012 Fellowship of Australian Writers National Literary Awards. Linda has worked as a magazine and newspaper journalist in Sydney, Melbourne, the Snowy Mountains, and on the Gold Coast. Her public relations business has provided her with perspectives on tourism, hospitality, food, horticulture, medicine, mining, dance, academia, media and the internet.
lindabrucesmith.com.au

Paul Williams is a British writer now living in Australia. He is best known for his study of 333 Jack the Ripper suspects and has contributed over 60 short stories to anthologies and magazines. *paulecwilliams.org*

Chisto Healy has been writing since childhood, but he only started following his dreams and writing full-time in 2020. On top of the award-nominated self-published novels from his earlier days, he now has over a hundred published stories. You can find out what is currently available to read at his blog or follow him on Amazon as there is new stuff constantly coming out. He lives in NC with his fiancé and her mom, his daughter, Ella, who has inspired stories that have been published, his daughter, Julia, who has been published alongside him, and his son, Boe, who thinks the world is his drum. *chistohealy.blogspot.com*

Sarah Jane Justice Sarah Jane Justice writes lyrical poetry, whimsical character pieces, and thrilling genre fiction. Her poetry has been featured in releases from *The Blue Nib*, *Capsule Stories*, and *Pure Slush*, and her short fiction has been published by *Hawk and Cleaver*, *Caustic Frolic*, and *Black Hare Press*. As a spoken word artist, she has won an array of competition titles, and competed at the Sydney Opera House as a national finalist in Australia's highest level of competition. In music, she is an accomplished songwriter, with three studio releases of original music to her name, as well as a science-fiction cabaret show that was featured in the 2016 Adelaide Fringe Festival. While currently managing the production of her mixed-media exhibition, *Cracks in our Shadows*, she continues to balance motherhood with an endless stream of new creative ventures. *sarahjanejusticewriting.com*

Michael Picco's a nice guy who writes about very bad things: things with sharp teeth and voracious appetites; things that lie in wait in dark shadows; things that chitter and howl and scream and slither. Things that make his readers check under their beds at night. Michael has been hooked on horror since he read *The*

Outsider by H.P. Lovecraft in third grade. Since then, he has contributed to a number of well-reviewed anthologies and has produced an award-winning collection of short stories: *Scenes from the Carnival Lounge*. His latest publishing credit (*Hey Nonny Ding-Dong, Alang, Alang, Alang*) appears in Craig Spector's Anthology: *Freedom of Screech*. He is currently working on a second collection of short stories called *Corpse Honey*. Michael lives with a menagerie of monsters in the Colorado high country. He finds beauty in odd things, making people laugh, and writing things that disturb his mother.
amazon.com/author/michaelpicco
michaelpiccoauthor.blogspot.com

Kurt Newton's fiction has appeared in numerous magazines and anthologies over the past twenty years. His more recent tales can be found in *The Black Beacon Book of Mystery*, *Nightscripts VI*, and *Dream of Shadows*. His third short story collection, *BRUISES*, is due to be published in 2021 by Lycan Valley Press Publications.

Cameron Trost is a writer of strange and mysterious fiction. He has published two collections, *Hoffman's Creeper and Other Disturbing Tales* and *The Animal Inside*, and a novel, *The Tunnel Runner*. He also creates puzzling cases for Oscar Tremont, Investigator of the Strange and Inexplicable, and is the founding editor of Black Beacon Books. Originally from Australia, Cameron now lives on the rugged coast of Brittany, where he enjoys nothing more than sipping a fine whisky by the fireplace while a storm howls outside.
camerontrost.com

Danielle Birch loves to write about tormented souls who have lost their path. Her short stories have been published in various anthologies and magazines and she is currently working on her first novel. She lives in a house filled with books in Queensland, Australia, with her husband, their little girl, and a spirited Kelpie.
daniellebirch.com

Indiana author **James Dorr**'s most recent book is a novel-in-stories from Elder Signs Press, *Tombs: A Chronicle of Latter-day Times of Earth*. Working mostly in dark fantasy/horror with some forays into science fiction and mystery, his *The Tears of Isis* was a 2013 Bram Stoker Award® finalist for Superior Achievement in a Fiction Collection, while other books include *Strange Mistresses: Tales of Wonder and Romance, Darker Loves: Tales of Mystery and Regret*, and his all-poetry *Vamps (A Retrospective)*. He has also been a technical writer, an editor on a regional magazine, a full time non-fiction freelancer, and a semi-professional musician, and currently harbors a Goth cat named Triana. An Active Member of SFWA and HWA, Dorr invites readers to visit his blog.
jamesdorrwriter.wordpress.com

Steve DuBois is a secondary school teacher from Kansas and is the author of over thirty works of speculative fiction and drama.
stevedubois.net

Karen Bayly is a writer, software tester, and author of the steampunk novel *Fortitude*. She writes in several genres but is most at home writing science fiction, horror, and fantasy. This is where her Ph.D. in biology and her research background best inform her writing. Her short stories and poems have appeared in journals such as *Black Hare Press, Toasted Cheese, Overland, Yellow Mama Webzine, Skive Magazine, Voluted Tales*, and *Every Day Fiction*. When not writing, you can find Karen dancing like a madwoman, or lying on the grass in her backyard watching birds, or staring at the stars and wondering where the hell the years have gone. She lives in Sydney, Australia with two indoor cats, a guitar, and a ukulele.
karenbayly.com

KG McAbee has had a bunch of books and well over a hundred short stories published, many of them quite readable. She lives in a 200-year-old haunted log cabin in South Carolina, takes her geekdom seriously and believes the words 'Stan Lee' and 'The Almighty' are interchangeable. She writes science fiction, pulp, steampunk, fantasy, horror and westerns. She's a member of

Horror Writers Association, Sisters in Crime, The Heinlein Society and International Thriller Writers and is an Artist in Residence-Literature with the South Carolina Arts Commission. Her awards include the Dream Realm, the Black Orchid, the Eppie, and an honourable mention from Writers of the Future. Feel free to drop her an email at *kgmcabee@gmail.com* or visit *kgmcabeebooks.com*

Paulene Turner is a writer of short stories, novels, and short plays. A former journalist, she is currently writing a YA series involving time travel. Her work has been published in anthologies and magazines in the US and Australia. She writes in a range of styles, from fantasy and sci-fi to romance and period mystery and has directed many of her short plays for Sydney's Short and Sweet, the biggest little play festival in the world. Paulene lives in Sydney. While not a mother of dragons, she is of twin daughters and twin pugs, which involves at least as much fire breathing.
pauleneturnerwrites.com

Robert Bagnall was born in Bedford, England, in 1970 and now lives in Devon, between Dartmoor and the English Channel. He is the author of the novel *2084 - The Meschera Bandwidth* and the collection *24 0s & a 2*, which collects two dozen of his thirty-plus published stories. He can be contacted via his blog at *meschera.blogspot.co.uk*

Kerilee S. Nickles has been freelance writing full-time for the past three years as she travels around with her international teaching husband. Her background writing work includes articles, blogs, columns, and more ranging from pets to travel to health to dating tips! She continues to write a monthly column about life overseas for her hometown newspaper in Pennsylvania but has moved on from short-form non-fiction writing. For almost two years now, she has been ghostwriting full-length historical romance novels and has ten already under her belt. She currently writes for four different publishing companies, and while she loves it, she is really excited to publish more work under her own name. Writing short stories has long been a passion of hers, especially in the genre of crime/mystery fiction. She is thrilled to be a part of this anthology! She currently lives in Lilongwe, Malawi in southern Africa.

kerinickles.wixsite.com/teaandtales

Also Available from Black Beacon Books

A short, stormy anthology designed to be read while the wind howls and the thunder booms. Batten down the hatches and take shelter!

For news, reviews, competitions, author interviews, and exclusive excerpts

Visit our website
blackbeaconbooks.com

Like us on Facebook
facebook.com/BlackBeaconBooks

Join us on Twitter
@BlackBeacons

Subscribe on Patreon
patreon.com/blackbeaconbooks